KU-450-611

3/23   LB of Hackney   F

9130001183208

THE SHADOW OF PERSEUS

Also by Claire Heywood

Daughters of Sparta

THE SHADOW OF PERSEUS

CLAIRE HEYWOOD

HODDER &
STOUGHTON

First published in Great Britain in 2023 by Hodder & Stoughton
An Hachette UK company

1

Copyright © Claire Heywood 2023

The right of Claire Heywood to be identified as the Author of the Work has been
asserted by her in accordance with the Copyright, Designs and Patents Act 1988.

All rights reserved. No part of this publication may be reproduced, stored in
a retrieval system, or transmitted, in any form or by any means without
the prior written permission of the publisher, nor be otherwise circulated
in any form of binding or cover other than that in which it is published and
without a similar condition being imposed on the subsequent purchaser.

All characters in this publication are fictitious and any resemblance
to real persons, living or dead, is purely coincidental.

A CIP catalogue record for this title is available from the British Library

Hardback ISBN 978 1 399 70266 9
Trade Paperback ISBN 978 1 529 33370 1
eBook ISBN 978 1 529 33372 5

Typeset in Plantin Light by Manipal Technologies Limited

Printed and bound in Great Britain by Clays Ltd, Elcograf S.p.A.

Hodder & Stoughton policy is to use papers that are natural, renewable
and recyclable products and made from wood grown in sustainable forests.
The logging and manufacturing processes are expected to conform to
the environmental regulations of the country of origin.

Hodder & Stoughton Ltd
Carmelite House
50 Victoria Embankment
London EC4Y 0DZ

www.hodder.co.uk

For Andrew,
A wonderful man.

'Perseus, renowned among all men'
Homer, *Iliad* 14.320

'son of Danae, who stripped away the head of fair-cheeked Medusa'
Pindar, *Pythian* 12.16-17

'son of Zeus, the mightiest Greek of his day . . .
gained glory which was held in everlasting remembrance from campaigns
waged in foreign lands'
Diodorus Siculus, *Library of History* 3.52, 4.40

Part I

Danae

CHAPTER I

Danae had a spring in her step as she made the steep ascent to the temple. She smiled as the wind pulled at her skirts, leading her on up the well-worn path that snaked its way along the rocky hillside. She could hear her handmaid Korinna panting behind her, and felt the sweat beginning to gather on her brow, but she pushed on. They were almost at the top.

'Not far now,' Danae declared, turning to her handmaid, but her grin dropped a little as she saw Korinna struggling with the heavy wine jar. 'Let me take that,' she offered, feeling suddenly guilty about the unrelenting pace she had set.

'Don't worry, mistress. We're almost there now, as you say.'

Nevertheless Danae dropped back and they carried the jar between them the rest of the way, each taking one of the clay handles. It might have been difficult, negotiating that weight between two sets of slender arms, but Korinna had been with her long enough that they knew how to move together. Just as when her handmaid dressed her in the morning, or fixed her hair in elaborate coils, or when the two of them set the loom with its colourful woollen threads, their bodies flowed around one another, each hand knowing where it was needed.

As the slope finally levelled out and the temple came into view, the two girls stopped to catch their breath. Though she had seen them many times before, those stone walls never failed to impress Danae. Each boulder was perfectly set, curving between its neighbours to create a great circle rising out from the plateau. It was no larger than her own home – smaller, probably – and yet there was an immovable solidity to those rocks that made the building loom beyond its stature. This was a place for gods, not men.

That feeling was undercut somewhat by the very mortal-looking attendant who appeared through the doorway. She and Korinna set the wine jar down on the gravel as the man stepped towards them, the morning light illuminating his pockmarked cheeks and balding head.

'Ah, Lady Danae,' he called, clasping his hands together as he strode towards them. 'You are welcome once again to the temple of the divine twins, Paion Apollo and Lady Artemis.' He glanced down at the jar. 'Another offering for the Lord Apollo?'

'Yes,' she gasped, still breathless from the climb. 'My father asks that Lord Apollo return a favourable answer in the question of his marriage. He asks that the shining god should reveal which bride shall provide him with a son, so that he may bring further glory to the illustrious city of Argos and pleasing gifts to the god who has been his patron in this matter.' She reeled off the words she had spoken each morning for the last two weeks, then took a lungful of air.

'Very well,' said the attendant with a gracious nod. 'We shall see that the libation is poured. May the shining god smile upon the king's request.' And with that he stooped to lift the cumbersome wine jar and carried it as ceremoniously as he could back through the doorway of the temple. Danae's gaze followed him under the stone lintel, trying to see into the centre of that mysterious building. She saw the flicker of fire, shadowy figures crossing its light, and then the door was closed.

She smiled. Let the priests keep their secrets. She had not hurried all the way up Larissa Hill to peer at altars and trade formalities with dusty old attendants. She hitched her skirts and strode straight past the temple, leaving Korinna behind as her eager feet almost sprang into a run, charging across the plateau, stones crunching under her sandals until . . . There it was.

Danae stopped herself, raised an arm against the sharp morning sun, and looked out on the object of her daily pilgrimage.

There in the distance lay the great glistening blue, stretching out to meet the sky. In all her eighteen years Danae had never left Argos. She could only imagine the worlds that existed beyond the sea, the vibrant people who inhabited them, the great adventures that might be happening right now on some distant shore. Her uncle told her such stories, when the hearth fire burned low and she and her cousins were huddled around him, drinking his words like honey wine. Stories of monsters and shipwrecks, of foreign kingdoms and great heroes. But even he rarely travelled. 'I have all I need right here,' he would say, gathering Danae and his daughters into his thick chest.

She loved those evenings, and the worlds he conjured with his deep, full voice. But sometimes she wished she could do more than listen. The view from Larissa Hill was the closest she came to stepping on those distant shores, to feeling their sand beneath her feet. It was worth the daily climb to stand here and take in the bay, to feel herself so close to the unbounded blue that connected her to a whole world beyond, to be buffeted by a wind that had shaken foreign trees and whipped unknown tides. She let the feeling of it soak through her.

'Should we not return now, mistress?' came Korinna's soft voice beside her.

Danae's heart sank. She could say no, and insist that they stay another few minutes, another hour, but it would only make her father anxious. She didn't want to risk putting him into an ill temper. He had been on edge these last weeks, awaiting the response from the oracle, and she knew that if she pushed him too far she might lose the freedoms she savoured. Taking one last lungful of the hilltop air, she tore her eyes away from the azure sea and began her reluctant descent with Korinna at her side.

They made their way through the city, attracting gazes and nods from the fishermen come to sell their morning catch, potters shaping their clay or bringing cups from the kiln, dyers filling the

street with mismatched aromas as they stirred their great vats –
earthy, sweet, then suddenly nose-pinchingly sharp. Between the
workshops and wagons, the stalls and stables, people gossiped and
haggled, each trying to be heard above the others. As Danae tried
to linger beside some of them, curious to hear something beyond
the usual palace talk, Korinna drew her veil over her head and
quickened her pace. But Danae knew they had no reason to fear.
No one in Argos would dare harm the daughter of Akrisios, nor
one of his slaves. So she smiled politely at those they passed, and
followed the path that was cleared for them.

As they turned on to the main street, another path was being
cleared further ahead. A wedding procession, from the torches
held aloft and the bridal hymn that filled the air. She could see the
timid bride, clutching her veil to hide her blushing face, stepping
carefully over the cobbles to avoid spoiling her fine saffron dress.
Danae felt for her in her nervousness, and yet beneath that there
was a twinge of envy.

Argos had no shortage of men hoping to marry Akrisios' only
daughter. But as each one presented himself, her father found a
reason to reject them. They were too fat, too thin, too poor, too
wealthy, too foolish, too clever. Danae knew the real reason for his
reluctance to let her marry. He already had one rival in her uncle
Proitos, and could not abide another.

Then a month ago, after years of trampled hope, Danae thought
her time had come. A young man, barely older than she was, had
come to stay in the palace with his father, a wealthy merchant
from Krete. Such a thing was hardly unusual – a little wine and
hospitality here and there was necessary for bringing new ships
into Nauplia, and new luxuries into her father's hands. But this
guest was different. Danae had been brought to dine with the
man, and with his son. And as soon as she entered the Hearth Hall
she had felt the weight of their collective gaze – heavier by far than
that of polite curiosity.

The boy had been quite unremarkable, with dark eyes and doughy cheeks. But even to be in the company of a boy her own age sent a warm tingle down her neck, and she felt her cheeks burn hot even though the fire was low. As she watched him over her cup, and as he watched her, and as their fathers spoke of wedding gifts and dowries, she found herself imagining the life they might share. There was a shyness in his glance that she found endearing, a curve in his lip that came and went as she caught him looking. Not a word had passed between them and yet she told herself that he was kind and decent. She had to believe it, if this was finally to be her chance to wed.

It had been going so well. The boy's father was wealthy but foreign. He had no stake to claim on the mainland, no power or loyalties to rival her father's. And the boy could hardly be a threat, young and unassuming as he was. He was the perfect candidate, she thought. And her father seemed to believe it too, nodding his black head as the merchant spoke of gold and silver, saffron and ivory. His heavy brows, always so closely knit, began to lift with each sip of wine, each deal arranged.

And then came the word she had heard her father speak so many times before.

'Impossible.'

His beard began to quiver and he leant back on his chair, face wrinkled with disdain. The merchant looked perplexed, glancing from Akrisios to his own silent son, and though his honeyed voice continued to flow, Danae's father had already set himself like a stone, arms crossed over his chest.

She hadn't caught what had passed between them. Some talk of inheritance, she thought, trying to recall the last moments in her ear's memory. But it was hardly worth the effort. She knew from her father's face that it was done. The boy would leave, like all the others before him, and she would have to close up her hope once again.

That had been the hardest one yet, Danae thought. It was cruel of her father to let her meet the boy. Not many had got that far. More often by the time Danae learned there had been a suitor at the Golden House they had already been sent away, and she would have to learn the details from gossip that spread through the palace like flies over ripe fruit.

Not two weeks after the boy had left, her father sent his men on a journey to far Delphi, to ask Apollo which girl he should marry to be sure of begetting a son. Perhaps it was a coincidence, though in the most sunken part of her heart Danae knew it was not. Her father had turned his eye to new prospects. Why pursue a marriage for her, when his own might yield so much reward, and bring so little risk? Yes, soon he would have an heir – a true, male heir – to put him ahead of his brother and secure the future of Argos for his own line. And what thought should he give to her future then? Even as she enjoyed her trips to the temple, bringing the pleasing wine for Apollo, she knew that she might be coaxing the very decision that would make her own life inconsequential.

Danae's throat was tight as she and Korinna watched the procession go by, but still she added her voice to the wedding hymn as it swelled and faded. Making a silent prayer for the bride's happiness, she watched as the veiled head disappeared among the crowd. Another girl gone to start her life, she thought, swallowing the bitterness on her tongue.

CHAPTER 2

The sun had reached its highest point by the time they returned to the Golden House. So called for the bright ochre of its walls, it had been built by her grandfather as a home befitting the King of Argos. Now two kings shared its cramped halls.

The great doors hung wide open, so perhaps her father and uncle had been giving audiences this morning. The thought slowed Danae's steps. It always left her father in a prickly mood, when he had been forced to lend space to his brother's words beside his own. Her grandfather had thought himself blessed to have twin sons and made both his heirs, to rule Argos with double strength. But he had not lived long enough to see the reality of it. She was glad, at least, that she had not been forced to spend her morning in the close hall, watching as the two kings clashed their judgements like shields, each pushing against the other until one was forced to relent. It was childish, really. Like boys matching the strength of their arms, biceps shaking as they tried to keep their faces smooth. And she could not blame her father alone. They were each as stubborn as the other.

A sour mood was all the more reason not to keep her father waiting, so Danae carried on past the guards with Korinna at her heels, through the atrium, across the small courtyard, and pushed against the heavy door of the Hearth Hall.

Just as she had predicted, there he was. Her father half arose from his throne as she entered, but sank back as he saw who stood in the doorway.

'It's you,' he sighed, without bothering to hide his disappointment. She smiled sweetly as if she hadn't noticed. Disappointing her father was nothing new to Danae.

'I thought you would like to know that your offering has been accepted by the temple. May the shining god bring you the answer that you desire.' She nodded dutifully, still standing in the doorway.

'We may as well have poured it down the well,' her father grunted, sinking further into his throne. 'Surely Apollo has moved the Pythia's lips to speak by now? Why have my men not returned?' he asked the hall at large, taking an impatient swig from his cup.

'Mind your words, brother,' came the steady voice of her uncle, seated on his own throne on the opposite side of the hall. 'We do not want the gods to think that we begrudge them their offerings.' He gave Danae a warm smile before continuing. 'Delphi is five days' travel at least. They will return in good time.'

It seemed her father didn't have any more to say, so instead he glowered at his brother over the rim of his cup, the hearth fire crackling between them. It was Proitos who broke the silence.

'Sit with us, Danae,' her uncle said, waving to an empty stool beside his three daughters. 'Your feet must ache after your journey to the temple.'

In truth she was not tired. She would happily climb the hill again given a cause, but she knew she would have to wait until tomorrow for her next glimpse of the beckoning blue. Though her father was becoming more irritable by the day, Danae secretly hoped that the Delphi mission would not return too soon. Each day that they delayed meant another trip to the temple.

Despite the stuffiness of the Hearth Hall, she was grateful for her uncle's invitation. She dismissed Korinna, who was still hovering behind her, and took up the empty stool with a broad grin.

'Come, Danae,' said Proitos jovially, wringing his great hands together. 'We have spent all morning in this suffocating hall. You must regale us with your tales of the outside. Is the city busy today?'

'As busy as always.' She smiled, shuffling her stool a little closer to her cousins. 'We saw a wedding procession.'

'Oh,' sighed Iphinoe. 'How wonderful. Was the bride beautiful?'

'Of course she was,' Lysippe interjected. 'What bride isn't?'

'When will you find husbands for us?' asked Iphianassa, who was seated closest to her father.

'When I think there are any worthy of you,' said Uncle Proitos, pulling Iphianassa towards him and kissing the top of her dark head. Like his twin brother, Danae's uncle had begotten no sons, and yet he did not seem to resent the fact. He doted on his three daughters as if they were the greatest gifts the gods could have bestowed. Though it made her smile to see his love for them, and theirs for him, she felt a familiar pinch in her chest.

'A marriage is not something to be rushed,' continued her uncle. 'Your mother and I have found great happiness in ours, and that is what I want for each of you,' he said, looking from one daughter to the next, and finally to Danae herself. 'Good things come in good time. And let us hope that time has come for our Lord Akrisios,' he said, raising his voice and his cup to his brother across the hall. Danae's father merely grunted in response and returned to his wine.

She frequently wondered how two brothers could be so different. Her grandmother used to say that they had quarrelled even when they were in the womb, and although Danae knew she was joking it didn't seem improbable. Where her uncle was warm, her father was distant. Where Proitos was joyful, Akrisios was bitter. The one was patient, the other rash. And yet as she studied her father over the light of the hearth, silver hairs shining amid the black, with thick brows sunk deep over his sharp eyes, she knew that she was being unfair. He was not always so morose. He was just anxious to receive his answer from the Pythia. In all his long years he had failed to produce a son, and a king without heirs was vulnerable. Danae's mother had died when she was too young to remember her, and though her father had remarried twice, both wives had been barren.

Now he hoped Apollo would help him avoid another wasted marriage.

'It has been a long morning,' declared Uncle Proitos, keeping his tone upbeat despite her father's sullenness. 'Shall we take some refreshment? I have a fancy for figs.'

The fruit was brought – cheese and bread too – but Akrisios took none of it. Her father had eaten little these past weeks, Danae observed, since he had sent his men to the oracle. His gaze flicked continually between the fire and the closed door of the hall, as if it might have opened while he looked away. Though Proitos continued in his light tone the smoky air was thick with anticipation, radiating from her father like the crackle of a storm.

Suddenly there was the creak of wood. Danae's head snapped round almost as quickly as her father's, quick enough to see bright sunlight spill across the floor as the great door yawned inward.

'Lord Akrisios.'

Her father was on his feet at once. Danae recognised his chief emissary, Aristides, as he stepped into the sun-filled chamber. He glanced around the room, and his eyes seemed to stop on Danae for a moment before returning to her father.

'Well? What answer did the Pythia give?' Her father took a step forward, filled with eager energy. All was silent except for his voice, ringing around the painted walls, but Danae could feel the held breaths and pricked ears. Even Proitos sat forward on his throne.

'Should we not offer Aristides a cup of wine first, brother? It is a long journey from Delphi.' Proitos waved to one of his attendants, but Akrisios held up a hand.

'I have waited long enough,' he snapped. 'Tell me. What did the oracle say?'

Aristides looked uncertain, his eyes passing once more over the inhabitants of the hall.

'Might we speak privately, my lord?' he asked quietly. The tremor in his voice made Danae uneasy.

'What is it?' demanded her father. 'Do the gods mean me ill? Tell me all that the Pythia said.'

Aristides held her father's gaze.

'The oracle foretold that you will never beget a son.'

Danae watched her father's face drop, as if the world had been sunk with those words. This was the answer he had feared.

'The gods continue to spite me,' he growled. He stepped back and fell into his throne, staring at the flames in the hearth. 'And that was all she said? There was no more?'

Aristides opened his mouth but hesitated.

'That was *not* all,' said her father eagerly, seeing the unspoken words on Aristides' lips. He leaned forward, eyes bright with renewed hope. 'Come. You must tell me what she said. What other prophecy did Apollo put upon her tongue? How am I to secure my kingdom?'

Aristides' eyes flicked from her father's to Danae's own, and the tortured apology she saw in them made her stomach twist.

'The Pythia foretold that your daughter Danae would give birth to a son, and that he would be your death.'

There was an instant chill, as if Aristides' words had thrown a shroud over the hall. Danae's heart thumped in her chest as she felt the faces of her uncle and her cousins turn towards her. Across the hearth fire, her father's eyes were like two pieces of charcoal, fixing her to her stool. She opened her mouth but it hung numb. What could she say against the words of a god?

CHAPTER 3

Danae paced across what had become her new chamber. Seven paces wide, and seven paces long. Sometimes six if she lengthened her stride. She had counted every knot of the wooden door, had traced her finger over every crack in the plastered walls. After less than two days in her prison, she had run out of ways to occupy herself.

And a prison is what it was. No windows and only one door, always closed. Father had chosen this room deliberately – until recently a storeroom for his fine wines and scented oils. A colossal oil jar still stood in the corner, half sunk into the floor and too difficult to remove. It was empty now, but she could still smell the pungent coriander that had seeped into the clay. Though pleasant at first, it was beginning to make her nauseous.

If she had known where she would be shut away, perhaps she would have made her feet drag more heavily. But as it was, she had been too dazed to resist. Half a month waiting for her father's oracle, and instead the Pythia had spoken of her. *Her* future. *Her* son. And the death he was fated to bring. Her chest felt tight at the memory, but she took a deep breath to loosen it. The words of an oracle were not always what they seemed – not least those of the Pythia, with their twists and tricks. She was not even married, or close to it. The thought of motherhood felt so far from Danae that any other consequence that might be tied to it felt almost comically unlikely.

She thanked the gods, not for the first time, for the modest hole in the centre of the ceiling, by which she could catch a little of the fresh air that blew past and watch the sun's rays as they crossed from one side of the floor to the other. If she stood in that sunny patch, and closed her eyes and opened her ears to the sounds of the city and the rustle of the leaves in the nearby olive trees, she could almost convince herself that she was on the hilltop again, the temple at her back and the unending ocean stretched before her.

As she stood imagining the far-off calls of the seabirds another sound brought her back to her cell: raised voices, muffled by the impenetrably thick wood of the door. She stepped closer and tried to pick out some words amid the din. One voice was her uncle's.

'He cannot just lock her away! I demand to see my niece!'

One of the guards replied in a low voice, and she struggled to hear what followed until her uncle raised his voice once more.

'He's gone mad! And you are mad to follow him!'

After that the voices seemed to die down until all was as quiet as it had been before.

Danae was grateful to her uncle for speaking out on her behalf, for trying to visit her, but she wished he wouldn't worry himself. Uncle Proitos knew as well as she did that Akrisios was slow to trust and quick to act. The Pythia's answer had scared him and he had hurried to protect himself in the simplest way he could fathom. By locking her in this room he could guarantee her chastity and prevent the grandchild he now so feared. It was drastic and unnecessary, of course – in truth he need only keep her from marrying, and he had done well enough at that so far – but she also knew that her confinement was only temporary. She reminded herself of the time her father had said she would never again be permitted to dine in the Hearth Hall, because she had spoken with one of the serving boys there. And the month that he had forsworn all bread, because he was convinced the wheat farmers were trying to poison him. She would endure her little cell for a few days – a few weeks even, if she must. But eventually her father would realise that it had been a foolish notion, like all his other notions formed in haste, and life would go on as it had before.

Looking around her square chamber, empty aside from her narrow bed, a chamber pot and basin, and the lonely oil jar, Danae sighed. If her uncle was ever permitted to visit her, she hoped he had the sense to bring her a spindle, a loom, a lyre – anything to stop her mind unravelling from boredom.

It was a week before Danae got her wish. As the sun was setting she heard the heavy bar on the door being lifted, and Korinna shuffled in carrying her evening meal – honeyed peas and a generous piece of bread. Danae smiled to see her friend, but the slave girl kept her eyes lowered as she set the dish down and turned back towards the door.

'Has my father said anything? How long will he keep me here?' Danae knew it was futile but she had to try, if only to know that her voice still worked. Korinna entered her cell twice a day to bring food and water, to empty her chamber pot and bring fresh clothes, but each time her lips remained shut tight. Danae knew that Father must have forbidden the girl to speak, and she didn't want to get her into trouble, but it was so unnatural to spend each day in silence. And what good did it serve? A maiden she may be, but Danae was worldly enough to know that talking to her handmaid would not put a child in her belly. She was beginning to think that her father really had gone mad.

Korinna turned her head and gave an apologetic smile. Danae smiled back, grateful for even that small communion. Then the girl turned and shuffled out, and Danae let out a sigh. But the door did not close. Instead Korinna re-entered, a broader smile on her face as she held up a lyre.

Danae beamed, hurrying forward to take it from her.

'Thank you,' she breathed, embracing Korinna awkwardly with the lyre between them.

The girl simply nodded and backed out of the chamber door, giving Danae one last glance as it closed behind her.

Danae sat on the edge of her bed, running her hand over the smooth stems of her new gift. The strings were taut and perfectly tuned, the tortoise shell body as beautiful as it was resonant. She experimented with a short tune, her fingers finding their place as if they had a memory of their own. It was a relief to hear those notes, to feel the vibration of the wood against her shoulder. Danae was surprised to find tears welling in her eyes as she played. However long her father's paranoia persisted, at least her days would no longer be silent.

CHAPTER 4

Another week passed, and still Danae was permitted no visitors. Korinna came and went as usual, her hesitant smile a welcome sight each time the chamber door opened, but then it would close again and Danae would be left alone.

The lyre had been a much-needed distraction, but it was no substitute for human company. She longed to laugh and talk with her cousins, to listen to her uncle's stories as they all sat beside the crackling hearth. She even missed her father.

Just a little while longer, she told herself, and forced her lips into a smile that no one would see.

This evening she sat playing her lyre, as always. Korinna had already brought her supper – a sad bowl of broth left uneaten in the corner of the room. Danae looked at it as her fingers plucked and strummed. Perhaps she should refuse all her meals. Perhaps then her father would see how unhappy she was.

Just then she heard a sound. She stopped the strings with her hand and listened. Had it been a bird? Or a voice borne on the wind through her little hole in the ceiling? She strained her ears, desperate for a voice, any voice from beyond her cell, but all was silent now. Danae returned her fingers to their position on the strings and was about to resume her playing when she heard it again. A grunt of exertion. Unmistakable this time, and close by.

'Hello?' she called, her heart suddenly beating quicker at the thought of another human soul so near. She put down her lyre and took a step towards the back wall, where she thought the sound had come from.

'Hello.'

Her head snapped up to see a grinning face appear through the square hole above. She stepped back, a little frightened by the sudden apparition.

'Sorry if I scared you,' said the face, his grin still spread wide between ruddy cheeks. 'I knew it was you.'

She studied him, a boy no older than herself, his dark curls blowing lightly in the evening breeze. His eyes were bright with excitement, but they held no threat.

'I wasn't afraid,' she said, straightening herself and setting her chin in what she hoped was a look of dignified nonchalance. 'I just didn't expect . . . Who *are* you?'

To her surprise the face disappeared for a moment, only to be replaced by two dangling legs, then a whole body as the boy lowered himself through the hole and dropped gracefully to the floor before her.

'I'm Myron,' he said in a half-whisper, sticking out a flour-covered hand. His grin dropped a little as he saw her perplexed expression, and he wiped the hand on his equally floury tunic before extending it again.

Though his frame was narrow, his limbs were muscular – his arms especially. Working arms, she thought, taking in the tan beneath the flour, the sun-kissed freckles that spread to his cheeks as well. His brown face shone from effort, brimming with an open, expectant energy. Danae felt a tickle across her skin, a stirring in her stomach somewhere between fear and excitement.

'I'm Danae,' she said, extending a hesitant hand to meet his. His fingers were rough with calluses, but had a warm comfort about them. She let go.

'I know who you are,' he said, lowering his voice even further as he eyed the door behind her. 'I told my brother Philemon it was you, when we heard your lyre. I've been listening every night. You play such melancholy songs – beautiful, though.' And there was

that grin again. She found her own cheeks rising in answer but
shook her head.

'But who are you?' she asked again, taking half a step back.
'Where did you come from?' She looked to the hole in the ceiling
as if it might provide a clue, but there was only the last glow of
sunset.

'My father's bakery is just across the street from here.' Myron
pointed through the solid wall behind him. 'We make bread for
the Golden House—' He stopped and she followed his gaze to her
supper in the corner, with its piece of bread untouched. 'Ah well,
perhaps it's not to your taste.' Danae felt suddenly guilty, but he
looked more amused than annoyed.

'No, it's not that,' she whispered. 'I just . . . I haven't had much
appetite of late.' She smiled weakly, and for the first time Myron's
expression became serious.

'Of course,' he nodded solemnly. 'I know about King Akrisios
locking you away. The streets are full of it. And what the Pythia
said, the oracle . . . ' He paused, eyeing her cautiously. 'I know he's
your father but it's not right what he's done, shutting you away.
You must be so lonely in here.'

Danae felt a sudden lump in her throat, to see this stranger look
at her with such genuine sympathy. Her father spoke of boys as if
they were callous creatures, selfish and grasping. But now that she
was here speaking with one he didn't seem cold at all. She could
feel the warmth of him, as if there were no space between them.
And as she stood looking into his brown eyes, she felt the resolute
wall she had built begin to crack, as a little of her own self-pity
broke through. Myron saved her from speaking.

'Those songs you play are so sad. I wanted to bring you something.' He reached to open the flap of a satchel, which hung from
his shoulder, and produced a slightly squashed barley cake. 'These
always make me feel better.' He watched her expectantly as he
held the cake on his outstretched palm.

Danae reached out and took it, still warm from the oven and smelling of honey. Her empty stomach growled and she could already taste the sweetness on her tongue. It was a small thing, and yet when her days held so little pleasure, even this felt like a great kindness. 'Thank you,' she murmured, and meant it.

'I can make more,' he said cheerfully, closing the flap on his satchel. 'There's always a little flour left at the end of the day. I can put some pistachios in next time, if you like.'

Danae was about to say that she was indeed fond of pistachios, when she stopped herself.

'Next time?' She stepped away from him again. 'I'm not sure you ought to have come at all. What if the guards catch you?' She didn't like to think what her father might do to that smiling face.

'Oh, they're not too bright,' he said casually. 'They never guard the back street. I don't think they even know it's possible to climb in here. Reckon me and Philemon are the only ones who've ever tried it.'

'You've been here before?' she whispered.

Myron's proud expression turned sheepish.

'Ah . . . yes.' He looked down, suddenly occupied with a bit of flour under his nail. 'Well, we used to drop in from time to time, and sample a little of your father's wine.' His eyes flicked back to hers, but Danae only laughed.

'It's a shame he took it all out before sticking me in here. We could have shared a cup.'

Myron laughed too, and for a moment Danae felt more light-hearted than she had in weeks. A noise from the corridor snuffed their smiles.

'You should go,' she urged, turning an ear to the door. Had the guards heard them? All was quiet again, but her heart still raced.

She put down the barley cake and linked her hands for Myron to step on, just as she had done for her cousins when they climbed trees in their youth.

'Will you come again?' she whispered, embarrassed by how desperate she sounded. But Myron only grinned.

'Pistachios next time.'

And with that he sprang up on her locked hands, pulled his lean body through the hole in the ceiling, and was gone into the night once more.

Danae half fell onto her bed and stroked the fine covers with preoccupied fingers. The chamber already felt colder, she thought, but now at least she had something to look forward to.

CHAPTER 5

For the first time during her confinement, Danae was relieved when Korinna closed the door behind her. The girl had brought her supper as always, just as the sun began to set, and Danae knew that no one would enter the chamber again until the morning. She had spent the afternoon fretting that Myron would come too early, but now she let herself relax. *He may not come tonight,* she reminded herself, and yet despite the risk she hoped he would. Their first brief conversation had left her almost giddy after so many hours alone. She had found her cheeks lifting as she nibbled the dense barley cake and thought about the boy who had dropped from the sky. Had he really been here? It seemed ridiculous, but the cake was real enough. She recalled the speckled tan of his arms, the easiness of his smile, and the giddy feeling began to rise again. Danae settled herself on the edge of her bed, lyre in hand, and tried to ignore the way her fingers trembled as they found the strings. *He may not come.*

The sun was fully set before she heard soft footsteps above her. Seconds later Myron's narrow frame had dropped through the hole.

'Pistachio, as promised,' he declared proudly, producing another little cake from his satchel.

'Shh!' Danae whispered, a finger to her lips. 'We must be quiet.' But even as she admonished him she took the pistachio cake from his hand, feeling her heart leap as her fingers brushed his. She was surprised by how natural it felt to see him again, to be so close to this boy she did not know.

'We can share this one,' she breathed, perching on the edge of her bed once more and inviting him to join her. He did so, leaving a respectful gap between them.

'Did your father teach you to bake?' she asked, breaking the cake in two.

'Yes, and my mother,' Myron replied, taking his half gently from her hand. 'I help her grind the wheat and barley, and I help my father work the oven.' Danae nodded. She realised she didn't have the first clue about how bread was made, though she had eaten it often enough – small rounds dipped in wine or oil, great brown loaves to accompany the meat and fish in the Hearth Hall, bread sweet with honey or salty with cheese. She had never given thought to the hands that made it. Not wanting to betray her ignorance, she let him continue.

'They want me and Philemon to take over the bakery, when they get too old. My mother already has pain in her hands, and her back aches from bending over the quern. I don't think it will be long before they hand the work on to us.'

'That's a good thing, isn't it?' she asked, surveying the shallow crease that had appeared in his brow.

He hesitated and took another bite of his cake. 'It's an honest trade,' he said thoughtfully. 'And the gods know there are those who would count themselves lucky to have it.' He took another bite, looking down at his knees. Despite her own privilege, Danae knew the truth of his words. She had seen those men on her trips into the city – women and children too – their faces thin and their clothes ragged. Korinna always ushered her quickly past, but she had seen their desperation.

'Haven't you ever wondered if there could be more?' Myron asked, turning towards her.

'More than what?' she whispered.

'More than *this*,' he breathed, spreading his arms wide, a few crumbs of his cake sprinkling the floor. Danae looked around the windowless chamber.

'Well, yes, I hope there'll be more than this.' She laughed softly. Myron laughed too.

'No, I mean more than the Golden House, more than Argos. There's a whole world out there, and I think I'd like to see some of it.' He beamed with an energy Danae recognised. She was sure she had worn just the same expression herself, while standing on that stony hilltop and gazing out at the boundless ocean.

'Where will you go?' she asked, leaning towards him.

'I don't know yet. I thought I might board a ship at Nauplia and see where it takes me. I could be a merchant, maybe – that way I'd sail all over.' His eyes shone as he spoke. 'I know my father might be disappointed, but I think a man must cut his own path.' He gave a little nod as if agreeing with his own conclusion.

'Oh, you're a man now, are you?' she asked playfully.

'Well, almost,' he said, blushing a little. 'Look, my beard is grow-ing!' He picked up her hand and put it to his cheek. 'See?'

She stroked the fine hairs, barely more than down, but then her eyes met his and she stopped, suddenly aware of how close they were. He let go of her hand.

'I'm sorry,' he murmured. 'I shouldn't have done that. I don't want you to think—'

'It's all right,' she said gently. 'I know you didn't mean any harm.' As she said it, she realised how ridiculous it sounded. What harm could possibly come from him holding her hand, or her touching his cheek? And yet all her life she had been guarded from such things, kept away from male servants and honoured guests alike, chaperoned at all times by Korinna on her rare trips beyond the doors of the Golden House. She had been almost unsurprised when her father had locked her in this pitiful cell – he probably wished he had thought of the idea sooner. Far easier to keep her from the world than the world from her, she thought bitterly. She almost laughed aloud to think of the look on his face if he could see her now, here with this boy in her very own chastity chamber. But then her amusement waned and suddenly there were tears in her eyes.

'I've upset you,' said Myron, his bright face clouded with concern. 'Honestly, I didn't mean anything by it. I'll go if you want me to.'

Danae blinked back the tears and smiled at him. Then she reached out and took one of his rough hands in hers. 'No, please don't go,' she said. 'It's nice to have a friend.'

CHAPTER 6

Danae lay on the floor of her chamber, watching the wispy clouds make their way across the sky and enjoying the afternoon sun on her skin. She had to savour the small pleasures, she told herself. In time she would be able to go out and enjoy the whole of that blue canopy, stretching in every direction, but for now her little square was enough.

Myron had continued to visit most nights. They talked of their families, of their childhoods, of the past and of the future – the places they might go, the things they might see there and the people they might meet. Even to talk about such things made her world feel larger. His excited whispers were a remedy to the hollowness of that chamber. Every word breathed life. And with every shared longing, every secret, every smile or sadness, she felt them grow closer. Danae realised she had never really had a friend before. A true friend. Not her cousins bound to her by blood and forced proximity, or her handmaid bound by servitude. Myron owed her no loyalty. He asked for nothing from her. And yet time and again his beaming face would appear through the ceiling and she would feel herself saved from an evening of desolation.

Sometimes they would both lie here on the floor, their elbows brushing, and Myron would point to the stars through the hole in the ceiling, and tell her their names and constellations and the stories of how they came to be. He had learnt them all, he said, for when he became a sailor. And Danae had told him of her trips to the temple, of the unbounded hope she had felt when looking out on that view, how she had remembered every detail of it, as well as she could, so that she could close her eyes and imagine she was there when it felt as if the walls of her cell were closing around her. Sometimes she would become sad, to think of the world beyond carrying on without her, and Myron would reassure her.

'It won't be much longer. Your father can't keep you here forever.'

Danae knew he was right, and yet her heart was beginning to doubt it. She must have been here a month or more – she had stopped counting the days. And her father had not even come to visit her. He had not given her the opportunity to commit herself to a life of maidenhood, if that was what he wanted, if that was what it took to live in the world again. It would be a bitter vow, but she would make it. If her happiness meant so little to him, if his fear was so great that she could have no life at all without those heavy words, she would speak them. She thought of strong-armed Artemis, of strong-minded Athena – great goddesses forever unwed, and no less respected because of it. Were they content, she wondered, to turn their spirits inward, to hone mind and body instead of devoting themselves to the will of husbands and the nurturing of babes? She might have thought so. She might have been able to convince herself of it, if she had not now come to know what two spirits could be when they began to intertwine. What they could unfold in one another, what comfort and closeness they could feel in simply being. It was a feeling not easily set aside.

But perhaps it would not come to that. She must only wait a little longer, she told herself, for her father's fear to cool and his mind to clear. She would be allowed to leave this cell, to return to her life as it had been. And then, in time, he might allow her something more.

Absorbed by the steady movement of the clouds, she was startled by the sound of the door bar being lifted. It was too early for Korinna to come with her supper. Danae sat bolt upright as the heavy door creaked open.

'Father!' It was as if her thoughts had summoned him.

'What are you doing down there?' His voice was edged with disdain, and yet Danae found she was pleased to hear it. She hurried to her feet, brushing down her skirts. *He's finally come*, she thought, heart racing. She had endured and now it was over.

'Good afternoon, Father,' she said, nodding reverently.

He nodded in reply before turning his attention to the chamber, surveying the small space with a sweep of his eyes.

'I trust you have been comfortable?' he asked, as if he were addressing a guest-friend. Danae opened her mouth to say that comfort had not been her chief concern of late, but decided that silence was safer. She nodded.

'And you've been eating well?'

She nodded again.

'Good.' Her father looked around the room once more. 'Good,' he repeated, almost to himself. He stepped towards her narrow bed.

'Would you like to sit down?' she asked, moving to arrange the sumptuous cloths and cushions that covered the bed. Her father merely inclined his head and perched himself on the far end.

'I'm glad you've come to see me,' she said a little breathlessly, taking a seat beside him. 'I've been hoping you would.'

He met her eager gaze. 'Yes, I know you've been lonely. I am sorry for it.'

Though his face remained neutral, Danae welcomed his words. It was just as she had thought. He was sorry for his cruelty and he had come to put it right. Her spirit began to lift with a fortified hope.

'You have enjoyed your lyre, my guards tell me,' he went on with the slightest smile, nodding to the instrument leaning against the wall. 'Is there anything else you would like for your chamber? I could have a loom brought in if you wish.'

'I have all I need,' she said calmly, even as she felt a heat rise up her neck. 'I trust I will not need to occupy myself for much longer, if you are to release me.'

'Release you?' Her father looked confused. 'My daughter, you are not a prisoner.' He smiled. 'I am keeping you here for your own protection.'

It was Danae's turn to look confused. '*My* protection? But the oracle said—'

'A child is a danger to its mother,' he said, still smiling in a way that made Danae afraid. 'You know this, my daughter. Your own mother died in the birthing bed. I only want to keep you safe.'

Danae looked into his smiling face and felt her fear turn to anger. She knew what the oracle had said. She had been there in the hall, had watched Aristides turn to her father and foretell his doom. *He will be your death. His* death, not hers.

'I will bear no children, then,' she said stiffly, her tongue resisting the words. 'If that is what you fear.' She took her father's hand in hers, squeezed his ringed fingers tight. 'Let me return to my old life, and I will never marry. You are my guardian. You have the right to refuse all suitors, if you wish. Or let me pledge myself to Artemis, before all of Argos, and swear my chastity to the goddess. I will devote myself to the virgin and to her temple.'

She imagined the future she was speaking into existence, and clung to it with heavy arms. Service to the temple would give her purpose. She needed that. She could be happy, she told herself, spending her days on Larissa Hill and looking out at the wide world. If she couldn't have a true part in it, let her see it at least.

She watched her father's face for some sign that her plea had moved him, but as he shook his head her hope sank.

'This is the only way, Danae. You may mean to keep your pledge, but the Fates are not so easily denied. By seduction or by rape they will see the prophecy fulfilled.' A new fear rose at those words, and Danae resisted a glance at the ceiling as she felt her cheeks burn hot. If Myron had found her, could other men? Men who meant her harm? Her prison was not as impenetrable as her father believed, and yet to tell him this would be to deprive herself of what little joy she had.

He withdrew his hand from hers and leant back, as if she were tainted. Her eyes stung with tears.

'You cannot keep me here forever,' she pleaded, throat tight. But he was already on his feet.

'No, not forever,' he said levelly. But before Danae's hope had chance to rekindle, he continued. 'You will remain here until your belly can no longer bear fruit, until your womb is shrivelled and your woman's blood has run dry.'

And it was then that she knew his true fear. He did not fear her but her body – the life it could bring, and the death. Its permeability, its fatal fecundity. This was no new threat. He had defended against it all her life. The oracle had only made his fear greater, the stakes higher. And with that realisation she knew she was lost.

Danae finally let her tears fall, her restraint broken by the image of her barren future. Her father's face was set hard, and she could feel her fingers slipping from the hope she had held so tightly these past weeks. What more could she say? How could she move him, when he held all the power and she held none? She clasped the hem of his tunic.

'Father.' Her voice sounded so thin. 'The gods,' she croaked. 'The gods will curse you.' But even as she spoke she did not believe it. What should they care for one lonely girl? Her father seemed hardly to hear her.

'I am sorry for the thread the Fates have spun for you,' he said gravely, looking down at her with what might have been genuine pity. He pulled his tunic from her shaking fingers and stepped back. 'You have done me honour by bearing it with dignity, and I hope that you will continue to do so.'

And with that he was gone, and Danae was left alone once more.

*

The tears continued to flow as day turned to evening, springing in fits of anger, of fear, of exhaustion, as Danae hammered on the thick door of her chamber, beating the wood until her palms were raw. She cried out to her father, to her uncle, to Korinna or the guards, to anyone who might hear her. But the reply was silence. Eventually she sank, dragged to the floor as she felt the last of her patient optimism collapse into bitter despair. Her father had forsaken her. Her guardian and protector, the very man to whom her happiness had been entrusted, had traded it for his own protection.

She thought of her uncle Proitos. Surely he would not allow this. He would stand against her father's cruelty and force him to release her. But if that were true, why had he not already done it? And though it pained her to let go of that last flickering hope, she knew the answer. As many times as she might have wished it to be true, Proitos was not her father. He did not have the right to decide what her life should be. In that regard he had no more power than she.

Danae forced herself to stand, limbs aching from the hard floor, and lay down upon the fine covers of her bed. The colours of the cloth were vibrant, the patterns beautiful as she traced her fingers across them, and yet she knew they would never change. They were fixed, immovable, like the four walls of her cell, like her own life trapped within it. She imagined the streets of the city outside, alive and bustling, different every day with new faces, new stories. She thought of the ships coming and going from Nauplia, how she had watched them disappear into the horizon, how the shining sea had seemed alive in itself, bright with colour and possibility. That world was lost to her now, she realised. She had been able to bear it before, when she thought that her father would relent, when she had imagined how she would appreciate her pleasures all the more once they were returned to her. But now she could see no end. Only the long years stretching ahead of her, until all her hope of joy had been spent. *Until your woman's blood has run dry*, her father had said. How long would that be? Thirty years?

Forty? The most part of her life, if she lived that long. It made her stomach sink to think of it.

Danae stared up at her square patch of sky, covered over with gloomy cloud. She could climb up into that dark night, couldn't she? As Myron did. And yet even as she thought it she felt so heavy, as if her limbs were weighted to the bed. For all its possibilities, the world out there was not the world that had been taken from her. No, the things she cherished most lay within the Golden House, so close and yet out of her reach. She longed to sit once more beside the hearth fire, to share food and laughter and song with the people she loved. Only her father could return those things to her, by opening the thick door of her cell and letting her rush back into that world of comfort. There was nothing her own hands could do to retrieve it. But even as she mourned for it, she could not give it up. Not in her heart, not yet. She could not pull her body out of its paralysis, could not bring herself to strive for a new life while the deepest part of her still ached for the old.

She turned onto her side, unable to gaze any longer into a world that was not really hers. But then, as if sympathetic to her misery, there was a gentle rumble and the heavens let loose their own tears to join those that had seeped into her pillow. Danae watched as they spattered onto the paved floor of the chamber, at first only a spot or two, and then more and more until all were joined in a dark glistening square. Across the chamber a torch burned in its bracket, and as the heavenly tears dropped past its warm light, they seemed transfigured, like a glittering shower of gold.

It was so beautiful that Danae felt fresh tears well in her eyes, to be given this tantalising glimpse of the world's majesty. She let the new wave overtake her, and sobbed and sobbed into the quiet night.

A noise from above made her turn her head.

'Danae?'

Myron was looking down on her through the ceiling hole, his hair lank from the rain. Realising suddenly how pathetic she must look, she sat up to wipe her eyes and heard his boots drop on the wet flagstone.

'Are you all right? What's wrong?'

He was looking her over as if for signs of injury, his face filled with fear.

'M-my father . . . ' she started, but the words caught in her throat. She realised she was shaking.

Without a word Myron sat beside her and put a tentative hand on her arm. She looked into his eyes and it was as if he had read it on her face.

'He's not letting you out.' His voice was tight with anger.

But then to her surprise his arm was around her shoulders, pulling her gently to him, so that her cheek leant against his chest. His tunic smelled of woodsmoke, damp and cool from the evening rain and oddly soothing. He held her there awhile, their breaths falling into rhythm, and Danae wondered at how comfortable she felt to be held in his arms. In all their evenings spent together they had never embraced like this, so close that she could hear the very beat of his heart.

She lifted her head from his chest and looked at him, his brown eyes warm with sympathy and something else too, which grew as she gazed at him. A shy uncertainty. Before he could apologise for touching her, she leant up and kissed him on the lips.

She felt his body stiffen in surprise, but then he kissed her back. Danae had wondered what it would be like, had thought about it more than once in those moments when she and Myron had sat together, when his eyes were lit with energy, when his broad grin was all she could see. But now she found she did not have to think at all. Like her fingers finding the strings of the lyre, her lips found his.

She felt him draw away.

'Is this what you want, Danae?'

His breath was hot, his mouth hovering inches from hers. She had felt the eagerness of his lips. Why did he hesitate?

'I know you're upset. But we can't do this. Can we? The oracle, Danae. You know where this could lead.'

She turned her head away, as if shaking off his words. She felt angry with him then, for breaking the spell she was so desperate to fall under. For taking away the warm oblivion of his kisses. She turned to him again, face ready with a scowl, but the concern in his eyes disarmed her. She wasn't angry with Myron, not truly. She was angry with her father.

'What should I care for oracles? What is the future to me, now?' She could feel a rippling heat rise up her body, flushing her cheeks and burning in her chest. Her fingers tightened on Myron's arms, grasping the one thing that felt solid. Here was happiness, she told herself. In that warm skin beneath her fingertips. In the kind eyes looking back at her from under that dark fringe, still wet with the rain. In that chest that rose and fell so steadily beneath the cling-ing wool.

'This is what I want,' she breathed, and found his lips again.

CHAPTER 7

'I could help you escape, you know,' Myron whispered one night as they lay together in the darkness. They had pulled the woollen cover from Danae's bed and laid it over the cold stone floor – a less comfortable choice but she had been afraid that the guard would hear the creak of the bed. She hadn't thought of it the first time – there had not been space in her head to think of anything but the feel of Myron's body against her own, the taste of his mouth, the tickle of his hair. The door was thick, she knew, and yet they must be careful.

Myron was regarding her, and she regarded him. The full moon shone through the hole above them, bathing his body in its pale light. She ran a finger down his flank, slick with sweat.

'I mean it,' he said, taking her hand and holding it against his chest. She felt the beat of his heart and looked into his earnest eyes. 'I could help you with the climbing. It's not hard when you know the way across the roofs.'

'And where would we go?' she whispered. 'My father knows of everything that happens in Argos.'

'Then we leave Argos,' he said, squeezing her hand tighter. 'We take a ship. We could go anywhere.'

'Leave Argos?' she murmured, drawing her hand away. 'But it's my home. My family is here, and yours.'

'All that's here for you is this chamber.'

'And you.'

He returned her smile but didn't let the subject go. 'I thought you wanted to leave. We talked of all the places we'd go.'

'I know we did . . . '

Words were one thing, and action quite another. The truth was that she was afraid. It had been exciting to imagine herself out in the world, but Danae realised that she had never really thought it would happen. She loved Argos. She loved her uncle and her cousins. She couldn't bear the thought of never seeing them again, and she knew that if she left with Myron, her old life would be closed to her forever. The wide blue had called to her, yes, but only ever at a distance. And always with the promise that it would return her home. To actually think of herself upon its waves, leaving behind all she had ever known, was more than a little terrifying.

'Perhaps my father will change his mind,' she whispered.

Over the past weeks, like a tiny shoot of green after a harsh frost, she had felt her hope begin to grow anew. Her father was fickle. He could not mean what he had said. Each day she imagined her uncle appealing to his better nature. Yes, these were the thoughts that tended that gentle seedling, that watered its deepening roots. If there was any possibility of keeping both her home and her happiness, she could not bring herself to turn away from it.

But even as she nurtured those roots, she poisoned them too. By sleeping with Myron, by following the thread the Fates had spun for her. She had taken the first steps along a path she might never be able to return from. She knew that in the depths of her mind, but each time the thought arose she pushed it down again. The future had become a dark place for Danae, cold and distant and conflicted. In the present there was comfort, and in these evenings most of all, lying beneath the stars with Myron's warm skin touching hers. One day she would have the strength to pull up the tangled roots from beneath her, to pull herself from her home. But for now she felt tethered, to Argos and to Myron. And the thought of unlatching herself from either one was enough to make her unravel.

'Yes, perhaps Akrisios will change his mind.' Myron nodded, though she could see he did not believe it. A thick silence spread between them.

They lay looking up at the patch of sky, stars winking. Danae ignored the unsettled feeling in her chest and tried to find the constellations Myron had taught her. Was that the Lyre or the Herdsman?

Suddenly he spoke again.

'If you want to leave . . . if you need to leave, I'll help you. You're not alone. I just want you to know that.'

Myron's voice was uncharacteristically heavy, and he squeezed her hand once more. But Danae kept her eyes on the sky.

CHAPTER 8

Danae lay on her narrow bed, fingers linked across her belly. She watched them rise and fall as she took deep, steady breaths. She had been feeling nauseous since breakfast – perhaps the milk had been off – and though the breathing helped, sometimes it would bring a waft of the coriander jar in the corner and her stomach would roll.

She sat up, thinking it might do her good to pace a little, but just then there was a sound from the door as its bar was lifted.

Korinna entered with her supper as usual and set it down in the corner. She smiled as she stepped back, and Danae saw that the plate held a large rib of beef. It was a rare treat – there must have been a sacrifice this morning – and yet as the smell of the roasted fat reached her she was not sure she could stomach it. Korinna must have seen her reaction.

'Are you all right, mistress?'

It had been so long since Danae had heard the slave girl's voice. Perhaps Father had finally permitted her to speak, or perhaps she had simply forgotten herself in her concern.

'You look pale.'

'I'm fine,' she said. 'Though I think the milk you brought this morning was sour. I'd like figs for breakfast tomorrow.'

Korinna nodded, and stooped to pick up Danae's worn clothes for washing. She paused.

'Have you still no rags to wash?'

Danae followed her gaze to the little pile under the corner of her bed, all clean and untouched since her last bleed.

'No, I—' she began, mouth suddenly dry. 'The blood was slow this month. It only began today.'

'Ah,' said the slave girl, with a small nod. 'That explains your paleness.'

But there was a crease in her handmaid's brow that worried Danae. It was a hurried lie, and a clumsy one. Had the girl noticed? The two of them had spent enough hours together that Korinna knew her as well as anyone. 'I'm sure I'll feel better with some food.' Danae tried to force a smile but could feel her cheeks trembling. She swallowed hard. 'Korinna . . . '

But the girl was already shuffling from the chamber, arms full with wool.

'I'll bring figs tomorrow,' she said in her small voice. But as the door closed Danae caught a glimpse of her friend's worried frown, and it made her afraid.

She sat on the bed, trying to think despite the blood pounding in her ears. How long had it been? But she had already read the answer on Korinna's face. Too long by far. Had the slave girl believed her lie? Or was she on her way to Father right now to report her suspicion? Though Korinna might call her 'mistress', and though Danae might have liked to call Korinna her friend, she knew that Father was the girl's true master. It would be dangerous for her to keep Danae's secrets.

Panic was rising in Danae's chest. She looked to the patch of sky above her and wished that Myron were here, that he could tell her what to do. She put a hand to her belly, as if she might be able to feel the truth there, but in her heart she already knew it. She had been so swept up by the exhilaration of Myron's visits, so wrapped in their balm-like comfort, that she hadn't thought what she would do when the inevitable happened. How stupid she was. No, not stupid. Desperate and lonely and afraid. A part of her had known what the consequence would be, and she had done it anyway. In spite of the oracle's words and her father's fears. To spite him.

And what now? Would he expose the child? Or perhaps his patience would not stretch that far. He might simply slit her throat and be done with it. She grew cold at the thought, and her nausea rose again.

She thought of Myron's promise. He had known they would have to leave, and Danae cursed the cowardice that had held her back. But it was not too late. Myron might come tonight, and they could be out of Argos and on a ship by sunrise. But what if he did not come?

Mind racing, she reached beneath the bed frame for one of the rags. Had she been foolish to lie to Korinna? Now the girl would expect soiled wool in the morning. But then, if that lie had been enough to delay her going to Father, it might just have bought her the time she needed. If Myron could not come tonight he would surely come tomorrow. She just had to convince them until then.

Danae scanned the room, and her gaze caught on the wooden tray Korinna had brought for her supper, and on the glint of bronze upon it.

She crossed the small chamber, light-headed from the suddenness of her movement, and stooped to pick up the knife.

Only a little cut, she told herself.

Hands shaking, Danae knelt on the stone floor and pulled the cloth of her skirt up past the knee to expose her white thigh. She grasped the handle of the knife, but as she brought it towards her skin a wave of nausea rose in her throat, and she had to wait until it passed. She took a deep breath and pulled the blade across her thigh.

It didn't hurt as much as she had feared, but the red blood bloomed quickly. The sight of it brought another wave of nausea but she swallowed it down, and remembered the rag in her hand. She pressed it to her thigh. Was that enough? She tried to focus on the jagged red line but it was as if her eyes would not obey her. She dropped the knife and put a hand out to the wall to stop the room from spinning. Somewhere in the distance she could hear voices, footsteps – but it was as if her ears were stopped with wool.

Then the chamber door opened. She tried to stand, to cover her thigh, but as her father stepped through the doorway the world went black.

CHAPTER 9

Danae's eyes were still blurry when she opened them again, the covers damp with sweat. They scratched as they clung to her. Strange, she thought. They had never seemed so rough before. Nor the mattress beneath her so hard. She twisted herself in search of comfort and felt a sting on her thigh.

She sat upright, blinking in the light of the feeble lamp beside her. Yes, she remembered now. The knife. The blood. She must have been carried to her bed, she realised.

But this was not her bed. These were not the walls she had stared at for so many weeks – even the dark shape of the door was wrong. Her head snapped upwards, and she felt her heart seize. There was no hole.

Myron's face swam into her mind. How long had she been unconscious? Without the sky it was impossible to tell. She imagined his bright smile collapsing as he saw the chamber empty. He would assume the worst, she thought. Or else he would look for her. Yes, she was sure he would. She imagined him scrambling over the roofs of the Golden House, peering through every hole and window. But how could he find her here, she thought hopelessly, staring at the solid walls, the smooth ceiling. Not even she knew where she was.

She sucked in a breath, chest shaking as she realised what it meant. She would never see him again. She knew it with a dragging certainty. Her father had discovered what she herself had known too late, and there could be no going back.

Danae grieved for the love she had known, felt the loss of it claw at her. She should have gone with Myron while she had the chance. The bitterness of that thought was enough to make her choke.

She rocked back and forth on the hard bed, heart split between pain and terror. Her hand moved to her belly, not yet changed as far as she could tell and yet full with a weight that seemed to anchor her. Though she knew the life growing there was the cause of her suffering, it was an odd comfort too, to know that she was not completely alone.

Danae could not know how much time had passed. With no hole above her she could not watch the moon grow and shrink. She could not even measure the passing hours by the sun's light, so instead she measured the months by the slow swell of her belly, and the days by the meals Korinna brought her.

She knew she should not blame the girl. They were each within Father's power, and they had each done what they must to endure it. Korinna's brief visits were more precious than ever – without the sun, without Myron, without even her lyre – and though the smiles that passed between them were fractured now, Danae would not poison those moments with hostility.

She thought Korinna was late coming today, but it was impossible to tell in the unchanging gloom of her lamplit chamber. Had the sun set? Danae's stomach rumbled, and her mind drifted to the barley cakes that Myron used to bring her. Though the memory of their sweetness made her mouth water, a painful twist in her chest made her push the thought away.

Just as she was considering whether she should call to the guard for some refreshment, she heard voices beyond the wood. She thought she could make out her father's low tones, but when the door opened it was two guards who blocked the corridor's light.

'You're to come with us,' said the taller, his voice gruff and his face unreadable. Danae's heart began to beat quicker, though she did not know whether it was with fear or hope. After these long months of silence, had her father finally forgiven her? Or were they simply moving her to a new chamber? Not wanting to consider the more frightening possibilities, she hastily threw on her mantle and followed the men into the corridor.

It seemed the sun had set, for the Golden House was dark save for a few flickering torches. She wondered how late it was. They passed no servants, and she could hear no voices from the Hearth Hall, nor from anywhere else. As they stepped out into the front court, all was still.

'Father?'

She recognised his frame, though his back was to her. And as he turned, the dark look on his face made her shiver.

'Come, Danae,' he said in a flat voice, and motioned towards the wagon that stood behind him. As she followed the sweep of his hand, she spotted the other faces illuminated in the darkness. Some stood beside the wagon, some were mounted behind it, their horses' tails whisking impatiently. She recognised all of them. They were her father's most loyal men.

'Come where?' she called, trying to keep her voice steady despite her rising fear. 'I'll not go with you.' She stepped back, only to find the broad bodies of the guards behind her.

'Come,' said her father calmly. 'Or be dragged.'

His voice was so cold he barely sounded like himself, and there were shadows beneath his eyes. These months had changed him somehow, she thought, and the realisation only made her fear sharper. What might this new Akrisios do, that the old dared not? Danae felt the guards reach for her arms, but she shook them off. She sent her father a piercing look, hoping she might break through to the man she had known. But his eyes were like stones.

'Very well,' she called, louder than necessary, and was satisfied to see the flicker of concern that passed over her father's face. Why travel at this hour, unless he did not want their journey noted?

She stepped forward, and felt the guards step with her. When her father put out a grey hand to help her onto the wagon, she ignored it, instead grasping the wood with one hand and cradling her belly with the other as she pulled herself onto the high step. Her father took the seat beside her, and they both set their gazes straight ahead as the great wheels creaked into motion.

The journey was slow and dark. Everything beyond the few torches held by her father's men was cloaked in inky blackness, so that Danae had no sense of how far they had travelled or where they might be going. Her father did not speak, and the faces of the men who walked and rode beside them told her nothing, their eyes avoiding hers or staring blankly back at her.

Eventually the wagon rolled to a stop. This time Danae was forced to take her father's hand as she jumped down, and was surprised as her sandals hit the ground with an unfamiliar crunch. She peered through the darkness, trying to see something beyond the dazzle of the torches, to find some hint of where her father had taken her, but there was only the wall of men about the wagon, and the sound of the wind rustling through the trees, in slow rhythmic sighs.

No, it was not the trees. Among the sighs there was the lap of water. They were at the shore.

Before she had time to take in any more, her father was pulling her by the elbow, leading her towards the sighing waves. And then she saw the boat.

Even in the lamplight she could see that it was of a curious design, quite unlike the sleek ships she had seen painted on the walls of the Golden House or watched gliding across the horizon as she looked out from the temple crag. No, this was little more than a large wooden bowl. There was no prow, no oars, no sail – only a stack of wooden planks on the sand beside it.

Her father came to a stop and grasped her arm with hard fingers.

'You all know my daughter's crime,' he called to the torchlit faces gathered on the shore. 'Her body is proof of her pollution. We must root out this evil before all Argos becomes rotten.'

Danae stared up at her father, tongue stiff in her mouth. He spoke as if she were a disease. And what was worse, all the faces, many of whom she had known since she was a child, were nodding in agreement.

'You know too that I am a pious man,' he continued, 'and unwilling to bring further pollution to our great city by murdering a child of my own flesh. Therefore I entrust her fate, and that of the bastard child she carries, to Poseidon, Lord of the Sea. Let him wash away their evil, and leave our hands clean.'

Danae tried to move her legs to run but her father held her tight.

'Bind her,' he said.

Thick hands seized her wrists and wrenched her arms forward. The rope was coarse, scratching her skin as she struggled against it. She heard animal sounds break from her throat, like a pig squealing at the sacrifice, the desperate gasps of a creature already dead. 'No!' she screamed, finding her tongue, but the rope was already tight, her wrists fixed painfully.

She almost fell as her father pulled her towards the boat. That beautiful blue that had called to her from the hilltop now felt like the dark maw of Hades, and she tried desperately to dig her heels into the sand, but two more men gripped her arms and pushed her down into the wooden bowl. As they stood over her, she braced her bound arms across her belly, knocked in the fall, and twisted herself to find her father's eyes amid the gloom.

'Father. Please.' Her voice sounded thin and pitiful, hoarse from her cries, but his face remained unmoved. 'Do not do this.'

One of the men bent down and she realised he had picked up one of the planks from the sand. In his other hand was a hammer. The first nail was in before she could react.

'Father,' she croaked, tears blurring the torchlight surrounding her. She tried to kick the next plank away, but another man grabbed her legs.

'Tie her feet,' came her father's voice, though she had lost sight of his face. Danae struggled against the grasping hands once more, but she hadn't eaten since dawn and began to feel light-headed with the effort. By the time her ankles were bound, the top of the boat was half covered with boards.

'Akrisios!'

The shout made the men stop their work. With their attention distracted, Danae rolled over and pushed herself up by her elbows so that she could see over the edge of the boat. Her heart nearly stopped as she saw the figure approaching on his horse, surrounded by a dozen others, their spear tips glinting.

'Uncle!' Danae cried, but just as his eyes found her, Akrisios stepped between them.

'This is no business of yours, Proitos. Go back to the city.' Her father's voice was almost a growl.

'This has gone far enough, brother. Did you think you could just steal her away in the night? There are still those at Argos who care for Princess Danae, and for decency.'

'Decency?' Her father's laugh was full of scorn. 'She has a bastard in her belly. I don't know how she did it, but that whore has betrayed me and polluted our house.'

Danae felt a bitter bile rise in her throat. How could he talk of betrayal after all he had done, and all he was yet willing to do?

'Or perhaps it was a god who visited her. Such things are known.' Her uncle's horse stepped sideways and she saw his earnest expression. 'Think, Akrisios. How else could she have got with child? You have had her sealed away all this time. If mighty Zeus begot the child, will he not punish us for its death? We should raise the child in honour.'

'Why should you be so keen to defend my daughter?' asked her father sharply, taking a step forward. 'Perhaps it is you who has lain with her.'

Danae's stomach lurched and she saw Proitos recoil, his mouth hanging in disbelief.

'You bribed my guards and dishonoured my daughter in my own house. You hope the child will be your heir, is that it? You wish to usurp me.'

'Enough.' Her uncle's voice cracked a little as he spoke, his face contorted in disgust. 'This is madness, Akrisios. Don't you hear your own words? The oracle has poisoned your mind.' He kicked his horse forward, looking around at each of her father's men, their hands still full with planks and nails. 'Do not follow him. Do not pollute yourselves with the death of innocents. Help me bring the princess back to Argos.'

Danae saw the men look at one another and then to her father, who drew his sword from its scabbard.

'Come any closer and you and your men shall die.'

The men around the boat abandoned their planks and drew their weapons instead.

'I do not wish to fight you, brother,' Proitos called steadily.

'Then leave.' Even from behind she saw that her father's body was tense with energy. 'Take your men and leave Argos. The city needs but one king, and she has it. Leave, or we shall spill your blood on the sand, and then I shall return to the Golden House and sell your wife and daughters for whores.'

Danae watched her uncle's face become pale. Father could not mean it. But Proitos was watching his brother, and what he saw seemed to scare him.

'You have lost your way, brother,' he said, shaking his head. 'And I cannot help you find it.' And as his shining eyes turned to Danae, and she saw the apology written in them, she knew her cause was lost.

'I'm sorry, Danae,' he croaked. 'May the gods protect you.'

She wanted to call out, to beg him not to leave her, but her throat was choked. She could hardly breathe as she watched him turn his horse and disappear into the night.

The men continued their work as if Proitos had never come, and Danae lay helpless as the last strip of torchlight was covered over. In the utter darkness she wept, sure that her father could hear her sobs and yet knowing they would have no effect. She was no longer his daughter – she had seen that in his dark eyes, just as her uncle had. All he could see was the threat of her life-filled body, and the means by which he might be rid of it.

There was a jolt as the boat began to move, dragged over the resisting sand. Danae could hear the grunt of the men as they pushed and heaved. Then she heard the splash of their boots, and the jagged movements became suddenly smooth. She could still hear their laboured breaths over the sloshing of the waves. Was her father among them, or had he kept his own boots dry? As she heard his distant shout, she had her answer.

'That's far enough. Poseidon will take her with the tide.'

CHAPTER 10

Danae shivered in the bowl of the boat, her stomach gnawing with hunger. There was no sound save the occasional slap of wave on wood as the undulating waters rocked her stiff body back and forth. She longed to stretch out, but the boat was only small – just large enough for her folded frame. She wondered what would happen if Poseidon were to send a storm, if he whipped up the waves and let loose his torrents of rain from the heavens. She would drown, just as her father intended. It was only a matter of time.

She thought of the girl who, only months ago, had looked out from Larissa Hill and marvelled at the smooth waters. How serene they had seemed, how inviting. Now she braced herself against their ceaseless beating, terrified breaths shaking from her chest. That girl had been a fool. Twice a fool, for she could have glided safely across these waves, she and Myron together, if only she had not been so afraid. What had staying brought her? Only death, here alone on the sea she had so loved. It would drag her body down in silence.

As Danae blinked back her tears, she felt a familiar twinge and moved her bound hands down over her belly. She waited a moment, and there it was again. A kick of life.

Not quite alone, she reminded herself.

'No, I haven't forgotten about you,' she whispered.

Danae drifted in and out of sleep. Each time she awoke the light had changed – from thick darkness, to bright slivers of sunlight flashing through the boards above her head, and into darkness once more. Her mouth grew drier and drier, until she began to think that her thirst might claim her before Poseidon did.

The baby moved restlessly. Danae thought to comfort it – and herself – with a song but could push no sound through her parched throat. She tried to swallow and found it painful. In her desperation, Danae found herself begging Poseidon to send a little rain, that she could catch some as it fell through the cracks.

As if in answer, there was a peal of thunder and the lines above were lit with a brief blinding flash. She felt the boat begin to rock, gently at first and then more strongly, tilting higher and higher until she was sure it would tip. Though drops of rain spat through the wood the movement of the little boat was too violent for her to catch any, and her stomach rolled with each terrifying swing. Wrists tied, she could do nothing to stop herself from being tossed back and forth, knees cracking painfully on the side of the boat with each jolt. She tried desperately to protect her swollen belly and winced as her knuckles scraped the wood. Her chest heaved with panic.

And then the rocking stopped. She could hear the storm raging on, but it was as if the boat was frozen, mid-tilt. It seemed impossible. Danae's ragged breaths filled the small space, her hair stuck across her face with sweat and rain. Was this some trickery of the gods?

'Ho! Look there!'

She thought she had imagined it, but the voice came again.

'What's that in the net?'

Danae's heart pounded. Should she cry out? Even if she wanted to, she wasn't sure her cracked throat would allow it.

'Haul it in!' cried another voice above the howling wind, and she felt the boat begin to move. Who were these faceless voices? What would they do when they discovered her? She had heard stories of wild satyrs, half man, half beast, who preyed on women with their unbridled lust, and of unscrupulous pirates who sold their captives for gold and bronze. Danae began to shake with fear and strained at her bonds. Her raw wrists seared in protest as her panic grew.

There was a scraping sound as the wooden hull moved onto solid ground.

'What do you reckon it is, Diktys?'

'Lost cargo, maybe. Here, give me your knife.'

They didn't sound like beasts, though their accents were a little strange. Danae stopped struggling and tried to calm her breathing.

There was a cracking sound above her head as one of the boards was prised free, and in its place there appeared the windswept face of a young man. She saw his eyes widen and his hand move to clasp an amulet that hung about his neck.

'By Poseidon's dark beard.'

CHAPTER 11

Twelve Years Later

Seriphos was a rocky place. At Argos, Danae had always thought it looked as if the rocks were breaking out of the landscape, peppering the sides of hills, forming little cliffs amid the trees. Here the rocks *were* the landscape, with tufts of green clinging on where they could, finding refuge in the sheltered places where wind and sea could not strip them away. Danae found she had an affection for those stubborn little plants.

She sat in Diktys' house, as she did every day, looking out across the bay. The waves lapped lazily at the stony shore, while above them green-specked hills tapered out to sea, where the fishing boats bobbed. She could make out Diktys in his hat, casting his net wide across the sparkling water. *What will he bring back?* she wondered.

Danae looked down at her work. She had already done most of the gutting but sighed at the small basket that remained. Wiping the sweat from her forehead with the back of her arm, she brought the next fish from the pile, laid it on the stone slab, and removed its head with one efficient cut. Another flick of the knife and the belly was open. She scooped out the innards with her fingers and dumped them in the pot for later, before splaying the flesh for drying. They already had more than enough fresh fish for tonight's supper – best to save the spare for a bad season.

Diktys' house was little more than a shack. It lay just off the beach, where the sand turned to soil, a single room with thin wooden walls and no flagstones, only hard earth beneath the rough woven rugs. The air inside was always thick with smoke and the smell of half-dried fish that lined the racks along one wall. As Danae worked, she would sometimes find herself thinking of her old life in Argos, and a quiet laughter would break from her lips. What fine dresses she had worn, what fine furniture she had sat on, what fine food she had eaten. Now there was only fish and barley. And more fish, and more barley. And she cherished every bite.

After all that Danae had experienced – her lonely confinement, her violent expulsion, her terrifying journey across the sea – it had taken her a long time to adjust. Slowly, cautiously, here in this smoky hut, she had come to remember that people could be good, that they could care for others and not just for themselves. Diktys had shown her that, on the day he and his fellow fishermen had plucked her from the sea. He said that she and her child had been sent to Seriphos by the gods, that it was his sacred duty to protect them. And so he had taken her in, given her a roof over her head, food to fill her belly, and work to busy her hands.

'Look what I found, Ma.'

Danae looked up to see her son's bright face, his attention captured by the little crab held delicately between his thumb and forefinger. 'What shall we do with it?' Perseus asked, watching its spiny legs flail fruitlessly.

'He means us no harm, so we shall do none to him. Go and put him back where you found him.'

He nodded obediently, his brown curls bouncing, and ran back down the beach. As she watched him place the little creature on a seaweed-covered rock, Danae thought of how Perseus had saved her as much as Diktys. Her son had given her purpose, even in the darkest moments. His safety and happiness were the beginning and end of each day, his growing spirit a vessel into which she could pour her love. She was not sure that she could have survived all that she had without him. They had grown into this new life together.

'Should I mix the paste now, Ma?' He came inside and took his usual place on the floor beside her.

'Not until we've finished these last few. We must add their guts to the pot.'

They got on with their work in contented silence, with Danae passing the gutted fish to Perseus for the drying rack. She could feel his eyes watching her as she worked, following the bronze knife as it sliced open each glistening belly and scraped the scales like slivers of opal. She supposed her son was old enough to use the knife now, but she kept that task for herself. The blade was sharp and the fish slippery. What if he should cut himself? But there was another reason too, a brutality in putting bronze to flesh, even to flesh already dead. His young hands were too gentle for that work.

When the last fish had been added to the rack on the beach, Perseus skipped back to the house.

'Did you put in all the little ones?' Danae asked, eyeing the paste pot. There were always some fish too small for gutting, but nothing was wasted.

Perseus picked up the heavy clay pot with a proud grin, tipping it so that she could see – and smell – its contents.

'All in there,' he beamed.

'And the barley seeds? And the salt?'

He nodded. She could see that his arms were struggling, so she took the pot from him and set it down inside the entrance of the house.

'Just the vinegar, then,' she muttered, tracing her finger along the stack of jars in the corner of the room. 'Ah, here,' she said as she found it. 'Do you want to pour it in? Not too much.'

Danae was surprised she could smell anything over the fish, but the sharpness of the vinegar cut through.

'All right, now you can mash it,' she said, putting the little jar back in its place.

Preparing the fish paste was a grim job, and yet Perseus seemed to like it. Even after all these years the mixture was enough to make her stomach turn, but in time it would ripen and, used well, could make even the blandest meal tempting.

'Finished already?'

Danae looked up to see Klymene returning from her trip to the village, with lengths of flax twine in her hand.

'You're even quicker than me, Danae!' she exclaimed, looking proudly at the rows of fish laid out to dry in the sun. 'Though I bet you helped,' she added, pinching Perseus' cheek affectionately.

Perseus brushed her off, though he was grinning from ear to ear.

Danae was grateful to Klymene, as always, for the warmth she swept with her. Not every wife would have welcomed another woman into her home, nor a hungry child that wasn't her own. Her friendship had been so precious to Danae in those early years, as they raised their children together, and now she felt they were almost like sisters.

'Well, you can help me fix the nets now,' Klymene went on, holding up the new flax.

The three of them sat together on the floor of the house, tying their knots by the light of the hearth. Perseus' small fingers were well suited to the task, and Danae smiled as she watched him, brow creased in concentration. It had taken her some time to get used to island life, to learn the skills and the rhythms of an existence so bound to the whims of the sea. But for Perseus it was all he had known.

'Tell me that story again,' he said suddenly, eyes still fixed on knotting the flax. 'About how I was born.'

She felt Klymene give her a sideways look that she ignored.

'Well, my love. It was a dark and lonely night,' was how she always began. 'And cloud-gathering Zeus saw how sad I was, and he decided—'

'Why were you sad?'

'I don't remember,' she lied. 'It doesn't matter now. Zeus saw me and he came from Mount Olympos in a shower of golden rain' – she fluttered her fingers, remembering how the drops had glistened as they fell past the torchlight on the night that Myron had come to her – 'and he put you in my belly.' She had to resist tickling him at this point, as she had done when he was younger. 'And then nine months later you were born, here in this house.'

Danae had told the story so many times she almost believed it herself. It was easier than remembering the truth, in all its stinging sweetness, and dwelling on what might have been. Her life was here now, and all that had gone before was best forgotten. And yet sometimes she would catch herself watching the ships that passed on the horizon, and wondering whether Myron might be aboard one of them. She imagined his grinning face sailing across wide seas, as he had dreamed of doing. And each time a ship dropped its anchors here on their rocky shore, there was a part of her that hoped to see his lithe form appear on the gangway. She smiled sadly.

'If Zeus is my father, should I not be more . . . special?' Perseus asked, his young brow furrowed.

'You are special, my love,' she said, leaning forward and kissing his curls. 'You'll do great things, I'm sure. The world is yours if you want it.' She smiled encouragingly, but his brow remained creased as he considered her words. He looked as if he were about to say something else, but there was a change in the light, and all three of them looked up to see Diktys standing in the doorway.

'Another good catch,' he declared, his tanned arms still wet from hauling the nets. He took off his goat skin cap and bent down to kiss Klymene. 'You managed to get the flax?' he asked, though he could already see the answer, and nodded with approval.

'I had to give them the best of the morning catch, but it's good twine.' She lifted a piece of the repaired net for him to inspect, and Diktys tugged on the flax, testing its strength.

'And how have you enjoyed your day, cooped up with the women, Perseus?' he said, ruffling the boy's hair. 'Look how pale you are. If we don't get you out on the boats soon, people will think you're a maid!'

Diktys laughed, but Danae saw her son's cheeks colour as he looked down at the net in his lap. Perseus loved Diktys like a father, and his words bruised all the deeper because of it.

'He's too young for that,' she said quickly. 'And besides, he's useful here. Have you ever seen tighter knots?'

Perseus lifted his head to give her a grateful look. She knew he enjoyed their days together as much as she did.

'Phokas and Anatole are not much older, and they have been fishing with me for two summers.'

Danae tried to keep her face smooth. She was tired of this argument, but she would stand her ground as always.

'How you raise your own sons is your concern. Allow me to raise mine.'

She was worried she had spoken too sharply, for the air of the smoky house seemed suddenly cool.

Diktys sighed and shook his head. 'A boy must learn to do a man's work. Klymene tells me you won't even let him use the fish knife.' She felt her friend's apologetic glance without needing to turn her head. 'You coddle him too much, Danae. You cannot hide him under your skirts forever. If you won't put him to proper work, then I will.'

Perseus' eyes moved between the two of them, and she could see the question in them. Whom should he believe, the mother who kept him safe and happy, or the man who told him that wasn't enough? He was still only a boy. She did not want to see his gentle nature hardened, as she knew it would be once he went to work on the boats. Here in their little house she tried her best to teach her son kindness, and patience, and love. What would the men on the boats teach him? She had seen what men could do. She had to push away the memory of their blank faces, nailing board after board as she pleaded for her life. No son of hers would be so heartless. She only hoped that she could keep him with her long enough that when he entered that world – as she knew he must – his spirit would be strong enough to withstand it.

'There is work enough for him here,' she said calmly. 'And I'll let him help with the gutting, if that is what you wish.'

Diktys was quiet for a moment, looking down at the three of them on the sandy rug. Perseus' slender fingers were still gripping the net, so carefully knotted. Danae put a hand on her son's knee, but just as Diktys opened his mouth again there was a flurry of movement outside.

'We're going to the rocks,' Phokas announced, poking his head through the door of the hut. He was almost as tall as his father now, though only fourteen.

'Who's going?' Diktys asked, before the brown face could disappear again.

'Me and Anatole,' Phokas said briskly. 'And the boys from the boats. We'll be back for supper.'

Danae knew which rocks he meant. The high crags in the next bay where the boys liked to fling themselves into the water below. She had been to watch them once, with Klymene, but her heart had never left her throat.

'Take Perseus with you,' Diktys said.

Danae saw her son's head snap up, bright with interest. Before she could raise a protest, Phokas had done it for her.

'Must we?' His voice was low, as if Perseus would not hear him in that small space. 'He cried last time when he cut his knee. The boys will laugh if I bring him.'

Phokas looked pleadingly at his father, but Diktys had seen his way to win the day.

'You'll take him, or you won't go. Brothers should stick together. You'd like to go to the rocks, wouldn't you, Perseus?'

Her son nodded in reply, though he glanced uncertainly at Phokas.

'But he isn't our brother,' the older boy said. Diktys would neither speak nor hear another word. He simply watched expectantly as Phokas, cloudy-faced, led Perseus towards the group waiting on the beach. Danae felt her heart follow them, tightening as she thought of her son on the high rocks. But he had seemed pleased to go. Diktys was right about one thing – she could not keep him in her skirts forever.

CHAPTER 12

It was a bright morning, and Danae was glad for the sea breeze as they made their way along the narrow path to a wide bay further along the coast. As its rocky arms opened out ahead of them, embracing rich blue waters, Danae took a moment to savour the beauty of it before making the descent to the shore.

The beach here was broad and flat – perfect for the festival. Though they were among the first to arrive, Danae watched as more and more of the islanders emerged over the surrounding hills, each carrying something to offer the god, or to add to the communal feast.

'Diktys!'

Danae took her eyes from the hills to see the tall figure striding across the sand to meet them. He embraced Diktys in his thick arms.

She knew Polydektes, of course, though he lived on the other side of the island and rarely visited their humble hut. Diktys' brother was Lord of Seriphos – the closest thing the tiny island had to a king – and had a large house overlooking the east bay. It was nothing compared to the Golden House, but she would never say so. He was such a gracious host, and called Perseus nephew just as he did Phokas and Anatole, for which she had always been grateful.

Seriphos did not enjoy the wealth that was found on the mainland, nor were its leaders destined by blood. Polydektes had been born a fisherman's son, just like his brother. But he had a way with people, a fineness of tongue, and a stature that inspired confidence. The island had chosen him as their lord, and he served them well. In her early years on Seriphos, Danae had wondered at how Diktys could be content to see his brother so risen. She thought of her father, of her uncle, of their noxious rivalry. To see Diktys and Polydektes embrace so warmly made her smile, though there was a sadness that tugged at her too.

'Have you added your offering to the altar?' Polydektes asked once he had released Diktys from his grip. They were like stretched versions of one another, Polydektes tall and broad, Diktys narrow-shouldered and wiry. But they both had the same arched nose, the same sea-blue eyes.

'Yes,' replied the younger brother, pointing to the great stingray they had carried over the hills, adorned with bright shells Perseus had gathered.

'Excellent. May Poseidon smile upon it.' Polydektes' grin extended to each of them before resting on Perseus. 'You're getting taller, my boy. Soon I'll be looking up at you!'

Danae knew his words were meant in kindness, but she saw the pained look that crossed her son's face and it made her heart twist. Perseus had always been small for his age, and she was sure the other boys teased him for it when she was out of earshot. She tried to put an arm around his shoulder, but he shrugged it off.

'Come,' Polydektes continued, clasping his great hands together. 'We must not keep the god waiting. It's time to start the contests.'

It took some time for everyone to arrange themselves. Danae took her place among the spectators, Klymene beside her, and tried not to let her worry show. Now that the boys were all lined up, Perseus looked smaller than ever. It was the first year he had been old enough to compete, and though he had been excited these last weeks, now he looked nervous, his bare feet scuffing the sand as he watched the other boys stretching their long, tanned limbs. Suddenly Polydektes' sonorous voice broke out over the crowd.

'Lord Poseidon, earth-shaker and storm-bringer, may you enjoy these contests that we perform for you, and may you give honour to those who prove themselves worthy of it.'

Then as each of the boys stepped forward, he announced their names.

'Nikomedes, son of Meliton. Lykos, son of Heliodoros. Philo, son of Timaios . . . '

Until finally he came to her own son.

'And Perseus, son of Danae.'

There was a snigger from the crowd behind her, which stopped abruptly as Danae turned her head. But when she looked back she saw that the boys on the beach were sniggering too, with sideways looks at the cringing figure of Perseus, his red face staring at the sand. And in that moment, amid her anger at the crowd and the protective love she felt for her son, she felt a great guilt seize her chest. She wished that her love alone could be enough, but a boy needed a father too, or at least his name.

The race was about to begin, and she saw Perseus sniff as he positioned himself, knees ready to spring.

'Go!'

Clouds of sand were flicked into the air as the boys left the line. Danae willed her son on, his pale arms pumping hard, but the long strides of the older boys soon left him behind. By the time he was rounding the rock to start the return leg, the leader was already celebrating his victory.

Next came the throwing of the spears. One by one the shafts streaked across the sky, disappearing into the brightness of the sun and back down into the sand. But when Perseus' turn came he mis-timed his throw, and the pointed spear went skittering across the beach. Danae held her breath for the painful laughter of the crowd, but instead there was only an embarrassed silence, as brows were creased and heads shaken. Perseus' shoulders slumped, as if he wanted to fold into himself. How she longed to run across the sand and hold him, but she knew it would only make his shame worse.

Finally there came the wrestling, and Danae was relieved to see that Perseus had been paired with Anatole. Diktys' son was only a year older, and the two of them had had their fair share of scuffles growing up. This was no different, she told herself. But as the match went on, and on, neither boy would concede. She could see that Perseus was exhausted, his arms trembling as they grappled one another, but his red face was set hard with determination. Then suddenly Anatole lost his footing on the shifting sand and Perseus was on top of him. The crowd cheered as he pinned his opponent, and Perseus was declared the winner. Danae saw her son's look of surprise as Polydektes came to congratulate him, and a shy smile spread across his shining face. He helped Anatole up from the sand, and the two of them went to join the rest of the competitors, gathered beside the altar now that all the matches were complete.

'A fine display,' declared Polydektes, as the crowd quietened down. 'And now, which of our glorious victors shall make the sacrifice?'

A channel was cleared through the crowd as a white goat kid was led by a thin rope around its neck. It looked around at the watching faces and roved its lips over the sand in search of any green morsels that might have pushed through. Danae saw her son following the goat's movements, smiling as it flicked its tail. When she looked up she saw that Diktys was watching Perseus too. Then his glinting eyes met hers and before she understood the meaning in them he was speaking into his brother's ear.

'Perseus,' Polydektes called. 'You shall have this honour.'

He spoke warmly, as if it were a gift, and yet Danae saw her son's face grow pale. He looked from Polydektes to the goat to Diktys.

Danae pushed her way to the front of the crowd.

'A generous suggestion,' she began, 'but perhaps one of the older boys—'

'Perseus has proven himself in the wrestling,' Diktys interrupted, taking a bronze knife from his belt and pressing the hilt into Perseus' palm. 'Every boy must draw his first blood.'

All eyes were on her son, as Diktys and Polydektes urged him on with encouraging smiles. The goat was led forward and Perseus gripped the knife with white fingers.

'One clean cut. That's all it is,' Danae heard Diktys murmur, as he put a hand on her son's trembling shoulder.

Perseus shot her a pleading glance, but she could say nothing more. Diktys knew she could not object to sacred rites. So she pursed her lips.

It was as if the whole beach were holding its breath. Perseus moved the blade closer, and Diktys held the creature still as it sniffed her son's hand. She saw him hesitate, arm shaking, as he looked into those curious amber eyes. His neck twisted round to Diktys.

'Phokas could do it,' she saw him whisper.

But Diktys tightened his grip on her son's shoulder. 'The sacrifice is yours. Come, I know you have the strength. A man takes what is his.' He guided Perseus' trembling arm back towards the goat, and a little of Diktys' certainty seemed to flow into her son's young body. He braced himself, teeth gritted, and drew the bronze across that white throat. Danae saw Perseus' face spread in horror as the hot blood gushed over his hand, but if either he or the creature cried out, she could not hear it over the cheer that erupted from the crowd. His glazed eyes were still fixed on the blood, but as Diktys clapped him on the back he seemed to come back to himself. As more and more hands patted their congratulations, she watched his terrified grimace melt away to be replaced first by a tentative smile, and then a full one.

By the time Perseus had made his way over to her, he was beaming.

'Did you see, Ma?'

'Yes, I saw,' Danae said weakly. The sight of his bloody hands made her feel ill, but she was saved from speaking further as Diktys strode towards them and put an arm around her son's narrow shoulders.

'We'll make a man of you yet!' he cried boisterously, as Perseus grinned up at him. 'Why don't you come spear fishing with me tomorrow? I'll bet you're a natural with those quick hands.' He squeezed Perseus tightly, and though Diktys' eyes met hers for a second, they were gone again before she could interject.

'Can I, Ma?' Perseus asked, his face bright and pleading.

'I . . . ' Danae's mouth hung open, but what could she say? Refuse and earn his resentment? She saw now that he was so desperate to prove himself.

'It'll do him good, Danae,' said Diktys in a low voice. 'You know I care for the boy. Let me help him.'

She looked into those well-meaning eyes, and felt her anger of a few moments ago sink.

'All right,' she sighed, turning to Perseus. 'As long as you're careful. And you must do as Diktys tells you.' But even as she said it and watched the excitement spread across her son's flushed face, her gaze fell again to the blood already turning black on his pale hands. Suddenly the words of the oracle whispered in the back of her mind, words she had tried so hard to bury and deny. They belonged to another life. And yet to see her son smile so broadly, still trembling from the violence he had done, made her skin prickle with fear.

Perseus rejoined the crowd, pulled into it by Diktys and the praising hands and mouths that had disdained him only moments ago. Was this what it took to gain their approval? A sharp knife and a bloody hand? But to see her son embraced by these people who had looked down upon him, laughed at him because of her, was a relief of sorts. She could not take that from him, not when he was without so much already. What was a little blood, if it bought him acceptance, pride – all the things she could not give him? That was what she told herself as she watched Perseus' beaming face. And yet she knew the true price was higher. It was innocence. It was gentleness. It was a son of her making for one of theirs.

CHAPTER 13

Six Years Later

There was a light rain in the air, as fine as ocean spray, which felt appropriate to Danae as they laid their gifts in the grave. She had gathered some of the bright yellow flowers that grew among the rocks and now laid them softly beside the gleaming triton shell Perseus had found. Finally, Klymene, eyes full and shining, laid her husband's fishing spear alongside his body.

Danae tried to avoid looking at the wound on his leg. Even now, with Diktys cold in his grave, it remained a sickening puce colour. He had brushed it off at first – a shallow cut soon healed in the briny waters. But then it had grown more painful, the skin around it hot and tight, and Diktys had become sicker and sicker until his eyes rolled in his head and then stopped altogether.

Danae could see Klymene shaking, her thin body racked by each violent sob, as beside her Phokas and Anatole lifted the cap stone. Perseus moved to help them, but Phokas shook his head. Diktys was their father, not his. He must let them do their duty.

With the stone laid down the brothers led their mother back down to the shore, and Danae followed with her own son. Perseus had not wept since Diktys' passing – not that she had seen, in any case. Deep furrows lined his young face and she worried for the pain he held inside, for the loss she knew he must feel. And she worried for herself too. What would they do now? It was Diktys who had taken her in all those years ago, who had shared his home and his family. But this was not her family. Nor was it her home. What had once belonged to Diktys now belonged to his sons. And it was their choice whether they should also inherit the burden of their father's charity.

'Danae,' came a soft voice from behind her. She looked back to see Polydektes stopped on the path. His figure, usually so imposing, seemed shrunken in its grief.

'Will you walk with me?' he asked, his tone sombre.

Perseus had stopped as well, but she nodded for him to go ahead. With a frown he obeyed, though she saw him look back once or twice as he went.

Polydektes extended a steadying arm, which she gratefully took, and the two of them resumed their slow descent of the pebble-strewn path, now slick with the insipid rain.

'I don't want you to worry, Danae,' he said, keeping his voice low. 'I see your fear, now that Diktys is gone.'

Danae was quiet.

'He was very kind to us,' she said eventually.

'I regret I did not have the chance to speak with my brother before the fever took him. But if I had, I know he would have asked me to take care of you, and your son. Please, Danae.' He squeezed her hand and looked across at her so that their eyes met. 'If you find yourself in need, you must come to me. I would not see you suffer.'

Danae held her tongue once more, unsure what shapes to form with it. She felt a hopeful relief rise in her chest and pushed it down, not wanting to overtake his meaning. Polydektes' words were meant as a comfort, but she knew they might only be that – words. He had the whole island to be concerned with. What were the fortunes of one outsider and her bastard? So she nodded awkwardly, and they continued their descent towards the beach.

That evening, once Polydektes and the other mourners had returned to their homes, Danae sat by the hearth. She had gone early this morning to trade the last of their ripened fish paste for a jar of wine – something she had rarely tasted during her years on the island. Phokas poured a cup for each of them, and one for the Thirsty Ones below.

'May you treat my father kindly,' he said, pouring the dark liquid onto the earthen floor.

Danae watched it sink in, and cradled her cup in silence. The hut felt different without Diktys' spirit to fill it. He had imbued their humble home with a kind of vitality, a living texture that flowed between the wooden walls and the sandy rugs and the ever-burning hearth, binding it all together, just as he bound them to one another. Now, despite the figures huddled in the flickering light, their shadows looming large in that cramped space, the hut felt strangely empty. The bare racks along the wall, that had once held so much fish, scared Danae now in a way they never had while Diktys lived.

She had seen Phokas watching her at the funeral, and felt his eyes upon her now. She looked up to meet them, and saw that his young wife was watching her too. Their son, only born last month, squirmed in his mother's arms, and she put her little finger in his mouth to stop him crying. Danae smiled at this vision of new life, remembering when her own son had been small enough to hold in one arm, but the faces that looked back at her were stony.

Perhaps Klymene sensed the tension filling the little house, for it was she who broke the silence.

'I go to my sister's tomorrow,' she announced, her voice hoarse.

Danae's head snapped round to look at her friend, her stomach sinking.

'For how long?'

'A season at least, maybe longer. Her husband's flock thrives. And they have fewer mouths to feed.' Klymene glanced around at the figures sitting in the hearth light, and then down at her lap. Danae expected one of her sons to raise his voice in objection, but they only nodded.

'You can't leave,' she said weakly. It sounded childish out loud, but she had to speak. Danae could feel the world she knew falling away beneath her. After so long on solid ground, it was happening again.

'She does what she must,' said Phokas, his voice quiet but solid. 'Poseidon has turned against us. The winter was harsh enough, but even now with spring coming the fish evade our nets. What little we can catch will only go so far.' He put his arm around his wife and glanced across at his brother, Anatole, before settling his eyes on Danae once more. There was a meaningfulness in his gaze that made her uncomfortable.

'If Diktys were here—'

'He is not,' said Phokas sharply.

'Watch your tone,' snapped Perseus. She felt his body bristle beside her, like a crackle of lightning in the brewing storm. Phokas leant forward, his gaze shifting to her son.

'Please. Enough,' came Klymene's weary voice. Her eyes were still red from weeping. 'It is a difficult time for us all. Phokas only means that we ought each to look to ourselves.'

'He means to drive my mother out,' growled Perseus. 'After all she has done for this family.'

'After all we have done for her,' shot Phokas, looking to his brother for support.

'If she leaves, so do I,' said Perseus. 'You need me to bring in the fish.'

'What fish?' asked Anatole, his voice softer than his brother's, but his gaze as firm. 'More hands just means more mouths. And we have Demetria for the nets and the gutting.'

Danae looked over at the girl, sitting silently beside her husband, her arms full with Phokas' firstborn. She would not get a moment's rest, poor thing, but at least her child would not go hungry. That babe was Phokas' blood, just as he and Anatole were Diktys' blood. It was a bond thicker than friendship or affection, thicker than eighteen years in a cramped hut. Such distinctions mattered less in times of plenty – they could almost have been forgotten. But things were different now.

'They're right,' Danae sighed, putting a hand on Perseus' arm. 'Diktys was kind to us, but we are not their kin. We must find our own way if we can.'

She tried to keep the fear from her voice. What way could there be? She could still feel her son's muscle tense beneath her fingers, but eventually it relaxed. Her words had cleared the storm, for now. Phokas looked satisfied, Anatole apologetic, Klymene numb, while Demetria's tired eyes looked between them all as she rocked her son close to her breast.

CHAPTER 14

Danae didn't sleep, but watched the embers glow and listened to the hushing waves. Before rosy-fingered Dawn had begun to spread her light, she knew what she must do.

She dressed quietly, into a simple woollen chiton – the finer of the two she owned – and slipped her feet into the well-worn moulds of her sandals. Even the babe was still sleeping soundly when she left.

The sky grew gradually lighter as she made her way along the coast path. Perhaps the journey would be shorter if she went inland, but she wasn't sure of the way, so instead she travelled above the rocky bays, looking down at each one as she went. She hadn't visited Polydektes' house in some time, but she remembered walking this path with Diktys, in happier times when Perseus skipped alongside her and Klymene fussed over her sons' mucky faces and uncombed hair. They had felt like a family then.

She had been walking for some time when a movement caught her eye. In the bay below her she saw two women, their hair and clothes as grey as the rocks they stood upon. Danae watched as they stooped to prise crusty limpets from the sea-beaten stone, before shuffling on and stooping again. The bags slung over their sagging shoulders were half full already, but Danae wondered how much of a meal the tiny creatures would make.

She had seen such women before. 'Kinless', Diktys had called them. Childless widows with no one to care for them. She had pitied them then, but now the sight of their hunched figures made her shiver with fear. She quickened her pace.

The sun was climbing the sky when she finally came in sight of Polydektes' house. It had two floors – a rarity on Seriphos

– and plastered white walls, making it impossible to miss amid the grey-brown landscape. As she approached she wiped her brow on her sleeve and tried to neaten her hair, swept wild by the journey. She calmed her breathing and set her expression steady. She had not come seeking pity from the Lord of Seriphos, only his help.

He must have seen her coming along the path, for he was at the entrance when she arrived.

'Danae,' he said warmly, gathering her hands in his. 'I did not expect you. I hope all is well?'

His eyes searched hers, and the concern Danae saw in them summoned the emotion she had been trying so hard to suppress. She swallowed the lump that rose in her throat.

'I . . . ah . . . I need to speak with you. May we sit?'

Polydektes gestured to a bench of stone.

'I had hoped not to need your help so soon,' she began, 'but you said that I should come to you.'

'What has happened?' His eyes were so similar to Diktys' that she found it difficult to return his gaze.

'Perseus and I are no longer welcome at the house,' she sighed. 'It's no fault of the boys,' she added hurriedly, seeing his brow harden. 'They are only protecting their family, and I must do the same for mine. I thought you might know of something . . . a boat in need of hands, a house unoccupied. I can gut fish and mend nets and spin wool, and Perseus is young and strong.'

She hoped she did not look too desperate as she gazed up at him. He wore a strange expression.

'Danae,' he said softly. 'I thought that you understood my meaning when I said that I would take care of you.' He took her hands in his once more. 'You must know that I have always admired you. When my brother plucked you from the sea I thought him the luckiest man on Seriphos. But he had his wife and I had mine. And now . . . '

Danae felt her mouth grow dry. Of all the things she had imagined he might say, of all the ways she had rehearsed this conversation on her long walk across the island, she had not anticipated this. She realised her palms were sweating and wondered if he could feel it.

'It has been more than a year since Melantha's passing, and I have no children living.' He leant closer. 'I would have you as my wife, Danae. To share my home and bear my children. You would want for nothing that the island can provide. And these fair hands need never gut fish again.'

He held her fingers and looked as if he might kiss them, but she drew them away.

'You cannot want me,' she said incredulously. She was past thirty-five, and tainted with another man's bastard. She loved Perseus more than her own life, but she had known from the moment she had washed up on Seriphos' rocky shore, her belly already big with foreign seed, that no man on the island would take her for his wife. And she had accepted her fate, grateful for the brief love she had known, and knowing that she would never be truly alone as long as she had her son.

'What of Perseus?' she heard herself asking.

'He would be as my own son,' said Polydektes, his expression sincere. 'He is a fine boy. Diktys tried to be a father to him. Let me do the same.'

Her head was spinning as she tried to take in what he was saying. She felt dizzy with the new visions he was offering, of a future she had never imagined, and yet at the same time she felt as if a comforting steadiness were coming to embrace her, reaching out with arms strong enough to bear all the weight she bore, if she would only let herself fall into them.

'May I have some time?'

Polydektes looked a little disappointed, but he nodded. 'Of course. Consider my proposal and give me your answer when you have it.' He paused, as if an idea had struck him. 'Will you dine with me tomorrow evening? You can bring Perseus as well. Please, Danae. Do me this honour.'

She smiled graciously. 'The honour would be ours.'

His tanned face beamed, and he clapped his hands together.

'Excellent. Excellent. And will you take some refreshment now, before you go?'

'Only some water,' she said with a grateful inclination of her head. 'I must get back before my son begins to worry.'

The journey back was only as far as the one she had taken that morning, but somehow it seemed longer, her mind distracted as it wandered far beyond the little track she followed.

She, a wife. There was a time when she had longed for it, and a time when she had been glad to be free of that burden. And now? She remembered the women she had seen that morning, picking their way across the rocks, wrinkled hands clasping blunt knives. Was that where her path would lead, without a husband to pluck her from it? No. She had Perseus. He would never abandon her to such a fate. But then she thought of Klymene, perhaps at this very moment making her way to her sister's house. Her sons were beginning their own lives, with their own wives and their own children. What would her place be, once Perseus was grown and had no more need of her? That time might come sooner than she imagined; by the summer he would be eighteen. Or what if something should happen to him? She rubbed the amulet she wore around her neck – a polished piece of stone in the rough shape of an eye – and thought of Diktys lying in his grave. A week ago he had been in full vigour. And unlike Klymene she had no sister to go to. No mother, no father, no cousin, no uncle. All she had here on Seriphos was what she could make for herself.

Danae found her pace quickening, as if spurred with new purpose. As she neared home she saw Perseus on the path ahead, charging towards her.

'Where have you been?' he demanded when they drew close, though he looked more worried than angry. 'You were gone half the day. Klymene has already left.'

A part of Danae sank, wondering when she would see her friend again.

'I went to Polydektes,' she said, struggling to meet her son's eye. 'I thought he could help us find new occupation.'

'And did he?'

Danae hesitated, but she knew she could not keep the truth from her son.

'He asked me to be his wife.' Even now the words sounded absurd.

Perseus' mouth gaped in confusion, but then his face darkened.

'He asked *you*?' A deep furrow grew on his brow. 'Should he not have come to me, as your guardian?'

Danae was surprised by his response. She supposed that Diktys had been her guardian all these years – she had lived under his roof, and he had treated her as family. With no father or husband, who else would have claimed that role? Even on little Seriphos a woman needed a man, a relative, to manage her property and arrange her marriage. But as Danae had no property, and as no one had previously shown any interest in marrying her, the matter of her guardianship had not been spoken of. And now? Should she truly be put into the hands of her son, when he was still a boy and she a woman grown?

'I'm sure Polydektes did not mean any disrespect,' she said. 'It is done now. The proposal has been made and we must decide how to answer. He has invited us to dine with him tomorrow evening. He seeks your approval as much as mine,' she added, though Polydektes had not said so.

'I will not give it,' said Perseus bluntly. 'There is no need for you to marry. I can provide for the both of us.'

'How? Where? We have no home and no boat. No family to support us. We should not dismiss what help the gods have provided.'

He clasped Danae by the shoulders.

'Have you not said that I am special, that I was born for greatness? I grew from the seed of mighty Zeus himself, did I not? If I cannot care for you, no one can.' He shook his head. 'I will not see you whore yourself to Polydektes.'

'Whore myself?' She twisted out of his hands. 'Marriage to Polydektes will give us respectability. No one will look down at you then.'

She saw a crack in his conviction, a flicker of fragility, quickly covered over as he raised himself to his full height – still no higher than her own.

'They look down because they know they should look up,' he said, setting his chin hard. 'They know I am more than they will ever be.'

'They look down because they know the truth,' said Danae softly. She took his hands in hers, meeting his eyes though they tried to look in every other direction. 'And you should know it too.' She felt him pull away but kept his hands wrapped tight in hers. 'You are too old for showers of gold.'

It was painful for Danae to remember the past, to think of her life before Seriphos and the events that had led her here. But she had spent eighteen years protecting herself from those memories. The child who had come with her across the terrifying sea was almost a man now. It wasn't fair for her to keep those things from him, for others to understand more of him than he did himself. So she set her pain aside for the truth that was rightfully his, and told her son the story of how he had come to be. She told him about Argos, about Akrisios, about the terrible oracle and the boy who had made her fate bearable, for a time. And he listened to it all, reluctantly at first, and then with a hunger she did not expect, drinking in every piece of the identity he had been without all these years. Danae's chest was heavy as she spoke, and yet somehow the memories became lighter in the telling. Now they were not only her history, but his too.

When the story was told Perseus sat down on a large rock beside the path, as if burdened by the weight of all he had heard. Danae perched next to him, watching his young face as it stared at the dirt.

'Did everyone know? Everyone but me?' he asked quietly.

'No. No, I only ever told Diktys and Klymene. It went no farther than them, as far as I know. But the others guessed enough. The fishermen – they saw my swollen belly when I arrived. And I never spoke of a husband, so they assumed that you were—'

'A bastard.'

His voice was bitter, and Danae stretched out a hand, hoping to absorb some of the pain she saw on his face. She had never told him otherwise, but she supposed being the bastard of a god was more palatable.

'I thought that I was special. The son of Zeus. You told me so.' There was an edge of accusation in his voice.

'This doesn't change who you are, Perseus. You are still *my* son. You are sweet and strong and—'

'It changes everything.' He was silent for a moment, his mind folded inward. Then his knotted brow seemed to shift. 'I could be a king, instead of hauling empty nets,' he said bitterly. 'I *should* be a king. Isn't that what the oracle meant? As Kronos overthrew his sire, and Zeus bested his. Young blood overthrows old, to take its rightful place. Isn't that what the gods teach us?'

His eyes were brighter now, but that only scared her. She tried to take his hand again but he rose suddenly from the rock, pacing back and forth.

'Akrisios deserves it, for what he did. And the oracle said that it would be so. He took my life from me, the life I should have had.

He wanted me dead, even though I was his kin. And that boy, my father. He left us. He should have saved us and he didn't. All this time I thought we had no family, but now I know they didn't want us. They didn't want me.'

His young face was twisted, eyes pressed shut.

'Myron could not have helped us. He never knew you existed. Or if he did it was already too late.'

But she was not sure he could hear her. His face was red, his whole body vibrating with what he had learned and all that it meant. Danae rose and stepped towards him softly, as one might approach a stamping bullock. He tensed as she touched his shoulder.

'Blood is not everything,' she said gently. 'Diktys took us into his home and you were as precious to him as his own sons.'

'And now he has left me too.'

He barely got the words out before his voice broke, and Danae's heart ached as she felt his shoulders quiver and he pulled himself away from her.

'I'm sorry,' she said. 'I'm sorry to have told you this tale and made it yours. But it is important that you know. Polydektes' offer is more than we could ever have hoped for, given our circumstance.'

Suddenly his body changed, no longer trembling but taut. He turned towards her, eyes filled with tears and yet set hard.

'We don't need Polydektes,' he croaked. 'We need nothing more than each other. I will look after you myself, or else we should return to Argos and reclaim our inheritance as the Pythia foretold.'

'The oracle promised no inheritance, only death. Our lives, our futures, are here on this island. We must make the best of it.'

But as Danae observed the flush of his face and the tension in his jaw, she knew that this was no time to argue. Perseus was upset by the truths she had told him. He spoke of Argos as if he might simply reach out and take it, and win all that he had been without. But her son was no killer – he knew it as well as she did, in his heart. And she had no intention of going back to that place.

For eighteen years she had put those memories far from her mind, and denied that the Pythia's words had ever been spoken. It had been easy here on Seriphos, where they seemed to mean so little. But now a tight feeling began to close around her chest. Had she made those words more real by speaking them to her son? Perhaps she should have left that part silent, but it was such a tangled thing, her history and his. How could she give him a piece of it and not the whole?

As she lay awake that evening, twisting under her blanket, Danae fought to push her fears down. She missed Klymene and Diktys. She mourned for the simple days they had spent together. But she could not dwell on the past, whether sweet or painful. Tomorrow they would dine with Polydektes. Tomorrow Perseus would remember that he was loved and wanted, and Danae would build herself a new life once again.

CHAPTER 15

It took some persuading for Perseus to join her on the long walk across the island, but once he realised that she would be going with or without him there was no more argument.

The sun was low in the sky by the time they reached Polydektes' door, left wide open for their arrival. The Lord of Seriphos emerged in spectacular raiment – a floor-length mantle sewn with golden sequins, a tunic dyed with purple murex. Danae pulled at the cloth of her shapeless dress, not dyed at all, but Polydektes looked as delighted to see her as if she had been wearing the ambrosial robe of Hera herself.

'I'm so glad you have come,' he said, opening his arms wide to them both.

Danae could feel Perseus stiffen beside her. He had barely spoken during the journey here.

'We are grateful for the invitation,' she said warmly, putting a hand on her son's arm as if to include him in her thanks. But he stood silent, regarding their host through narrowed eyes.

'Come, the food is almost prepared,' continued Polydektes, oblivious to that intense gaze, or choosing to ignore it. 'You will want some wine after your journey.'

The dining chamber was the size of Diktys' house, with walls richly painted. Danae took in their vibrant shapes – plants and animals flowing around the room – and felt suddenly homesick, remembering the painted patterns of the Golden House.

As soon as they were seated the wine was brought and Danae cradled her cup with tense fingers, breathing in the fragrant herbs. She could feel Perseus' sullen presence beside her, sweeping his disinterested gaze around the walls. She smiled politely at their host.

'Your home is as lovely as ever,' she began.

But just as Polydektes returned her smile, Perseus cut in.

'Did you know that my grandfather is King of Argos?' he said, swilling his cup lazily with one hand. 'His halls must be much grander than this.'

Danae froze, unable to look at Polydektes' reaction.

'King of Argos? I had no idea.' His tone was light, curious, and Danae felt his eyes upon her. 'Your mother is full of secrets, and I hope to learn them all, in time.'

She looked up to see his lips curl graciously, and she thanked him with a silent nod that he pressed no further. No doubt Perseus had hoped to follow his insult with a reminder of what Polydektes already knew, that she had come to Seriphos as an unwed mother, and an exile. If Polydektes was concerned with such things he would never have made his proposal, but Perseus was testing him.

'How did your wife die?'

'Perseus!'

Her son's tone had a callousness that shamed her, and she shot him a reproachful look, but he did not turn his head to meet it. He was watching Polydektes over his wine cup.

'Melantha died in childbed,' said their host, a sadness passing over his face.

'And the child?' asked Perseus.

'She lived,' said Polydektes stiffly. 'But only until the winter sickness took her.'

Danae wished she could extend a hand of comfort, but the table between them was broad, and she did not want to agitate her son further.

'It seems the gods do not favour this house,' said Perseus, with what might have been sympathy but sounded more like spite. 'And when my mother dies, will you marry again?'

'Enough, Perseus,' Danae snapped. She had been wrong to bring him here, so soon after yesterday's revelations. His whole bearing seemed changed somehow, spreading into his chair as if he were already imagining himself upon his grandfather's throne. She had seen him angry before, had seen him hurt, defensive, but this new cruelty was something that worried her.

'You have told him of my proposal?' Polydektes asked.

Danae nodded, almost apologetically. How could she not? And yet, had she known he would react this way she might have held her tongue.

'Should your mother agree to marry me, I would do everything to ensure that—'

'It is my agreement you should be seeking,' Perseus interrupted. 'As her guardian.'

He pinned Polydektes with a challenging gaze, which was met with equal intensity. Danae looked between them, wondering which would look away first, but as the food was brought in, the clatter of dishes on wood severed the tension.

Danae could see that Polydektes was aiming to impress. Bowl after bowl filled the space between them, their warm aromas making her mouth water. There was a steaming lamb stew, a whole roasted rabbit, parsnips with cumin, broad beans with capers, plump prunes, pickled olives, honeyed chestnuts. After weeks of stretching out their meagre catches, Danae knew that Perseus must be as ravenous as she, and yet she could see him feigning disinterest.

Thankfully the meal was enjoyed – by Danae and their host at least – without further incident. Their talk moved away from the subject of marriage, on to the affairs of the island, the preparations for the spring festival, and memories of Diktys. Perseus remained quiet, pushing the delicious morsels around his plate as if they were barley gruel. His venom seemed to have run dry, having gained no reaction from Polydektes. Or perhaps her son had been humbled by the sumptuous array, knowing that for all his talk of providing for her, he was far from being able to. Danae did not want him to feel so. She knew that all he wanted was to take care of her. But the world was bigger than just the two of them.

With the meal finished and Danae's belly fuller than it had been all winter, Polydektes poured them each another cup of wine.

'I've had the guest chambers prepared for you,' he announced casually.

'Guest chambers?' Perseus suddenly sat upright. 'We are not staying here. We'll return to our house.'

'The sky is black,' said Polydektes. 'You cannot cross the island at this hour.' He looked at Danae expectantly.

'He's right,' she said, putting a gentle hand on top of her son's. 'It is too late to go back.'

'We'll take a torch.'

'It would not last the journey. And in any case,' she said, turning to their host, 'we should be grateful for the hospitality.'

'My home is yours for as long as you would have it,' said Polydektes warmly, though she could see he was still watching Perseus with a wary eye.

Her son paused, his hands clenched.

'We need only one chamber,' he said eventually. 'My mother's honour must be protected.'

'Of course,' said Polydektes seriously. 'On that we are agreed.'

Perhaps Perseus was disappointed by Polydektes' calm assent, for his fists seemed to clench tighter. If their host was vexed by the insinuation, he did not show it. His broad face was like the still surface of his wine cup, while Perseus' began to match its dark colour. It was like watching a cub spar with a lion.

CHAPTER 16

They stayed with Polydektes the next three nights, despite Perseus' protests. He could not drag his mother back across the island, nor would he leave her there alone. So they stayed. But although Danae had won a victory of sorts, Perseus would not give up the battle and made full use of the greatest weapon at his disposal: his presence.

Wherever Danae was, there he was too. If Polydektes asked her to go for a walk with him, Perseus insisted on coming along and would follow them like a shadow. At dinner he would interrupt their conversations, or make them icy with some impolite comment. And yet despite this Danae felt as if she was getting to know the man who might be her husband. He had a steady confidence she found appealing, an ease of character that came from the comfort in which he lived. And yet he did not hold himself above the people of Seriphos but with them, for them. He arranged their festivals, promoted their trade, settled their disputes, welcomed their children and honoured their dead. And of course he gained a share of the island's prosperity in return. There was little that happened on Seriphos without his agreement, and yet now it was he who must gain approval. Danae suspected he was not used to the feeling.

Though he masked his frustration well, Danae could feel a tension growing, like a bowstring pulled gradually tighter. Polydektes' smiles had grown stiffer, his responses to Perseus' goading questions more terse. Danae was afraid that he would give up his suit altogether, just as Perseus no doubt intended.

She had tried to excuse her son, to herself at least. He was still a boy, she told herself, and he felt slighted by Polydektes, who had treated him as such. He was afraid to lose her, like all those other people who had left him, rejected him, abandoned him. He was still grieving the loss of Diktys, the only father he had known, and was not ready to accept another. He was adjusting to a new sense of himself too, shaped by the truths she had put upon him.

Danae knew all this. And yet she also knew that if he succeeded in pushing Polydektes away, if they were forced into poverty and isolation and dishonour, her love for her son would always be bound up with a bitter resentment, eating at her heart like a maggot. She feared that future most of all.

On the third morning she woke early. The chamber was still dark, with Perseus snoring on the floor beside her bed. With silent feet she stepped around him and threw on one of the dresses Polydektes had given her – the wool a vibrant red, soft against her skin. Checking to see that Perseus' eyes were still closed, she opened the chamber door and stepped out into the central court. With dawn barely broken it was not much lighter outside, but she was glad to breathe the cool air. It felt like an escape of sorts, to be out here alone. Perseus had not left her side since their journey across the island, and now she knew she must not waste her opportunity.

She crossed the courtyard and rapped gently on the door of Polydektes' chamber. Silence followed, but just as she was about to walk away the door opened.

'Danae? What is it? Are you well?'

His eyes were bleary, his broad chest bare. She stepped back, suddenly embarrassed.

'Oh. Yes, everything's fine. I . . . I just wondered if we could talk. Alone.' She gave an awkward smile and saw him look out into the courtyard behind her. He blinked sleepily, but then understanding seemed to spread across his face, and it brightened.

'Yes. Yes, of course. Give me one moment.'

The door closed softly and she waited, listening as the first birds began to twitter. A moment later Polydektes appeared, fully clothed.

'Lead on,' he said, his voice barely more than a whisper, and extended an elbow for her to hold. She placed her fingers lightly upon the cloth of his sleeve and they left the courtyard, out onto the path overlooking the bay.

'I'm sorry for how Perseus has behaved,' she began. 'I did not expect him to react this poorly. And you have been so kind to us.'

'He is young,' said Polydektes simply. 'He wants to be treated as a man but does not know how to act as one.'

'He grieves for Diktys,' she added.

'Perhaps,' was Polydektes' reply. 'Though I think that, even if my brother were yet living, your son would object to anything that took you from him, or he from you.'

Danae was silent.

'Perseus has always been at your skirts, Danae,' he said quietly, glancing across at her. 'Diktys tried to make him a man, to give him strength and courage and pride. But while he clings to you he will only ever be a boy.'

She met his gaze. Was it true? She knew her son better than anyone, but perhaps she had been too close, all these years, to see how she was stifling him. An uncomfortable feeling rose in her chest.

'I have only tried to be a good mother,' she said, her throat suddenly tight. 'To raise him with love.'

'Of course, of course,' said Polydektes softly, stopping to gather her hands. 'You have done admirably. He's a fine boy, a fine boy.' He squeezed his warm fingers around hers, his sea-blue eyes catching the first rays of the morning sun. 'But a boy needs more than his mother's love if he is to become a man. He must prove himself, discover himself. He must meet with his own challenges and defeat them.'

Danae regarded him, taking in his steady expression. He spoke with such surety. And perhaps he was right. After all, what did she know of manhood? Diktys had told her much the same, and though she had been afraid to send her son out with the fishermen, she could not deny that he had grown stronger from the experience, not only in body but in spirit. He had a boldness now that she could never have taught him.

'What do you propose?' she asked.

'If he were my son –' he looked at her seriously and then turned his gaze towards the bay below – 'if I really wanted to build his character, I would put him on a merchant ship. Let him make his own way for a while, let him see more than this craggy island.'

'You mean send him away?' she asked, as her cheeks dropped.

'Only for a season. A few months, a year at most.'

'A year? I have not been without him a day since he was born, nor he without me.' Already she could feel a rope pulling at her chest.

'But don't you see that's the problem?' said Polydektes, locking his eyes with hers once more. 'While you are together, neither can grow. He needs to begin his life so that you can live yours.'

She took a step back, understanding his true meaning.

'I will not send my son away so that we can marry. I respect you greatly, and I am grateful for all that you offer, but you must know that I will place my son's interests above my own.'

'No, no. That is not my intention. It is for the boy's own good.'

'I cannot send him away. So soon after losing Diktys . . . He is fragile.'

'That is why you must do it. A few months on the sea will strengthen his spirit, toughen him up. He will leave a boy and come back a man, and he will thank you for it.' He paused, stepping towards her and taking her hands once more. 'I know you are afraid for him. I can ensure he sails with an experienced crew. I will tell them he is my own son and ask them to look after him. I care for Perseus as I care for you. I only want what is best for him, for all of us.'

Polydektes was right on one account. She was afraid. That wide sea still held a terror for Danae. She still awoke sweating in the night, from dreams where she was tossed back and forth by the rolling waves, the rain pouring through the cracks above her, filling the boat, her throat, her lungs. She had known when she landed here on Seriphos, Diktys' baffled face blinking down at her, that she would never leave the shore again. And she had been content and grateful to live the rest of her life on this little island, for it was no more constrained than her life in Argos had been. But Perseus did not possess the same fear. He had no such limits. Should he not have the opportunity to visit distant shores, as she had once dreamed of doing, as his father had dreamed? A small life was not always a safe one – Diktys had shown them that – so why not offer her son something bigger?

She could see Polydektes watching her, searching her face for an answer. But another fear tugged her.

'Where would he sail? Not to the mainland. Not to Argos.'

Polydektes could not know the true reason for her concern, but he reassured her nonetheless.

'No. No, we will send him east, if that is what you wish. Let him trade copper and spices for a season. What danger can there be for him in that?'

There was always a danger in crossing the waves, Danae thought, but Polydektes' answer had given her some comfort. If her son must be far from her, let him be far from Argos too. Let him leave that shadow behind and find something new for himself out there in the wide world.

'All right,' she said with half a sigh. 'But let me speak with him. He will not listen if it comes from you.'

★

'You're sending me away?'

Danae had anticipated anger, objection, argument, but the hurt she saw on her son's young face disarmed her.

'No, my love,' she whispered, sitting beside him on the bed of their chamber. 'It is an opportunity. To prove yourself, to become a man. Think of all the things you'll see, all the stories you'll have to tell.' She tried to smile.

'You want me gone. You don't need me now that you have Poly-dektes looking after you.' His voice was bitter, but it had a choked quality as if he was holding back tears.

'I'll always need you—'

'This is his doing,' he murmured darkly. 'I have seen the way he looks at you. He means to drive us apart and take you for himself.'

Danae wasn't sure what to say.

'You must guard your honour,' Perseus continued. 'He cannot marry you without my permission, but you must promise not to give yourself to him while I am away.'

She felt a flicker of annoyance, to hear him speak of her honour as her father had, to have him instruct and warn her as if she were a child. But she pushed the feeling away and nodded vaguely.

'Does this mean that you will go?' she asked, pressing his hand.

'If that is what you ask, I will go.'

He met her gaze with steady eyes, but Danae could see a sad-ness in them, and perhaps a hope that she would take back her request and beg him never to leave her. Her lips parted, and she could feel the words rising, like mother's milk summoned by a babe's cry. But he was a babe no more. She remembered Poly-dektes' words and pressed her lips together. *It is for his own good.*

And so when the first ships of the season arrived the following week, Polydektes enquired with their captains and found one in need of a boy. Danae packed him some food – almonds, dried mutton, a jar of wine to ingratiate himself with the crew – and warm clothes for the cold nights at sea. Though her arms shook as she hugged her son farewell, she smiled bravely. And that night, when his face filled her thoughts, wounded and fearful as it looked out from the departing ship, she turned over in her bed and reassured herself once again. *It is for his own good.*

Part 2

Medusa

CHAPTER 17

In the low light of early evening the serpent crown gleamed. Medusa turned it in her hand, watching as her torch brought the writhing creatures alive, golden bodies entwined, shining heads alert. She could almost hear them hiss. Even after two years it was still a great honour to place that crown upon her head. She felt the weight of it, as heavy now as it ever had been, and thought of the woman who had worn it before her – the woman who had saved her life.

Crown in place atop her cropped black hair, Medusa approached the rugged altar, little more than a large rock in a small clearing. She added fresh lotus fruits to the wrinkled ones already there – not yet taken up by the goddess – and unstrapped the jar from her back. She untied the sheepskin lid, drew out one of the fat toads she had caught this afternoon, and cast it into the pit at the centre of the clearing. It was as if she had sprinkled water onto a hearth. A great hissing erupted, and she leant over to watch the smooth bodies uncurl. As her first offering was snapped up and swallowed, she produced a second toad, and a third – one for each of those dark roving heads – until all was silent once more. Then, amid the orange dust of the pit floor she spotted another figure, like a ghostly apparition beside its corporeal sisters: a shedded skin.

With the snakes sated and sluggish, Medusa took her opportunity. She picked up the stick that lay beside the altar, its curved end polished smooth, and dipped it into the pit. As gently as she could she hooked the brittle skin and brought it up into her hands. Medusa smiled to see that it was intact. *Yes, it will serve us well*, she thought, and silently thanked the goddess for her gift. She traced her finger over the translucent scales, hard and delicate at once. What marvellous creatures they were, flicking their tongues at her from beneath the earth. Ever growing, ever renewed. She looked down at her own flesh, smooth and soft, and remembered the cuts, the bruises, the scabbed wounds that had once marked her. She did not push the memory away, but embraced it. Like the snakes, she had been reborn.

She coiled the snakeskin into the now empty jar, and covered it over once more. With it safely stowed under one arm, and her torch held aloft by the other, she left the clearing.

The cave gaped before her, twice as wide as it was high. She often thought it was like a great eye, looking out over the trees and rocks, and further out to the sea. That was how it felt as she sat beside the fire, admiring the lingering glow of sunset, the quiet rustle of the bushes, the chirruping of the insects. From here she could look out upon the world but be safe from it.

The snakes helped, of course. Even the hyenas feared their hiss, and the deadly bite that might follow. Scorpions, lizards, vipers – all kept their distance from those mighty cobras. And any evil not cowed by their fearsome guardians would be warded off by the fresh snakeskin she had laid beside the beds. She would sleep soundly tonight, she thought, and yet there was something troubling her.

Euryale was late. She was their finest hunter, and more than able to look after herself, but Medusa could not help worrying. She was usually back before sunset, with something slung over her shoulders or hanging from her waist. Perhaps she had shot something different today, too large to carry alone. Stheno was always offering to go with her, but Euryale liked to hunt alone, like the stealthy cheetah. Light-footed and willowy, she could make herself invisible among the trees, whereas Stheno's substantial presence was more suited to wrangling sheep and chopping wood than stalking prey. They each had their strengths, even the Grey Ones.

Medusa watched them across the fire, spinning coarse wool to fine thread, preparing devious snares, grinding roots and leaves for healing salves. They had barely an eye and a tooth left between them, but Medusa had learned more from their wise mouths and practised hands than all the world could teach her.

And what was her strength? What role did she, Medusa, perform? She was their guardian, their priestess. She kept the snakes so that the snakes might keep them. She honoured the goddess to earn her favour. They had no need of queens here in the cave – no woman was above another – but when Medusa spoke her sisters listened. Gorgo had seen something in her, and had encouraged the others to see it too.

The glow was gone from the sky now, and the fine hairs of Medusa's arms stood on end. She could not leave Euryale to the dark night.

'Stheno,' she called, seeing that her sister already had a flaming torch in hand. 'We will go together.'

No more words were needed. The two of them left the yawning canopy of the cave and strode together across the open plateau into the trees. They walked without speaking, ears keen to every sound around them. They knew Euryale's route and traced it backwards through the wood. Medusa was thankful for the bright moon, but her breath still shivered. With every step she begged the goddess to keep her sister safe, and though she could taste the dread on her tongue she knew her silent companion was battling a greater fear. Stheno's steps, usually so sure, crunched uneasily as she crossed back and forth across the trail, sweeping her torch at shadows.

'We should go separately,' Stheno whispered. 'We will cover more ground.'

'No, we must stay together.' *In case we have to carry her*, she would have added, but stopped herself. Her sister knew what might be. There was no use in tightening her heart.

Suddenly Stheno stopped.

'Do you hear?' she whispered.

Medusa made herself still, tuning her ears to the breeze. Amid the rustle of the black leaves there were voices. One had Euryale's woody pitch; the other was unfamiliar. But before Medusa could hear any more, Stheno was pushing ahead through the trees and Medusa had to run to keep within her light. It was not long before two figures emerged from the darkness.

'Sisters,' Euryale breathed, smiling broadly. Her large eyes glinted as she looked between them. 'You scared us. But you look as if you have been scared too.' She sent her gaze to Stheno, warm and reassuring. 'Forgive my lateness. I found something I did not expect. By the blessing of the goddess, this is Halla.' She stepped aside to reveal the smaller girl, her round face scrunched up in the bright light of the torch. Surprised by the suddenness of their meeting, it took Medusa a moment to notice the bundle clutched in the girl's arms.

'By the goddess indeed.' Medusa smiled with relief to see that no one appeared to be harmed. 'Come,' she said, ushering the squinting girl as Euryale and Stheno embraced. 'There will be a time for talking but we must not linger. I'm sure you are tired and hungry. Come.'

They walked back through the woods in silence, ears listening. The round-faced girl stayed close by Medusa's side, her arms wrapped around the gurgling bundle, while Stheno and Euryale led with the torch, their hands brushing one another as they picked their way over stones and branches. The journey back felt so much shorter now that Medusa's fear had settled, and they soon saw the gaping mouth of the cavern ahead of them.

The girl ate in silence but smiled gratefully at each thing she was offered – cheese, dates, a little meat. She looked thin, and Medusa wondered how long it had been since her last meal.

As soon as she had finished eating, she opened her dress to feed her baby, who seemed as hungry as she was. It had been a long time since Medusa had seen such a sight, and she was surprised at the feeling of sadness that flickered in her chest. She looked away to stoke the fire.

'What did you say your name was?' she asked over her shoulder.

'Halla.'

'And your tribe?'

'The Psylli.'

Medusa saw Stheno nod. She had travelled far.

'She wants to join us—' Euryale began.

'I can't go back.' Halla's brown eyes were wide and desperate. 'My mother spoke of the women of Green Mountain, but she did not know your tribe. I know that you may not accept an outsider, but I had to—'

'We are Psylli,' said Medusa, holding the girl in her gaze. Halla's brow wrinkled in confusion. 'And Nasamones, and Auschisae, and Asbystae, and Augilae, and Giligamae.' She looked around at her sisters gathered by the fire. 'We were all these things once. But now we are our own tribe. The Gorgons. Sisters in spirit, though not in blood. We welcome any woman who seeks our protection, and who pledges to protect her sisters in turn.'

Halla's face was full of wonder.

'And my daughter?'

Medusa smiled. 'We welcome her too, of course.' She tried to hide her relief that Halla had not said *son*.

The girl's young face shone with gratitude. She let out a long, shaking breath, as if she had been holding it for days.

'Thank you,' she breathed. Her babe was still nestled against her breast and she stroked the dark wisps of hair that covered the child's head. 'She's the reason I'm here. I had to leave. I couldn't let them . . . '

Suddenly Halla's eyes were glistening. She swallowed hard, her cheeks flushed in the heat from the fire.

A Gorgon was never pushed to tell her story. Some were too painful, best forgotten. Some were told many years later, once pain had dulled and wounds had healed. Some, like Medusa's own, were written on the body, half told before any words were spoken. But she sensed that Halla's story was one straining to be free. Her dark eyes were welling and her lips trembled. Medusa wondered whether words or tears would spill first.

'My people have a saying,' the girl said quietly. '*The snake bites one already bitten.* The Psylli do not fear the snakes of the sand, for they will not bite a man who knows he will not be bitten. It is difficult to explain but . . . this is what my people say.' Halla stroked her daughter's head once more. 'They say true Psylli, those of pure blood, are born without fear. And so when each child is born they . . . ' She paused, staring into the fire. 'They put it before a viper. If the babe is truly one of the Psylli, it will show no fear and be unharmed. But if it is not . . . '

Medusa remained silent. She already knew some of what the girl had said, but knowing it was different to living it. It was best to let the girl speak.

'I knew the rites. Of course I did.' Halla's breath was ragged now. 'But when it came to it, when I had my own warm babe in my arms, I couldn't let them take her. I begged my husband, but he said it must be done. When I refused they said I knew the child to be impure. They said I had lain with an outsider. My husband knew it was not true, but he did not speak for me. He said I had shamed him, brought doubt on his house. And when I fled he did not follow.'

There was a sadness amid Halla's anger. Medusa had seen it many times before. The girl still mourned the life she had fled, even as she rejected it, grasping desperately for a new one. It was grief and betrayal and rage and hurt. It was the face of a Gorgon.

'You are safe here,' said Medusa in a soothing tone. 'You and your daughter will be cared for. We will show you our ways, and you will find your own strength. Welcome, Sister Halla.'

And like an echo through that vast cavern, the voices of the Gorgons joined as one.

'Welcome, Sister Halla.'

CHAPTER 18

Medusa rose early the next morning, her limbs springing with energy. It was rejuvenating to have a new sister in the cave, and one so young. Halla was the first arrival since the winter before last, when Stheno had come to them wide-eyed and quivering like a beaten dog. How strong she had grown now, how skilful, how sure. She had found her spirit here among the Gorgons, just as Halla would.

Medusa herself had been no older than Halla when Gorgo had found her. How many years had it been? Five? Six? Her life before the cave felt more distant than any number of years could measure.

Once she had helped the Grey Ones prepare breakfast, she set off to check the snares. She performed this duty every other day, retracing the familiar path through the trees, looping around behind the cave, onto the slopes of Green Mountain, then down towards the shore, and back again to the wide opening in the rock. She remembered where each snare had been set and checked them in turn, collecting the unfortunate creatures that had happened across them. Medusa took no pleasure in death and was careful to take only as many of those little lives as were needed, to feed the snakes, to keep her sisters safe, to please the goddess who brought the rains and nourished the trees and gave abundance to the land. They each must play their part, she thought, as she placed another limp shrew gently into her bag.

The sun had crossed the sky and was beginning to dip as she knelt down to replace the final snare. Even with her fingers busy she always kept her ears sharp, and so when the twig snapped, she heard it.

Her bow was drawn before she had risen to her feet. She turned in silence, watching for movement, a flash of fur. She expected a gazelle, feared a wolf, but what she found was altogether more surprising. There between the trees, barely a stone's throw from where she stood, was a young man. Though she ought to have feared this sight more than any wolf, she found her bow lowering in bafflement. The boy – for he was barely a man – was stepping backwards, feeling out the ground with his feet, while his eyes were fixed on a small bronze shield he held in front of him. She watched him with curiosity but could make no sense of his behaviour. Was he mad, perhaps? Too long exposed in the midday sun? He did not have the look of a Libyan. By his clothes and complexion she would guess he came from the islands of the Great Green, and she had heard that the sun shone less fiercely there. Eventually her curiosity overcame her wariness and she stepped towards him.

'What are you doing?'

His feet froze, but he did not turn his head.

'Who's there?'

She had guessed right, for he spoke the Greek tongue. It had been some years since Medusa had spoken it, but she was pleased to find that her mouth remembered.

'Why do you hold your shield so?' she asked, ignoring his question. She moved closer, her bow forgotten at her side.

She saw his eyes flicker a little, but still he did not turn his head.

'There is a terrible creature that haunts this forest. With great wings and snarling tusks and shining hands of bronze. Its gaze is deadly to all who look upon it.'

'Is that so?' Medusa was quite amused now but tried to keep the laughter from her voice.

'If I look at the beast only through the reflection of my shield it cannot harm me.' He spoke with conviction, and yet she could see his arms tremble a little. She stepped towards him again.

'And must you avoid my gaze also?'

He paused, and his chin twitched.

'I . . . I suppose not.' He lowered his shield and finally turned towards her.

His face was youthful, unbearded, but his shoulders were muscular despite the slightness of his frame.

'What is your name?' she asked.

'Perseus. And yours?'

'Medusa.'

He stood regarding her for a moment, curious green eyes moving over her face, her clothes, her bow, and back to her cropped hair. Medusa doubted he had ever seen a woman such as her.

'You should not be in the woods alone,' he said. 'Does your husband not fear for you?'

'I have no husband.'

'Your father, then.'

'I have none.'

To her surprise he nodded, as if with sympathy.

'Still, it is dangerous. There are snakes and wolves and . . . not to mention the beast.' His body took on a renewed tension as he said it, and she could see he was trying to resist glancing through the trees.

'What is the name of this beast? I have lived in this wood for many years and have seen no such creature.'

His brow creased.

'Why, you must have heard of it? It is notorious in this land.' Perseus dropped his voice to a whisper. 'The fearsome Gorgon.'

This time Medusa could not hide her amusement.

'Why do you laugh?' asked Perseus, his expression earnest. 'It is a terrible foe. It has claimed the lives of many men hereabouts. Its gaze turns their very blood to stone!'

His eyes were wide, his fingers gripping the edge of his polished shield.

'Tell me, then,' she said, leaning towards him a little and speaking softly. 'How is it that any man knows what the creature looks like?'

He paused, mouth half open. She tried not to smile as he searched for an answer. Eventually he gave up and his eyes sank to the ground between them. Medusa almost felt sorry for him. There was a peculiar charm in his naivety, and she felt as if she had fractured it.

'Why did you come if you feared the Gorgon so?' she asked gently.

'I thought . . . ' He sighed. 'I thought that if I could kill it . . . ' His boots scuffed the dirt. 'I have been with a merchant ship almost half a year. They call me boy but give me no opportunity to prove myself a man.' He shook his head bitterly. 'Some of the crew have journeyed inland to trade with the silphium growers but would not let me go with them. What gain is there in travelling the world if I see no more than a few stony beaches?'

He looked up as if expecting her to answer, but she stayed silent.

'Now I see that the local men lied. That there is no Gorgon. No doubt they all had a good laugh about it when I left. And I will have no trophy to show my crewmen.'

A part of Medusa wished she could tell Perseus the truth, that he had at least partly succeeded in his quest, but she knew it would be foolish to do so. The more people who believed her and her sisters to be deadly fiends, or not to exist at all, the safer they would be. They already had to deal with the occasional threat, men curious to see how they lived, to steal their livestock, to take advantage of women unguarded by men. But they defended themselves well enough. Even now Medusa's quiver was filled with arrows, their flints painted with just enough venom to paralyse a man, though not enough to kill him. Death only brought more death, but a man was unlikely to brag of how he had lain in his own waste as a woman stripped him of his belongings.

Occasionally a stranger – a woman most often – would approach alone, unarmed with hands raised, or bearing a sick child. They came for medicine, for advice, when desperation outweighed fear. And the Gorgons gave what help they could, and accepted goods in kind, things they could not find or make themselves, even things from across the sea. This was the way things were done, the way they kept themselves safe.

'You should return to your ship,' Medusa said quietly. Though the encounter had been an amusing diversion, it had run its course. The boy's hip glinted with a curved dagger, and Medusa knew she could not allow him to wander so close to the cave.

Perseus looked disappointed.

'May I not walk with you? Or see your home? I could help you with – ' he glanced at the leather bag she carried – 'whatever you're doing. I need not return while the sun is so high.'

Medusa shook her head. 'I'm sorry—' She stopped, her attention caught by a movement in the sparse undergrowth. The slender form of a viper slid over the stones, right beside Perseus' foot.

He followed her gaze and jumped back, taking the curved blade from his belt.

'Do not move,' she whispered, putting out a hand as if to hold him still, but Perseus was swiping his dagger back and forth at the creature. Its dark head was raised, watching the blade, watching him.

And then it struck. Its fangs were sunk into his ankle before he could step back. Perseus cried out and raised his blade.

'No!'

But he had brought it down before she could shout. The viper's head still clung to his flesh while its body dropped into the dust.

She darted to him and unlatched the fangs as carefully as she could.

'You fool. Now the poison will be twice as strong!'

But he wasn't listening. Perseus fell to the ground, screaming in agony as he clasped his leg, eyes wide with terror. Already she could see the skin around the two terrible holes darkening. There was no time to lose.

Medusa untied her belt and wrapped it around his bare leg, halfway up the calf, tying it tightly. Perseus cried out with fresh pain, but she ignored him. Kneeling beside him, she closed her lips around the wound and sucked the deadly venom from his flesh. When her mouth was full she spat the bitter blood onto the earth and sucked again, and again, until Perseus' leg began to look pale. She glanced at him, to see whether his eyes were clear, and saw that he was staring back at her, his face still lined with pain and yet frozen in awe, confusion, disgust – she could not tell which.

After a moment Perseus seemed to remember his agony and looked back to his oozing ankle, sweat gathering on his brow. She had done all she could to remove the poison, but Medusa could see that it had taken a hold on his body. He began to clutch at his throat.

'I'm so thirsty,' he croaked. 'Please. Am I going to die? Please help me.'

She could see his wide eyes welling with tears, though he held them back.

'You won't die,' she said, hoping her tone was steady enough to be convincing. She picked up her ostrich shell, unslung when she had removed her belt, and brought it to his lips. It was half full with water, and though he gulped it down his fingers still raked his throat.

'Come,' she said. 'Can you stand?'

Medusa helped him from the ground and bore half his weight as they set off through the trees.

CHAPTER 19

As Medusa approached the cave she could see the Grey Ones sitting in its shade.

'Enyo,' she called, as she half dragged Perseus, moaning with pain, to one of the closest beds. The stooped woman was at her side before Perseus had lain down. 'A thirst snake,' Medusa explained, though she needn't have bothered. The Grey Ones knew most bites by look alone.

Enyo pressed the flesh around the neat holes on Perseus' ankle, making him cry out. She sucked her teeth.

'Silphium,' was all she said, and she shuffled to the back of the cave. She returned with a handful of the pungent root.

'Boil this with vinegar,' Enyo instructed, pressing the silphium into Medusa's hand and turning back to examine Perseus' wound once more.

When the brew was ready Enyo drained off the steeping liquid for Perseus to drink. His face twisted at the smell, but he lacked the strength to resist. Then the softened roots were mashed to a paste and smeared over the darkening ankle. Enyo set the leftovers aside.

'If the pain continues, mix this with a little lotus wine and have him drink it. It will quench the flame in his blood.'

'He'll live, then?' Medusa asked.

Enyo simply nodded. Then she crossed the cave to rejoin Deino and Pemphredo, their grey heads bowed in conversation. Enyo had asked no questions, made no hesitation in saving Perseus' life, and yet Medusa sensed disapproval in her terseness, or at least a reluctance to spend any longer in the company of their unexpected guest. The Gorgons did not welcome visitors, and certainly not strange men carrying sharpened bronze. But Medusa had done what was right, what any civilised person would do. Life was a sacred thing and, seeing Perseus' drenched body finally begin to relax, she had no regrets.

As she watched his chest fall into a steady rhythm, an unfamiliar voice spoke.

'How do you know these things?'

Halla sat on a nearby antelope skin, nursing her daughter. She eyed Medusa with curiosity. 'My people know the ways of the snakes better than any. They told me that other tribes are ignorant. But the grey-haired one . . . And you – that is your belt around his leg, yes? You drew the bad blood with your mouth?'

Medusa smiled, pleased to see that the girl was impressed.

'We know the ways,' she nodded humbly. 'Our leader, Gorgo, was of the Psylli.'

Halla's eyes widened in surprise, but then her young brow fell.

'I have not heard of this Gorgo.'

'She fled the Psylli many years ago. Before you were born. Before even your mother was born, I would think. She took others with her – Enyo was one of them – and they found this place, this green land blessed by the goddess. They built a life here, and a tribe.'

Halla listened, nodding reverently. 'I am proud to share blood with her, then,' she said in a tone that sounded serious beyond her years. 'And I shall be proud to be a Gorgon.'

Beside her Medusa felt Perseus stir. Suddenly his eyes were open, his hand gripping the curved dagger he still carried.

'Gorgon!' he rasped, looking about with an unfocused gaze. He tried to raise himself, but she put a hand on his chest. She could feel his heart pounding. Medusa doubted he had understood their conversation – the language of the tribes was rarely spoken outside their lands – but evidently one word had caught his attention.

'Hush,' she murmured. 'There is no beast here.'

But Perseus pushed her hand away. He sat up, dagger raised, and Medusa saw Halla's face spread with fear, clutching her daughter to her breast.

'Enough,' said Medusa sharply. She prised the bronze hilt from his fingers and held his chin so that he looked at her. 'There is no beast. Only us. We are the Gorgons. We women here.' She gestured across the wide cave, and his gaze followed, able to take in his surroundings now that the worst pain had passed. He looked back at her and she smiled gently. 'Are we so terrifying?'

She watched his expression carefully, as it turned from fear to confusion.

'But you have no tusks,' he said vaguely, examining her face as if she might be concealing them.

She gave a quiet laugh.

'No. Nor wings. Nor . . . hands of bronze, was it?' She turned her hand in front of his face, so that he might verify for himself. 'Nor will we turn your blood to stone.'

The mention of blood seemed to jar something in his memory. Perseus looked down at his ankle, then back up at her. She realised his eyes were on her lips.

'You . . . '

But then his face creased in pain. He made a whimper and she lowered him back down onto the animal skins.

'Don't move,' she ordered, and to her relief he obeyed.

It only took a moment to mix the silphium with the lotus wine, just as Enyo had instructed.

'Drink this,' she urged as she returned to his side. This time he did not hesitate but drank thirstily. When the bowl was drained he lay back, his eyes closed and his jaw tight. Medusa put a hand to his forehead – still hot, but no longer slick with sweat.

'You must rest,' she said softly.

The wine was strong and he was soon asleep, his young face smooth and untroubled. It was only when Halla spoke that Medusa realised she had been staring.

'You speak the foreign tongue,' the girl said.

Medusa looked up and found Halla's expression to be equal parts awe and suspicion. 'I learnt it many years ago,' she replied, answering the question that had not been asked. 'My village traded with those across the sea.'

Halla looked impressed.

'What tribe are you?'

Medusa smiled. 'Only Gorgon.'

She did not like to speak of the past and hoped her unease did not show. Thankfully Halla had greater concerns.

'I have never seen a man such as him,' the girl said, her eyes roving freely over Perseus' sleeping form. 'His clothes are strange,' she mused. 'And where are his tattoos? Do his people not honour him?' Her gaze came to rest on the curved dagger Medusa had taken from him, now abandoned on the floor of the cave. 'What did he say? Has he come to harm us?'

Medusa smiled reassuringly and shook her head.

'He is only a boy far from home. We will make him well and then he will return to his people. There's no need to fear.'

Halla looked relieved, and held her daughter a little less tightly.

'The Gorgons are blessed to have you as their guardian, Medusa.'

But there were those who disagreed. When Stheno returned from herding the flock late in the afternoon, her eyes were filled with fire.

'And you brought him *here*? To our home? With a knife in his hand?' She kicked the blade as if it were a deadly scorpion, and it skittered across the cave floor.

'He would have died, Stheno. I had to help him.'

'You did not,' her sister bit back. 'You could have left him. It was not your doing. He would have been bitten whether you were there or not. You should have left him to die, if that was what the goddess willed.'

'You don't mean that,' said Medusa quietly, and yet the hardness of Stheno's gaze told her that she did. She looked at Perseus as if he were a feral dog, a terrible plague, an invader come to rape and pillage and kill. The Gorgons had cause to fear men, of course they did, but Stheno's fear was closer to hate. Her husband had been a cruel man and her pain was still fresh. She had not shed her scars as Medusa had.

'He is harmless, Stheno.'

'He is a man,' her sister growled.

'He is a boy,' Medusa replied, laying a gentle hand on her sister's arm. 'He is not like the others. He is young and innocent. He means us no harm.'

Stheno paused, looking over at Perseus' bed, separated from the others at the far end of the cave.

'Whether he means it or not, he is dangerous. We must send him away.' Stheno's dark eyes met hers, steady and immovable.

'As soon as he is well,' Medusa agreed.

And though her sister's head eventually nodded, Stheno's eyes remained as hard as they had ever been.

CHAPTER 20

By the morning Perseus seemed much improved, though he
was a little unsteady on his feet as he followed Medusa about
her tasks. His limbs were still weak from the venom, and his
punctured ankle was an angry red beneath the salve. She kept
him close, both out of concern for his recovery and out of
respect for her fellow Gorgons. She had brought this stranger
into their midst, and now he was her responsibility.

It was a curious feeling, she realised, to have him trailing after
her, looking to her as they moved from one chore to another.
He had learned his lesson from the snake, perhaps, for he did
exactly as she told him. Medusa had grown used to leading
women, to having their ear and their trust and their gratitude.
But it felt different to have Perseus beside her, almost a man
grown. No man had ever listened to her, or looked at her, the
way that he did.

Stheno had milked the goats that morning, and so now Medusa
sat in the shade of the cavern, straining the curds through a fine
woven basket as Perseus watched.

'Have you never made cheese before?' she asked light-heart-
edly, seeing his expression as he eyed the dripping basket. To her
surprise he shook his head.

'My family—' he began, but stopped. 'My people are fishermen. We live from the sea.'

Medusa nodded, though in Libya it would be counted strange
indeed to live without even a goat.

'You have eaten it, though?' she asked.

'Of course.'

'And the whey?' She held up the bowl in which the cloudy liquid had gathered. Perseus looked uncertain. 'You should drink some,' she said encouragingly. 'It will bring back your strength.'

He took the bowl with cautious hands and sipped a little from the edge. She watched him contemplate the flavour, and was pleased when he tilted the bowl for another mouthful.

'Thank you,' he said, passing it back. She saw him look around the cave, at the gentle fire, at the Grey Ones scraping skins for leather, at the baskets of food stacked along the back wall, and back to the white curds still dripping their whey. 'You live well here,' he concluded. Medusa could not help smiling at the surprise in his tone. 'And you are women only?'

She nodded.

'But who protects you?'

'We protect ourselves.'

'Who do you marry?'

'We do not marry.'

Perseus looked thoughtful for a moment. Then he leant towards her, his voice lowered.

'Then how do you have children?'

She saw his eyes drift to Halla, her babe strapped to her chest as she swept the cave floor.

'Each day the world gives birth to another wronged woman,' Medusa said quietly. Gorgo had spoken those very words to her years ago, when she had asked the same question.

Perseus turned his eyes back to her and smiled faintly as if at the wit of her reply. And she knew that he did not understand, that he could never really know the truth of those words. And yet, just as when they had first met, it was Perseus' naivety that drew Medusa to him. There was no place for naivety among the Gorgons, no space for it in the minds of women who had seen the world in all its cruelty. But Perseus was different, intact and untrodden. Medusa found herself enjoying the company of this wide-eyed boy, who had the luxury of fearing imaginary monsters instead of real ones.

'How old are you?' she asked.

'Eighteen.'

Yes, she thought, surveying his smooth chin, his bright eyes, his thick arms. She supposed that sounded right, but it was strange to think that he was only a few years younger than herself.

'And where is it that you come from, this land of so many fish?' She gave him a playful smile, but it faded as she saw the twinge in his cheek.

'Seriphos. Though it is not my land really,' he added quickly. 'I am heir to the kingdom of Argos.'

He watched her as he said it, perhaps to see if she was impressed.

'I do not know these places,' she said slowly, breaking his gaze to press the curds. 'They must be very far away.'

She saw his brown curls nod at the edge of her vision.

'And what is the heir to a kingdom doing on a merchant ship?' she asked.

'It was my mother's wish,' he said stiffly. 'That I may see something of the world.'

'But the crew, they did not take you with them on their journey inland? They must mean to keep you safe. They will worry if you are not there when they return.'

'I doubt it.' He laughed, then shook his head. 'No. No, they leave me behind because they do not respect me. I have not proven myself yet. But I will. The gods themselves have foretold that I will do great things.' There was a sparkle in his eyes as he looked at her, but it was not the brightness of youth that she had seen there before. What should she say to that? Medusa had little care for the gods of men, so she smiled and returned to pressing her curds.

'Tell me of your travels.'

'I have been on the sea many months,' he began. 'We travelled first through the islands, then around the great circle of

Oceanos – from Kypros to the coast of Canaan, along to the green banks of Egypt, and now here to unending Libya. I had been told of its vast wastes, and yet I am surprised to find it holds much beauty also.'

Medusa could feel his eyes upon her, different somehow to the way they had felt before. A strange sensation began to creep up her neck, pleasant and tingling, as if the wind had brushed her. She looked up.

'The goddess has blessed this land,' she said softly. 'Here on Green Mountain all things grow, and we have everything we need.' Her words were as true as they had ever been, and yet she felt her lips falter a little as those green eyes looked back at her.

'Who is this goddess you worship?' Perseus asked. 'Hera? Artemis?'

Medusa shook her head. 'She is our own goddess. We do not speak her name, for it would demean her. She is light and life. She is in all things.'

Perseus hung on her word, his face full of curious wonder.

'And her temple?'

'We keep a shrine for her, here in the woods. Or rather, I keep it. I tend to the offerings so that we may keep her favour.'

'You are her priestess?'

She could see that he was impressed, and felt the curious warmth spread from her neck all the way up to her cheeks.

'Will you show me the shrine?'

She hesitated, swallowing as he regarded her. The shrine was not for outsiders. And yet Perseus was different, wasn't he? She had told her sister so, and she felt it more certainly now. He was not like other men. He wanted nothing from her. Not to use or command her. Only to know her, and the life she had built. And here, under his gaze, Medusa felt different too. She saw herself as something different. Something to be admired.

'Come with me.' Her lips were moving before her mind knew that the words would be spoken. She let the impulse spread to her limbs, and left the cheese in its basket as she took Perseus' hand to lead him through the trees.

She could not enter the clearing without the serpent crown, so she took it from its hole, carefully covered with leaves, and unwrapped it from its goatskin cover. She was pleased to see the look of awe on Perseus' face as she lifted it into the light and placed the gleaming snakes upon her head.

'You look like a queen,' he whispered, and she felt her face grow warm again. She realised how close he was, how his hand hovered in the space between them, and stepped back.

'The Gorgons have no queen,' she said.

For a moment she thought they ought to turn back. Was she foolish to trust this boy? But here amid the trees she felt a strange intimacy emerging. Almost childish, like the secrets she and her friends had treasured in their carefree youth. That feeling drew her in and made her want to share some part of herself, some part of her life that was special and private.

As soon as they entered the clearing the cobras began to hiss, anticipating whatever morsel Medusa might have brought them. They knew her scent, the vibration of her step. Beside her Perseus froze.

'What is in there?' he asked, staring at the pit with fearful eyes.

'The snakes, of course,' Medusa said simply. She had had no time for catching toads, so she bent down and took a handful of locusts from the box beside the shrine. She cast them into the pit, prompting another chorus of hissing.

'Snakes?' Perseus took a step back. 'Why would you keep such foul creatures?'

'They are not foul—' she began, but as she turned and saw the perplexity on Perseus' face, she realised that it must seem an odd custom.

'The snakes protect us,' she explained. 'By the very danger that gives you dread, they keep other dangers at bay. Their venom can kill a man or cure him, set his flesh afire or soothe it. One only has to know the ways. How to handle them, how to take their venom and how to use it. Like us they are complex creatures, worthy of our reverence, as well as our fear.'

Perseus' gaze moved between her and the pit, his expression still cautious, but thoughtful.

'I can bring one up to show you,' she offered, but he shrank back.

'No!'

Medusa laughed, but she saw Perseus wince with embarrassment and stopped herself.

'I'm sorry,' she said, stepping towards him. 'It is wrong of me to tease you. I forgot my fear of the snakes long ago, but you are fresh bitten. Forgive me.' She reached out to press his hand and he smiled, though his cheeks were stiff.

'What happens when the rains come?' he asked, looking up through the leaves and back down to the pit. 'Will they not drown?'

Medusa tilted her head, surprised by his concern for the creatures he so feared. She had been right to trust him, for how could a spirit so gentle be dangerous?

'The snakes could no doubt escape their hole,' she said, imagining their powerful bodies climbing the earthen walls.

'Then why don't they?' Perseus asked. 'They could go now and be free.'

'Why should they want to?' Medusa replied, her brow creasing at the notion. 'Here they are fed and cared for and respected.'

Perseus paused, his eyes on the pit. He shook his head. 'It is not natural for them to live in such a way.'

Medusa gave a quiet laugh, and Perseus' eyes rose to meet hers.

'Nature is cruel. Here they are safe.'

CHAPTER 21

When Medusa returned to the cave, with Perseus at her side and the sun low in the sky, Stheno and Euryale were there waiting.

'Go and sit by the fire,' Medusa murmured to her companion, seeing that the burning look was back in Stheno's eyes. Then she walked with her two sisters to the far edge of the cavern and they sat upon the rocks there, Euryale resting a steadying hand on Stheno's thigh.

'He is still here' was Stheno's curt opening.

'He is not yet healed,' Medusa replied calmly.

'He looks well enough to me,' she said, glaring over at the centre of the cave, where Perseus sat awkwardly poking the fire. 'You should have sent him away this afternoon, while there was still enough light to travel by. Now we will have to wait until tomorrow.'

'What danger is there in one more night?' Medusa asked. 'If he meant us harm he would have done it already.'

'He may be gathering information,' Stheno whispered, her body filled with an urgent energy. She leaned forward. 'He may be counting our numbers, watching our habits, finding our weaknesses. And when he has all he needs, he will return with more men to take all that we—'

She stopped, her gaze distracted by something.

'You are wearing the crown,' she said slowly.

Medusa put her hands up and felt that it was true. She had forgotten to remove it after they left the clearing.

'I . . . ' she stuttered.

'You have shown him the shrine?' Stheno asked, more disbelieving than angry. Beside her Euryale gasped, looking between Medusa's eyes and the crown above.

'Is it true, sister?' she asked quietly.

Medusa hesitated before nodding. The reproof in their eyes was painful.

'I only wanted to show him how we live. There was no harm in it.'

'But you could not have known that,' said Euryale, her large eyes full of worry. 'He could have desecrated the shrine, stolen the crown, harmed the snakes. He could have harmed you.'

Medusa shook her head. 'He wouldn't—'

'A Gorgon knows the danger of men, and she keeps her guard,' Stheno interrupted. 'You have forgotten the pain that should protect you.'

'And you feel yours too strongly,' Medusa snapped back. 'You see enemies everywhere.' She looked hard at Stheno, fists gripping the leather of her skirt.

'I see them so that I do not suffer them,' her sister replied coolly. 'My fear keeps me safe. It keeps those I love far from harm.' She took Euryale's hand and laced their fingers together. The two of them shared a glance and drew their heads close in a way that made Medusa's chest feel suddenly heavy. 'You must think of your community,' Stheno said after a moment.

Medusa felt a flame of anger rise inside her. It was easy for Stheno, who had all she needed, to send Perseus away. But his presence had sparked something in Medusa, like a light illuminating the hollow places within her. A need for companionship, for affection, for that singular bond that she would not find among her fellow Gorgons, that she might never have the opportunity of finding again.

Or perhaps that was not what she needed, not truly, and not from Perseus. Perhaps she only needed a little time in the presence of this boy who did not make her afraid, to feel powerful beside him, admired under his gaze. It was a feeling she had not looked for, a feeling she had not imagined possible – from a man, or even a boy – and yet she felt it trickling through those hollow places, nourishing a thirst she had not realised was there.

She knew though that to follow that feeling, that missing something, to let it pull and lead her as it had today into that most sacred place, was to risk all that she did have. She could feel the tension of that string already, and knew that if she pulled it any further it might snap. Stheno was right – the Gorgons wore their pain like armour, their fear like a shield. And for good reason. They would never allow a man to live among them. It did not matter that Medusa had seen women act as cruelly as men. It did not matter that Perseus was different, that he was gentle and naive and well-meaning – the Gorgons would never see it. They held to what they knew. And what all Gorgons knew, without exception, was that men were dangerous.

Despite her hardness, Stheno sat watching Medusa with apprehension in her eyes. Euryale too, her slender fingers gripping Stheno's callused ones. And Medusa felt her own anger, her envy, flow out of her. These women depended on her, feared for her as they did for themselves. They had not confronted her out of spite but out of love, and a desire to protect what they had built, this haven that they had all helped to create and which they each had a responsibility to maintain. It was bigger and more important than any one of them.

Suddenly Medusa felt like a foolish girl, clinging to a boy she hardly knew – and for what reason? Because he had made her feel beautiful? Because he was something new and rare, a distraction she did not want to give up? It was embarrassing, to see herself through her sisters' eyes.

'I'm sorry,' she said eventually, looking between them. 'You're right. Of course you're right. I've let down my guard. Forgive me.' Medusa reached out with both her hands, so that they were all three united. 'He leaves tomorrow.' She nodded her head decisively and felt the weight of the serpent crown upon it as she did.

Stheno and Euryale sighed with relief, and each rose to embrace her.

But as the two of them parted from her and walked to the back of the cave, to the bed they shared, Medusa felt her chest grow heavy once more, to see their hands entwined, their low voices breathing words only they would hear. She took a breath and dragged her eyes away, over to the fire, and to Perseus who sat waiting for her. He smiled as he saw her approach, an easy, carefree smile she could not match, and yet despite herself she found her cheeks lifting, her chest lightening. And though she knew it was foolish to indulge what she could not keep, Medusa let herself fall into that feeling, let it fill her and warm her, before she had to cast it away forever.

CHAPTER 22

By sunrise Medusa had hardened her resolve for what must be done. Perseus' visit had been a pleasant diversion, but now it was at an end. He would have left sooner or later, gone back to his ship and away across the sea, so it was better that they part now before familiarity grew to deeper feeling.

Before he was awake she had baked them a flatbread each on the fire, spread with a little fresh cheese. She brought them over to where Perseus slept, but hesitated before rousing him. He looked so peaceful, his brown curls fallen across his cheek. How could Stheno fear him? But it was not him she feared, Medusa knew. It was the world he came from, where men had power and women had none, where a woman's life was worth less than a man's honour. Medusa feared it too. It was a world they must shut out.

'Perseus,' she whispered, shaking his shoulder gently. His face wrinkled and a green eye squinted back at her. 'The sun is risen.'

He blinked and pushed himself up. 'Thank you,' he croaked, accepting the bread she offered. 'What is our task this morning? More cheese?'

He smiled brightly but she shook her head. 'We must check the snares. If your ankle is well enough healed.'

He glanced down at the wound, flexing his foot back and forth. 'I can barely feel it now. I should be glad to be on my feet again.'

Medusa felt a twinge of disappointment and realised that a part of her had hoped he would need more time to recover.

'Good,' she replied, forcing a smile. 'Finish your bread and we will head out.'

She took him on her usual route, wide around behind the cave and back down in a slow arc towards the sea. It gave them time to talk, and to share the silence as they walked between the trees. She tried to savour the lightness of his company and ignore the weight that sat in her chest.

When she could see the soil turn to pale sand ahead of her, Medusa stopped. Perseus looked around at the bushes, his brow creasing.

'Is there a snare here?'

She hesitated just long enough for him to know that something was wrong.

'Medusa?'

'The sea lies just beyond these trees,' she said, trying to keep her breath steady. 'From here you can follow the beach back to your ship.'

He stood looking at her for a moment, as if he had not comprehended her words. 'You want me to leave?'

She felt her neck twitch but kept his gaze. 'You are healed now. There is no need for you to stay.' She hated how cold her voice sounded and tried to soften it. 'Your people will be waiting for you.'

'It has only been three days,' Perseus protested. 'They will not return from the silphium fields for another three at least. Can I not stay with you until then?'

There was a pleading look in his eyes, but she shook her head. 'It is impossible.'

'Because of the broad one? The one with the scar on her cheek?'

He had seen Stheno watching him, then. She had made no attempt to hide her distrust.

'Not only her,' Medusa said quietly. 'You know our ways. We cannot allow a man to live among us.'

Perseus opened his mouth as if to protest again, but it hung silent, his face frozen in thought. 'You could come with me,' he said suddenly.

It was such an absurd idea that Medusa laughed aloud. 'As what, your wife?'

'I don't know. Maybe.'

There was a sincerity in his look that made her smile crack a little. He was serious. This boy who knew so little about her, who did not know what he was asking of her. She could not return to the world. From the day she had come to the cave, she had known that she would never leave. No matter how faded her scars became, no matter how dull her pain, her fear would still hold her fast to the safety of that cavern, and to her sisters who had seen the world as she had, who had known the same terror and licked the same wounds. But she also knew that there were no words, in his language or hers, with which she could make him understand that, so she simply shook her head.

'You would rather live here?'

She was surprised by the incredulity in his tone. 'Yes,' she replied. 'Here I am safe and free and respected. You said yourself that we live well.'

'Well enough for exiles in a cave. But you could have a real life.'

'More real than this?' She smiled and spread her arms, looking up at the trees, the sky, breathing in the fragrant, salty air.

'Bigger than this,' Perseus said quietly, stepping towards her. 'Come with me,' he urged. 'There is a whole world we could see together.'

'I have seen enough,' she said soberly. 'The Gorgons are not exiles. It is we who have cast out the world.'

But she wasn't even sure he was listening. He stood looking at her, green eyes sparkling with the optimism of inexperience. It was a look she had grown fond of, a look she envied, but she could not allow herself to be drawn into it.

'You don't understand these things,' said Medusa, shaking her head. 'The world out there belongs to them. To men. You don't know what men can do. You don't know what they are.'

His bright eyes darkened a fraction. 'But I am a man.'

'By what measure?' she laughed. 'No, Perseus. You are as fresh to the world as a stumbling gazelle.'

'I have lain with women,' he said, raising his chin a little.

Medusa was surprised to feel a beat of disappointment knock her chest, to learn that this naive boy was not as untouched as she had thought.

'In your homeland?' she asked.

'At the ports. My captain paid for the first, to make me a man.'

Medusa felt her lightness disappear, stripped away by a flash of anger. 'And did it? Taking some desperate port girl who could not refuse you?' She could hear her voice tightening and tried to calm it. She let out a slow breath. 'A man should lie with one who wants him.'

Medusa's sudden anger had wrapped around her like fog, but as she breathed again it began to clear, and she saw that Perseus wore a strange expression. His eyes were on hers, his lips slightly parted, his cheeks flushed. He was embarrassed, she thought. Ashamed. It was a relief to see that in him. To know that she had not been wrong about him.

But then he leant forward, and kissed her.

She pulled back. 'What are you doing?'

'What we have both wanted. Since I met you, since you saved me. Since you sucked the black blood from my flesh.' He clasped her shoulders, eyes fervent, lips smiling. 'Don't you see, Medusa? We are bound together. I am yours and you are mine.'

'I am not yours,' she said, twisting out of his embrace. She stepped back, but he grasped her wrist.

'Medusa,' he said softly, but his hand was hard like a chain, so much like that other hand that her heart began to pound and she wrenched herself free. His face was all confusion now.

'But I thought . . . ' He looked down, staring at the dirt. When he looked at her again his eyes were shining with tears. He swept an arm across them, as if it were a shield, and suddenly Medusa was reminded of their first meeting, of the clueless boy stumbling backwards through the woods.

'I'm sorry, Perseus,' she whispered, and stepped towards him, but he recoiled, arm still braced across his face. She could see his lip trembling, could feel his hurt, his embarrassment, and yet what could she do? *I cannot be what you what you want me to be. I cannot give myself to you, to anyone.* But those were not the words she spoke. 'I cannot go with you,' she sighed. Perhaps one day he would understand what held her back, once he had seen more of the world he offered. Medusa shook her head. 'You're just a boy.'

Something seemed to change in Perseus. His shielding arm took on a new tension, muscles tight, fist clenched. As it lowered, her eyes finally met his, still shining but somehow hard beneath the tears. He trembled with a different energy.

'Perseus—'

'You don't have to say any more,' he murmured, his voice low and hollow. It barely sounded like him at all. 'You don't want me so I'll go.'

'Perseus.' Medusa's chest was tight. She felt her own tears rise but held them back, and swallowed the lump that choked her voice. What could she say anyway? That she wished he could stay? That she could go? That the world was not so cruel nor she so damaged by it? The world and she and he could only be as they were. It was better not to agonise him with visions of what might have been.

'Do you know the way?' she asked, imagining him stumbling across the sand in the dark. She had no idea whether his ship lay to the east or west.

But he did not speak again. He simply turned on his heel and strode away from her, his polished shield strung across his back and flashing in the dappled sunlight.

Medusa stood rooted to the dirt, cheek quivering as she watched him go.

CHAPTER 23

An orphan learns to take what is given. Staling bread, spoiling fruits, a spare portion from a pitying mother, a place by the fire on a cold night. All these things Medusa learned to take in those lonely years after her father's passing. She would sit by the beach, hugging her bony knees, watching the sea grow and shrink, the ships load and unload. She would greet the sailors as they passed, ask where they had come from, where they were going, if they needed a hawker or a porter or a messenger. Sometimes she would get work for an hour, an afternoon, or sometimes she would get only a passing smile, sometimes nothing at all. She took what was given.

And when the priest came, offering friendly words and a hot meal, she accepted his charity, thankful that the gods had smiled upon her that day. She followed him to the altar, beyond the village, where the animals were sacrificed and their flesh roasted. Her mouth watered as she walked, imagining the smell, the taste of it, the fat dripping from her chin. Her stomach, silent out of habit, began to growl.

But when they came to that sacred place there was no meat. The altar was empty, the fire pit cold. She opened her mouth in confusion, only to find it stopped by an invading tongue. She pulled away, brow creased, touching her lip where he had bitten it, but he only laughed. Even now she remembered the sound of that laugh, of the voice that asked, 'What else did you expect?' She turned to go but a hand grasped her. And another. He was in her before she could scream.

When she found her voice, he choked it. When she clawed his arms he barely noticed. And afterwards, when she cried, he spoke no words but left her alone in the dirt. The sun was setting as she walked back through the village, her feet stumbling on the stones, her face streaked with tears. She took the sleeve of a kindly-looking woman, one who had fed her more than once, and tried to speak of what had happened. Her throat was dry, her voice raspy from his squeezing hands, but she forced out those terrible words, barely more than a whisper. And the woman's face changed. Her eyes narrowed, her mouth wrinkled in disgust. She pulled her sleeve away, stepped back into the entrance of her tent. And Medusa stepped away too, eyes stinging, but now the woman was speaking to her husband, now her neighbour, and there were whispers all around her, and eyes glaring and fingers pointing.

The priest was called and the matter resolved. She had seduced him, offered herself for bread and meat. There were many who attested to her baseness, her vagrant living, her dealings with sailors, and now she had corrupted their priest and defiled their altar. She had no belongings to pay for her crime, no offering to appease the gods, so they took the only thing she did own: her beautiful hair. Uncut since birth, long and shining, black as ebony, they sheared it from her head. Not to use, not to offer, only to spoil and reduce and shame. She felt the bronze blades slice her scalp, watched with burning eyes as her dark tresses fell into the dust. But when it was done the crowd remained, still glaring, still unsatisfied. One man pulled at her dress, then another, tearing it in all directions, until she had to cover herself with her hands. And then the first stick struck her flesh. A tentative bat, but it was soon followed by more, and as the confidence of the crowd grew so did their spite, meted out in searing lashes of wood and leather. She watched through guarding arms as faces that had once looked upon her with pity, even kindness, twisted with rage, with revulsion, with desire, with righteousness. They threw words like spears. 'Polluter!' 'Defiler!' 'Whore!' And all the while her body screamed, her soul wailed, though her lips remained silent.

The next morning Medusa awoke lying on a bed of her own hair and blood, like the nest of some foul beast. Through the slits of her swollen face she gazed at the dusty earth, the blue sky above, barely believing that she was still alive to see it. She struggled to keep her gaze focused, but a movement caught her attention. A donkey stood beside the well, with patchy fur and one eye and raw flesh beneath its too-tight tether. It looked as broken as she. She forced herself to stand, every limb crying resistance, and dragged her feet towards the pathetic creature. It shied at her advance, but as she put a shaking hand to its face it seemed to recognise her as a kindred spirit and sniffed gently at the dried blood of her arms.

Her hands were untying the rope before she had even thought to do it. The creature did not run but stood as if waiting. And so they left together, Medusa slumped along the donkey's back, her cheek against its musty fur. She could recall little of the journey, drifting between agonising wakefulness and numb oblivion, and yet her companion had known the way to go. He had brought her to Gorgo, and to the cave.

The Gorgons had cared for her. They had treated her wounds and rebuilt her spirit. Even now they nurtured it, helped her to learn and grow. But there was a part of her, beneath her mended flesh and her gleaming crown, that still felt scarred. 'Polluter', they had called her, as if she were a poison. But if she were the poison then surely he had been the snake. And yet he had not been exorcised. They had not shaved him and shamed him and broken him. Only her.

She could have let that anger make her monstrous. She could have hated the world and everyone in it. She could have taken revenge on those who had wronged her – even now she could. But why become what they had tried to make her? They had degraded her, dehumanised her, taken her beauty, her honour and her spirit, but she had been reborn, not as a monster of their making but as a woman free. She kept her hair short not because they had made it so but as a reminder that her past was hers to control, as her present, as her future. Her body, her life, was hers alone.

CHAPTER 24

It had been two nights since Perseus' departure, and life at the cave continued as if he had never been there. Medusa made herself busy, keeping the memory of him distant enough that it would soon drift away. It was better that way, she told herself. How could she expect the bruise to fade if she kept pressing it? Instead she let herself enjoy the new ease that had settled throughout the cave, the brief smiles Stheno now granted, the silent looks from the Grey Ones that told her she had regained their approval.

Halla was settling in well, Medusa thought, though she was as exhausted as any new mother. Medusa had noted the dark patches beneath her eyes, the tiredness of limb that she tried to hide with sweet smiles. She needed something to strengthen her, and Medusa knew just the thing.

Stheno had not moved the animals out to graze this morning, so Medusa went to where they were penned, at the edge of the wide plateau that opened out before the cave mouth. She climbed over the wooden fence and stepped calmly towards the nearest nanny goat, making a low clicking sound with her tongue. She recognised the nanny by the dark stripe down her back, the one they called Lightning for her wicked kick, but who was gentle enough if you knew how to handle her – a lengthy scratch between the horns usually did the trick. She had only one kid this season and was always overfull with milk, so she let Medusa take a little without complaint. Straight into the ostrich shell it went, warm and frothy.

When Medusa returned to the shade of the rocky canopy, she took a jar from the back wall, filled with glistening black locusts, dried in the baking sun, and crushed a few of them to a fine powder that she sprinkled over the milk. It was Euryale who had

taught her this method, common among the Nasamones, for producing a drink that would restore lost vigour. Medusa had drunk
it herself many times, in those early days when she had lain in the
cave half dead. She was convinced that the vital drink had saved
her, in body at least.

She brought the frothy mixture over to where Halla sat and
pressed the ostrich shell into the girl's hands. Halla smiled dis-
tractedly, her attention still on her daughter who was sleeping
soundly on a sheepskin. Despite the peace of the scene, Halla's
young brow was heavy with worry. She took a sip from the shell
cup without asking what was in it.

'Have I done the right thing?' Halla asked, turning her gaze at
last. 'Bringing her here. It was right to do, wasn't it?'

'Your child is safe. You are safe,' said Medusa softly. 'What
could be more important?'

Halla smiled as if she were reassured, but the crease in her brow
remained. 'Yes, you're right,' she said vaguely. 'But . . . ' She bit
her lip. 'If I had allowed them to perform the rite, she may have
been safe anyway. What cause would the snake have to bite her?
She would not have been harmed, and she would have grown up
among her kin. She would have married and had children of her
own one day. I have robbed her of that life.'

'And given her this one,' said Medusa gently. 'No worse for
being different.'

'Do you really believe that?' Halla asked hurriedly, her eyes
suddenly sharp, desperately searching Medusa's own. 'Do you
feel full? Whole? Without family, without children? I . . . I need to
know that my daughter will be happy.'

Medusa looked into those wide brown eyes, and down at the
sleeping child, sucking obliviously on its tongue. There was a time
when she had imagined herself becoming a mother, and a time
when she had come close to it. She still knew the place where she
had buried them, down near the sand where the waves hushed

and sighed. It had felt like the right place, as right as anything when life had become death. It seemed cruel that they should have been allowed to survive her scourging, only to perish once she had recovered, torn from her body before their time in a stream of terrifying blood. She had held them, afterwards, each no bigger than her palm, and she had wept for them, and for herself, and for the mother she would never be. Though the seed had been hateful, the fruit had been hers.

That pain was many years past, almost forgotten until these last few days. Feelings long buried had been tilled like fresh soil, brought up to weigh on her chest. But they would soon settle. She had been happy before and she would be happy again.

'It is a full life,' she said, with a surety that was as much for herself as for Halla. 'Family is ours to make. The Gorgons are my mother, my grandmothers, my sisters, my children. And I promise – ' she took Halla's hands in hers – 'your daughter will find as much love, as much happiness here as anywhere on the wide earth.'

She meant what she had said, and felt it in her heart as she spoke the words. There were things she would never have, but in their place so much more, so much that a helpless orphan girl could never have imagined. And there would always be more. As life rolled on, the cave would grow and change as she did. More sisters would come to enrich her life, to join her family, and Medusa would be there to welcome every one of them, to teach and protect them.

She smiled, and Halla smiled too, her shoulders sinking with relief.

'Thank you,' she breathed, squeezing Medusa's hands. 'I didn't want you to think me ungrateful. I just . . . I needed to know.'

Her eyes returned to her daughter and she was silent for a moment.

'I've been thinking about her name. It's time she had one, and I wondered whether . . . Do you think your sisters would mind if I named her Gorgo?'

The corners of Medusa's mouth twitched, with happiness and with sadness, as she remembered the woman, fierce and gentle, who had saved her.

'They are your sisters too,' she reminded Halla with a smile. 'And I think they would be honoured.'

Yes, she thought. *And we will raise Gorgo together, as she raised us*. There was a roundness to it that satisfied her, and yet her sadness lingered too.

She left Halla to finish her milk and made her way into the trees alone. It was not yet time to feed the snakes, but Medusa suddenly felt a need to be near them, to ground herself in the quiet of the wood, to be away from that chubby-limbed child that filled her with such hope while scratching at a deeper sorrow. There was a comfort in the snakes, who bore their own contradictions so naturally. They were beauty and dread, safety and danger, their venom a toxic tonic with the power to heal as well as harm. Those writhing creatures were conflict embodied.

As she walked through the trees Medusa realised that a part of her hoped she would see Perseus there. She found herself search-ing for a glimpse of his shape through the leaves, her mind drifting back to how they had stood so close in the clearing, the way those green eyes had looked at her. She shook her head. It was a girlish dream, no more. She was ashamed to cling to it, to feel those mem-ories tug at her like warm fingers. She had not even known him, not truly. No, it was the idea of him that lingered, the doubts he had raised, the sense that his leaving had taken more from her than their brief acquaintance. She had been right to send him away, she knew that. She only wished that her churning belly would settle.

You are Medusa of the Gorgons, she told herself, almost speaking the words aloud. She needed time to remember that, a space to gather all the parts of her that had been ripped loose.

The snakes hissed softly in their pit as Medusa lay down beside them, golden crown and aching limbs pulling her towards the earth in their heaviness. She lay looking up at the rippling leaves, at the clear sky above, and drew her fingers through the dirt. This was where she belonged. She felt her chest rise and fall, listening to her breath, to the snakes, straining for the sigh of the waves, too far away to reach her here. She imagined Perseus' ship upon them, cutting through the crests, bearing him away. It was for the best. It was for the best. With her mind drifting on the Great Green, watching as that smiling face became smaller and smaller, she fell into an uneasy sleep.

When she awoke, Perseus was staring back at her.

She blinked, thinking herself still dreaming. But there he was, as real as she, his eyes alive with desperation, his teeth gritted. There was sweat on his tanned brow. Was he hurt? Had he been bitten? She tried to sit up but realised he was straddling her.

'Perseus?' she mumbled stupidly, lips numb with confusion. And then she felt it. A pressure at her navel. She looked down to see his curved dagger pressed against her goat leather. 'Wh—' she started, but couldn't form the words. It didn't make any sense.

He gritted his teeth harder and shut his eyes tight, his face lined with tension.

'Perseus,' she whispered, raising a hand to his cheek as if to smooth it. 'What are you doing? This isn't you.'

She was surprised by how light her voice sounded, though her heart beat so hard it felt as if it would break through her chest. The weight of him brought back an ancient fear, pinning her to the dirt, seizing her limbs. But she forced herself to focus on his face and pushed the memory away. This was another time, another place. Perseus was not that man, she told herself, and she was no longer that girl. Her throat was dry and she swallowed, watching him, breathing his hot breath.

Perseus opened his eyes, bright with anger, narrowed in pain.

'You . . . You . . . ' But his voice was thick, too choked to speak. She watched a tear well and drop, and knew that he was the same boy she had found hunting shadows. He held the dagger with shaking fingers and looked as if he would sooner let it fall.

'You don't have to do this,' she breathed, hand still holding his face. 'You don't have to do anything.'

Though his eyes were blurred with tears, something in them seemed to clear, and he stared at her. It was as if there were two of him within that gaze, each wrestling the other – the gentle boy she knew and a stranger she did not. She held her own gaze steady, willing him to see her, to remember the woman who had sucked out his black blood and brought him into her home. She could feel him bearing down on her but fixed herself upon those green eyes, drawing back the tender boy she had sent away.

It could only have been a few moments but it felt like an eternity to Medusa, locked in that embrace, the dagger's tip quivering against her belly. And then Perseus relaxed. His face, his shoulders, his shaking arms went slack. He sat up to draw in a great shuddering breath and closed his eyes, forcing more tears to spill down his cheeks.

Medusa's heart was still pounding, but she lay still. Now that his anger had cleared he was Perseus once more, her Perseus, just a frightened boy whom she had hurt. She had not known how deeply she had wounded him, and she was sorry for it. But in her relief she found herself smiling.

'I knew you were different,' she sighed. He opened his eyes and looked down at her, brow furrowed. 'I knew you were not like the other men.'

In an instant Perseus' face was transformed, stretched in a terrible grimace, eyes wide, teeth bared, spit flying from his trembling lips. And there it was, carved in every line. The rage, the pain that his sweet face had masked. It had been there all this time, if she had only wanted to see it. Medusa knew now what would come, but it was too late. Her mouth opened in a voiceless scream, and for a moment they were frozen, two Gorgons facing one another.

He drove the hard bronze into her flesh.

Part 3

Andromeda

CHAPTER 25

The water was still warm. Andromeda let her fingers glide through it, enjoying the sensation after the cold night. Dawn was breaking, and soon the oasis would be full with its usual hum – braying animals, bartering merchants, gossiping men and chattering women – but for now there was just her and the clear water.

Of all the springs at the oasis, fresh or salty, trickling or profuse, this one was surely the strangest. They called it the Fountain of the Sun and Moon, hot at night and cool in the day. Her mother had told her the reason for its fickle nature when Andromeda was a young girl, and the story had always stuck in her mind.

'The great Ammon, god of the sky, has two wives, you see,' her mother had said, smiling as Andromeda poked at the curiously warm water one evening. 'The Sun, his first wife, is with him in the daytime and enjoys his company on her long journey from east to west. But at night she must make way for Ammon's other love, the shining Moon, and so the Sun waits here on earth, in the waters of the fountain, making them bubble with her great heat, until day comes again and she can rejoin her husband above. When she rises, the water cools, and the cold Moon comes to dwell in the fountain instead, until the night comes again. And so Ammon shares his affection equally, with neither wife being neglected.'

She remembered the satisfied smile on her mother's face, pleased at a story well told, and yet Andromeda had not smiled. She had wondered how each of them felt, the bright Sun and the shining Moon, trapped in these waters as they watched their husband spend his hours with another. Even now as her fingers rippled the still-warm waters, she imagined the Sun rushing to embrace her lover, while the Moon resigned herself to another lonely day.

It was not a life Andromeda would wish for herself, nor one she would accept. No, when she married she would have a whole husband, not half. Just as he would have a whole wife. It had suited her mother and father well enough. And soon she would follow in their footsteps. Very soon.

It was the day of the bride fair. Andromeda had witnessed it before. Dozens of men seeking a wife, as many girls waiting to be chosen. They came from all across the wide oasis, some even from beyond – the true nomads, the southern traders, those without a tribe of their own. All were welcome at the oasis, as long as they brought flocks and goods and civil manners. The Ammonians themselves were, after all, a tribe of migrants. Wanderers from Egypt in the east, from Nubia in the south, from the western sands and the northern coast, they had sought prosperity and nourishment and found both beneath the shady palms. Andromeda herself had been born here among the springs, like her parents and her grandparents, and though she liked to spot the outsiders who came for the fair, to see new faces and exotic wares, she would not be the bride of any but an Ammonian. The oasis was her home and she would not be taken from it. Its waters ran through her as if they were her own blood.

Now that the sun was in the sky, Andromeda spared a thought for the abandoned moon and made her way back to her family's tent, where her mother stood waiting. Her foot tapped impatiently on the sandy ground.

'You would choose today, of all days, for a morning stroll.' Her mother clicked her tongue. 'Come, quickly now. We must have you ready. Sitammon has already finished her daughter's hair.' She looked over to the neighbouring tent, her eyes narrowed as if she might spy on their progress through the goat hide.

Andromeda tried not to smile. Her mother had always harboured a competitive nature, and her children were one of the only means she had for pursuing it. Andromeda's siblings had all found good marriages and lived prosperously in various corners of the oasis. Now it was her turn.

'You have such beautiful hair,' her mother said, unwinding the long braids from around her head – the way that Andromeda preferred it – and letting them fall down her back. 'You must let people see it.'

Andromeda felt her mother's skilful fingers untie the bottom half of each black braid so that she could thread polished beads among the hair. When the first was finished, Andromeda drew it over her shoulder to admire the colours – bright turquoise, warm carnelian, pale amethyst – not glass but real stone. She had seen her mother buy them from an Egyptian trader three moons ago. No extravagance was too great for the daughter of Kassiopeia.

Once all the beads were in place, Andromeda changed into the dress her mother had laid out and fixed it at the shoulder with a neat pin of ivory. The skirt fell to her ankles, with an open slit to reveal her tattooed shins. Her patterned arms, too, were left bare, and all limbs rubbed with sheep's butter until they shone. Next came the jewellery, thin discs of hammered gold, rattling at her wrists, circling her throat. And finally some thick kohl for her eyes, and a daub of red cinnabar for each cheek, a complement to the fine tattoos at her chin and forehead. Once she was married her cheeks would gain permanent marks of their own, but she was not a woman yet.

When all was done her mother stepped back, surveying the product of her labour. After a careful appraisal she nodded and allowed herself to smile.

'A true beauty,' she breathed, her plump cheeks full. 'I myself had five suitors, you know.' She dropped her voice as if it were privileged knowledge, though Andromeda doubted whether there was anyone left in the oasis who had not been privileged with that fact. 'I'm sure you will have as many. Maybe more.' She clapped her hands giddily, turning away to prepare her own outfit for the fair, and Andromeda smiled to see her so happy. She was glad to please her mother, but she was also glad for herself. The more suitors the better. Not for her pride but for her freedom. She wanted the power of choice, to have a husband who would respect her, who was kind and intelligent, who would not try to rule her. That above all. She knew what it was to be a wife, the freedoms she must give up, the responsibilities she must take on, but she would not make herself a slave. Her mother had chosen wisely, and so would she.

When they were both ready they waited under the large citron tree that stood in front of the tent. There was a breeze rustling through the oasis today, and Andromeda took it as a good omen, a blessing from Ammon. As the sun rose higher she felt her anticipation grow, a tingle that started in her belly and spread to her limbs. It was a nervous feeling, but it was not fear. For Andromeda fear dwelt in the uncontrollable, in power-lessness and weakness. Today she would decide her future, and she prayed to the all-knowing god of the sky that the right path would be clear to her.

Eventually her father emerged from the tent, dressed in his ceremonial robe of antelope skin, fine patterns dancing across its surface. His black hair was braided like hers, though neatly cropped so that it did not touch his shoulders. Another thick braid curled past his ear on either side, longer than the rest and twisted with shining beads like her own. From the top of his head bloomed two ostrich feathers, carefully fixed among the braids, and Andromeda smiled with pride to see them. Her father was not one for ostentation, but neither would he hide his status when it mattered. Today he would look as splendid as any of the other lords of the oasis.

'Kepheus.' Her mother's face lit up to see him so finely dressed, and she hurried forward to take his free arm – the other being occupied by three rolled goatskins. The two of them set off together, leaving Andromeda to carry the large basket of almonds they had prepared.

By the time they reached the marketplace her arms were aching, and she set the basket down with the other contributions for the feast. There was already an impressive array – fruits and cheeses and several clueless goats tethered to palm trees. No rams, of course, for they were sacred to Ammon, but the goats were not so lucky.

Father found a spot in the shade and unfurled the goatskins. As Andromeda settled onto hers she felt several heads turn in her direction but kept her own gaze lowered.

'Good,' said her mother. 'Men like a demure wife.'

Andromeda heard her father laugh. 'Is that so?'

'Ignore him,' her mother tutted, waving a distinctly un-demure hand at her husband. 'Today is your day, Andromeda. I have held you back long enough. Can you blame a mother for clinging to her youngest?' She squeezed Andromeda's knee. 'But you are in your prime now. Play the game right and you may get a better match than even your sister. Did you know that Karomama's husband keeps thirty asses?'

Andromeda nodded, though she wasn't sure that her mother's idea of a good match was entirely the same as hers.

As she continued staring at the sand, two feet stepped into view, ankles shining with bands of gold. Remembering her mother's words, she resisted raising her head.

'Kepheus,' came the voice from above. 'I trust your daughter will be participating in the fair this year?' Andromeda knew the deep voice that spoke. It belonged to Osorkon, one of the lords of the oasis.

'Yes, yes,' her father replied. 'We are sad to let such a treasure go, but we cannot hold on to our children forever.'

'And her dowry?'

Her father shifted on his mat. 'The same as for her sister,' he said levelly.

'More than generous,' her mother interjected, 'considering my daughter's obvious charms. And she weaves and she cooks – the best stew you have tasted. I have taught her all myself.'

'Enough, wife,' her father murmured beside her. Andromeda thought she heard Osorkon's tongue click. 'And what of your son, Nabis? Is he among the suitors?'

'Like a lion among hyenas,' Osorkon replied, and Andromeda had to bite her lip to keep from laughing. She had known Nabis since she was a girl. He was rather squat, with small eyes and a sneering smile. When they were young he had called her Camel for her skinny legs and encouraged the other children to do the same. Luckily she had no fear that he would deign to choose her at the fair, though she pitied the poor girl that would become his wife.

The sun was halfway up the sky now, and the wide marketplace was thronged with bodies, shuffling past one another, trying to find spaces beneath the trees. Eventually a call rang out, and Andromeda spotted Wayheset, the priest and elder, who must have climbed upon the large rock at the heart of the marketplace, for his torso was raised above the crowd.

'Clear the centre,' he called, and the bodies obeyed, shrinking back like blown leaves. Once he was alone on his rock, Wayheset called again. 'Bring the brides forward.'

It was time. Andromeda stood, smoothing her split skirt. She felt her mother's hands briefly touch her hair, straightening the beaded braids, and then her father was leading her by the hand into the centre, where Wayheset waited. Other girls emerged from the crowd, each led by her father, and then with one last squeeze of the hand the men departed, leaving their daughters in a nervous huddle. Andromeda was no less nervous than the rest of them, though she tried not to show it. She looked for her father, but his plumed head was already lost amid the watching eyes. She did spot her mother, however, speaking to this person and that, men, women, those she recognised and those she didn't. *What is she saying?* Andromeda wondered, but she could guess well enough.

'Isn't my daughter beautiful? See how her skin shines. Look at those cheeks. Oh yes, real stone, not glass.'

Andromeda smiled and rolled her eyes. Her mother could brag all she liked. There were more important things at hand, and Andromeda needed to keep her focus. But as her mother's whispers continued, she felt more and more eyes upon her, and her face began to warm. Suddenly she was all too aware of her body. Was she standing straight? Did her arms look awkward? Should she look at the sand or meet the gaze of the crowd? Luckily it was not long until Wayheset spoke again.

'Let the suitors come forth,' he called from behind her, jolting Andromeda out of her self-consciousness.

And in a moment the men had appeared, hovering in a scattered ring around the bundle of brides at the centre. The drums began, and then the pipes, and the suitors started to pace slowly around the girls, some circling in one direction, some in another, all with keen eyes.

Some of the girls began to move to the music, raising their arms and swinging their hips. Andromeda remembered her mother's words. *Play the game*, she had said. And so Andromeda began to move as well, though only a little so as not to make a fool of herself. The men watched as they circled, their eyes moving from one girl to another. It was not long before a suitor cut a decisive path to the centre and took one of the girls by the hand. Andromeda watched the two of them as they rejoined the circling figures, the man looking back as he led his potential bride behind him. The girl's eyes were locked to his, assessing him just as he had assessed her. She seemed to find something she liked, for she did not let go, and the two of them continued circling together.

Perhaps encouraged by the success of the first suitor, others began to make their way into the centre, taking girls with them as they rejoined the circlers. Some girls let go quickly, shrinking back into the pack. Others took a circuit or two before deciding against the match – perhaps after seeing a shake from their father's head amid the crowd. A few, like the first, seemed content, or simply relieved to have been chosen, and kept their hand clasped to the one that led them.

Andromeda had seen many eyes look her way, some fleeting, others lingering. Then, as she watched the girl next to her be led away, she felt a hand grasp hers.

The suitor was tall with dark lustrous skin and golden eyes. She found herself entranced by his beauty as he led her into the circling throng, and flattered that he had chosen her, but she could not forget her purpose. It was clear from his attire that he was a trader from the south. No doubt he would give her fine children, but she could not think of leaving the oasis. With an apologetic smile she let his hand drop and returned to the centre.

Barely a moment later her hand was taken up again, this time by an Ammonian boy, though she did not recognise him. He had kind eyes, and smiled at her hopefully as he led her along, but she could see that his robe was worn, his scarce jewellery copper not gold. She had to think of her family as well as herself, and when they passed her father she saw his answer. It pained Andromeda to see the boy's cheeks drop as she unwound her fingers from his.

She did not even reach the centre before the next hand clasped hers. The jolt of it startled her, and when she turned to face her bold new suitor, her surprise only grew.

Nabis held her hand as though he already owned her, marching through the throng as if all were gathered for his wedding. His ears and wrists dripped with gold, though it only served to make him look dull by comparison. How could he think that she would accept him? His father was rich, of course, but Nabis was a cruel boy and would make a cruel husband.

She tried to let go of his hand, but he held it tight. She pulled harder but he gripped tighter. He was beginning to hurt her but he didn't seem to care, smiling triumphantly out at the crowd as he dragged her behind him. Eventually she lost her patience.

'Let go of me!' she yelled, digging her bare feet into the sand.

It was louder than she had intended. The musicians faltered, and it felt as if all eyes were on her, on the two of them frozen in their awkward tableau. Nabis looked back at her, his small eyes blinking in surprise. He let her hand drop.

There was a hum of chatter from the crowd, and a ripple of laughter somewhere to Andromeda's right, but among all the watching faces the one Andromeda saw was Osorkon, with brows low and jaw tight.

It was not long before the music restarted, and Andromeda made her way back to the dwindling huddle in the centre. One of the girls made a joke and Andromeda tried to smile, but she could still feel Osorkon's burning eyes upon her.

Eventually the tightness in her chest relaxed a little, and she began to watch the couples again. There were now far fewer empty-handed suitors amid the throng, though Andromeda liked to think that those left were simply the most discerning. The selection of a wife – or a husband, for that matter – was one of the most important choices one could make, and worthy of careful consideration.

As she swayed to the music a broad figure appeared before her, and she looked up to find another face she recognised. It was the son of one of her father's friends, though she could not remember his name. He smiled nervously but did not grasp her hand. Instead he extended his for her to take. One of the girls laughed at his strange behaviour, but his gaze remained steady, watching to see what Andromeda would do. She let her lips break into a smile and placed her hand in his.

His eyes barely left her as they made their way through the throng. They were a warm brown, with an intelligent light. Open and curious. She liked the feel of his hand around hers, the way they fitted together so neatly, and though he walked ahead he did not pull her with him. They simply fell into step. There was something about the balanced confidence of his stride, neither shuffle nor strut, that made her want to follow, to learn more, to keep her hand in his. And before she knew it they had circled the rock once, twice, three times.

As they completed their fourth circuit, her rational self rushed to justify the decision her instinct had made. He was the right age – no more than a year or two older than herself, and too young to have another wife. He was from a respectable family, and not lacking in prosperity from the look of his fine robe. Like her, he had been raised by the waters of the oasis and would not take her from her home. And it seemed that he cared more for her approval than for his own pride, if his unusual gesture had been anything to go by. *Yes*, she thought to herself. *A good prospect.*

And so she squeezed his hand, and he squeezed back. And once their circling was ended and both fathers had approved – as she knew they would – the promise was made. At the next full moon they would be wed. Andromeda, daughter of Kepheus, and Phineus, son of Belos, would begin their life.

CHAPTER 26

The breeze that had begun so pleasantly grew stronger over the following days, until the whipped-up sand began to scratch at Andromeda's skin. The people of the oasis were used to sandstorms. Every spring they came and every spring they were endured. But it was summer now. This wind paid no heed to season, tearing down from the north to blight their crops and choke their livestock. Unnatural, unrelenting, inescapable. No matter how tightly Andromeda wrapped her scarf she found her skin stripped dry, her ears and nostrils filled with sand. She had never known a storm so bad. Even the spring storms lasted no more than a day at a time.

On the evening of the third day, a meeting was called. The lords of the oasis were to gather in the Great Tent, and Andromeda's father asked that she accompany him.

'You know my hearing is not what it was,' he said as he wrapped himself against the scratching wind. 'If the men speak too quietly you can tell me what they say.'

Andromeda was pleased to go with him. The oasis was her home as much as anyone's, and she was anxious to know what would be done to preserve it. Nor did the other lords go alone. Many of them brought sons or brothers, and though Andromeda felt a few eyes rest on her, no one stopped her from entering the Great Tent and taking her seat among the men. They had greater concerns.

The tent was cramped. Usually a gathering such as this would be held outside, but the storm made that impossible. And so here they sat, hot bodies pressed against one another, voices buzzing like flies. Eventually Wayheset, High Priest of Ammon, cleared his aged throat and a pregnant hush fell.

'Three days we have suffered the winds of the north. Our flocks die in their pens, our crops are ripped from the earth. I have consulted with the oracle of great Ammon, so that we may know the cause of this disaster.'

Wayheset paused to swallow and lick his cracked lips. No doubt his throat was as dry as Andromeda's, but she couldn't help feeling impatient as she waited for him to continue.

'The great god is angry,' he said eventually. 'It is we who have brought about this anger, by an excess of pride. And now Ammon of the wide sky sends his winds from the sea in the north, to punish us for our conceit.'

There was a quiet muttering around the tent as the revelation was digested. Andromeda turned to her father to see if he had heard the priest's words, but the many wrinkles of his forehead told her that he had. He gazed at the central fire in solemn thought.

A movement caught Andromeda's attention, and across the tent she saw long-faced Osorkon rising from his mat. His son, Nabis, remained seated, though he cast his small eyes about the room, with heavy lids narrowed. Afraid that they would fall on her, Andromeda looked instead to Osorkon as he adjusted his ostrich feathers. She had not seen Nabis since she had rejected him at the fair and did not want to meet his piercing gaze.

'This is grave news indeed,' Osorkon began, shaking his head so that the ostrich feathers swayed. 'But now that we know the cause of Ammon's anger we can make reparation.'

There was a murmur of agreement. *The sooner the better*, Andromeda thought. Even now she could hear the wind howling, the sand hurled against the thick hide of the tent.

Osorkon paused, apparently deep in thought.

'One hundred goats,' he said eventually. 'Would this be a worthy sacrifice?' Osorkon turned to the priest Wayheset, who looked back solemnly.

'Yes,' he croaked, his grey head nodding. 'One hundred goats would please the god. We shall ask one from each of the wealthiest families.'

There was a ripple of nods from the assembled men. Though a loss, they would lose far more than one goat if the storms continued.

'Yes. Perhaps, perhaps,' Osorkon murmured, stroking his braided beard. 'But is it not right that the one who transgresses should make amends with the gods? When a man spills blood, he must make it right himself. He does not ask his neighbour to make a sacrifice in his stead.'

Andromeda saw faces turn to one another, some muttering agreement, others wrinkled in thought. Across the tent a lean man rose to speak.

'This is not one man's problem. We all suffer from this blight on our land.'

'And yet we have not all caused it,' came Osorkon's level reply. 'It can be no coincidence that the winds began the day after the bride fair. Many of you were there.' He looked around the tent, drawing men into his gaze. Andromeda felt the sharpness of those eyes, just as she had felt them that day, glaring at her across the circling suitors. An uncomfortable feeling began to grow in her stomach. 'You saw the same thing I did. Heard it with your own ears. Unbridled pride. Shameful. Shameful.' He shook his head heavily. 'And from the mouth of a woman.'

He said the last word as if it were a piece of grit on his tongue, and Andromeda's skin prickled. A hum of chatter broke out around the tent. Her father asked what had been said, but she didn't have time to relay before Osorkon raised his voice to continue.

'Kassiopeia. Wife of Kepheus.'

Now all eyes were on them. Andromeda took her father's hand as if to shield him.

'She touted her daughter's beauty as if it were wrought gold, her words an overflowing spring of conceit. Ammon sees and hears all, and he has seen that woman's wicked pride. Now he punishes us for her excess, but should we be made to suffer twice over? To lose our wealth in paying for her crime? I say that it is he who must pay.' Osorkon's arm shot out, pointing across the circle. 'Kepheus, who has let his wife run wild. He must give one hundred goats to great Ammon, to rid us of these storms.'

Her father's hand was tight around hers now.

'How much?' he asked her. 'How much did he say?'

'One hundred goats.' She wasn't sure if he could hear her above the din that had erupted around them, but as his face sank she knew that he had. One hundred goats. It was enough to ruin them. They would have to trade away their sheep too just to make that number.

'Let he who has angered the god pay the reparation.' Osorkon's deep voice sounded above the clamour, and other voices rose in assent. As Andromeda looked upon their faces in horror, upon the self-preserving smugness of their folded arms, she felt anger boil inside her. These men traded with her father. They sat at his fire, drank the honey milk she mixed for them. And now they clung to their own fortunes and let his sink. As she looked about her, hoping for a dissenting face, she noticed Osorkon watching her, his hard eyes glinting in the firelight. And there beside him sat Nabis, his lips curled with a satisfied smile.

Before she had thought about what she was doing, Andromeda was rising from her mat, legs trembling beneath her skirt. She could not let Osorkon send her family into ruin. Not when it was she who had provoked him, not when her mother was not here to defend herself. By the time she was on her feet the tent had fallen silent, with baffled faces turned towards the girl who dared to stand among men. They did not seem angry but curious. Andromeda's heart pounded in her chest. She could see them asking the same question she was: what would she say now that she had their attention?

'My uncles,' she began, her voice quavering a little. It was a term of respect, and yet now it felt too familiar. She cleared her throat, and when she spoke again her voice was stronger. 'Lords of the oasis, you ask that my father give all he has to save us from the storms. And he would do it.' She looked down at her father, his plumed head set stiff with resignation. 'You know him as a man of honour, of loyalty. He would give his life for our tribe if it were asked.' Around her, heads nodded with respect, and Andromeda felt emboldened by them. The words were coming easily now, the path before her revealing itself as she spoke. 'But what use is there in his sacrifice, if it is not the *right* sacrifice?'

At this Osorkon stepped forward, his long face thrown into relief by the fire.

'High Priest Wayheset has already said that one hundred goats would please Ammon.' He drew a breath to continue but the elderly priest knocked his staff on the ground.

'All sacrifices please the gods,' he rasped. It felt as though the whole tent leaned in to hear his thin voice. 'But even I cannot know the desires of the great god. I can tell you only what has been revealed to me by the oracle. Beyond that nothing is certain. Perhaps this sacrifice would bring an end to the storms, and perhaps it would not.' Wayheset sucked what were left of his teeth, his expression meditative. 'I would like to hear what this girl has to say.' He turned his grey head towards Osorkon, as if daring him to speak again, and then gestured for Andromeda to continue.

Surprised and honoured, she gathered herself quickly.

'When a crop fails, we bless the ground so that it might nourish us the next year, yes?' Andromeda paused as the men nodded their dark heads, before going on. 'And when an infant dies, we cleanse the mother so that she will not bring forth death again.' The heads continued to nod. This was all well known, of course, but she was glad to see that they were listening. The answer was so clear now. She could save her family, save the oasis. She just had to convince them. 'Does it not stand to reason then, that for the sacrifice to work we must go to the source of the evil. If we hope to turn Ammon's winds away from us, we must make our sacrifice on the northern shore, from whence the great god sends his wrath.'

There was a murmur from the crowd, stopped almost immediately as Osorkon raised his voice once more.

'Foolish girl. You open your mouth and speak only nonsense. How are we to transport one hundred beasts to the edge of the Great Green in the midst of a sandstorm? Take your seat now, and save your father any further disgrace.'

But Andromeda did not sit. She planted her feet, toes pressed into the sand, and spoke again.

'We do not need to transport the beasts. I will be the sacrifice.'

CHAPTER 27

She felt her father grip her skirt.

'What are you doing?' she saw him ask, but she could barely hear him. The tent was full of shouts, of objections, of laughter too. Even Wayheset struggled to gain quiet. Eventually, as the priest raised one arm, the voices lowered to a whispering hum.

'Daughter of Kepheus,' he said firmly, gripping his sacred staff. 'The great Ammon has never demanded such a sacrifice, nor would it please him. The gods abhor the spilling of human blood.'

His words produced another eruption from the crowd, and Andromeda waited for it to die down before speaking.

'I do not propose to sacrifice my life, only my pride. As my beauty has been the cause of this calamity, so it will be the remedy. I will travel to the northern shore and expose myself to the sea, and to the sight of all-seeing Ammon. I shall give my body up to him for one night and one day, for him to lash with wind and wave, and so degrade the object of my mother's conceit.' The crowd murmured and Andromeda saw heads turn to one another at the edges of her vision, but her eyes remained fixed on Wayheset. 'Would this satisfy the great god and bring an end to his anger?'

The old man flexed his fingers around his staff, his chin buried in his neck. After some moments of contemplation, he finally looked up.

'I think it would.'

There was a collective exhalation from the watching men, and the tone of their murmurs changed, from sneering outrage to relieved approval. The god would be appeased. The storms would end. And they would have to give nothing of their own to achieve it. Even Osorkon looked satisfied. He had sought to ruin her father for the embarrassment she had caused him, and no doubt for her denial of a profitable union between their families, but she supposed that the ruin of her own dignity was compensation enough. She noticed Nabis' beady eyes upon her, and felt that he was already imagining her bare flesh exposed. Though her skin crawled under his gaze, she did not shrink. She had won a victory, of sorts, and held her chin high.

'I understand if you need to end the engagement,' Andromeda said before Phineus had opened his mouth. The meeting had ended not long ago, and now here he was in her tent. His father had told him, of course, about what she had said, what she had pledged, and she did not blame him for wanting to break his promise. She knew that in giving herself up to Ammon she was sacrificing not only her dignity but her value as a bride. A woman's nakedness was for her husband only, in the privacy of their tent. What man would want a wife who had exposed herself, who had spoken of it before all the lords of the oasis? He would make himself a laughing stock. So no, she did not blame him, could not blame him. And yet it stung to think that she had held happiness in her grasp. He would have made her a good husband, but nothing was more important than protecting her family.

'Andromeda. Are you listening to me?'

She had turned away to continue packing their supplies for the journey across the desert. And to hide her face from him. She did not want him to see her cheeks trembling, but now he took her hand and turned her towards him.

'Did you not hear what I said?' She was surprised to see that he was smiling. 'I said I'm coming with you. To the northern shore.'

Andromeda blinked at him. Her expression must have amused him, for Phineus' smile broadened.

'My father was very impressed by your commitment to the tribe. And to stand up before all the lords . . . I wish I had seen it myself. He told me what a good match I'd made, but I knew that already.'

Her mouth twitched, but she still wasn't sure what to say. His face was bright, his chest full as he looked at her. He took her other hand in his.

'I can't let you go without an escort. Your father says one of the merchants has already offered to guide you, but you'll need protection as well. I'm no warrior,' he added quickly, 'but my father taught me to hunt and I can handle a bow well enough.'

He looked at her expectantly, and she looked back at him. His shoulders were broad, his arms thick. Warrior or not, she would feel safer with him at her side. Her father's fighting days, if he had ever had them, were well behind him.

'Thank you,' she breathed, finally finding her tongue.

It was still dark when they set out, though a glow had come upon the sky – enough to see by with eyes accustomed to the black night. They travelled light, taking a donkey each and two for the supplies. Most of their weight was water – goatskins and ostrich shells full to the brim. Food was less important, though they took enough to see them through the journey. Andromeda, like her mother and father, had dressed in a long woollen robe, her arms and legs thoroughly wrapped against the violent sand and withering wind. She had wrapped her head too, with only a narrow slit through which to see the world ahead. On her lap was a shawl for the donkey, to protect its eyes and ears from the worst of the storms. For now the air was relatively still, but she knew it would not be long before the wind rose again.

It was a strange feeling, to leave the oasis. That swathe of green had sheltered her all her life, and she could not help looking back as it shrank behind her. Ahead there was only sand and sky, open, vast, and more than a little frightening. Andromeda was glad of the other donkeys plodding beside hers and tried to cast her mind beyond the horizon, to the far north and the Great Green. It would be a wondrous sight, she told herself, though she could not ignore the uneasy feeling in her stomach. When they reached the shore, she would have to do what she had promised. With the wind so low, a part of her hoped that the storms had ended, that the god's anger had abated and they would be able to turn back. But in her heart she knew it was not so. Ammon must be appeased.

By the time the sun had reached its height the winds had risen too. The sand lashed at her clothes, scratching at any strip of skin that wasn't covered. They pushed forward, clashing head on with the gusts from the north. Andromeda had to close her eyes to keep the grit from them, and so she was as blind as the donkey beneath her, its head wrapped with the shawl. She could only hope that they were keeping to their path. Every now and then she would open her eyelids a sliver to check that the others were still beside her, and when she did she witnessed the sand racing over the ground in an endless stream, the air so hazy that it was no longer clear where the earth ended and the sky began. It was bewildering, suffocating, so much worse than the storms had seemed at the oasis, amid the trees and the tents. Here the winds had nothing to stop them, tearing across the barren plateau and whipping up every grain in their path.

Even when the wind dropped again there was little talking among their party. Their throats were too dry, their mouths too muffled by their shawls. Andromeda had imagined conversations with her husband-to-be, an opportunity for them to grow more familiar, but now that they were out on the sand the only goal was to cover as much distance as they could. While there was light in the sky they pushed on, quickly when the wind was low and more slowly when it was high. Their nights were brief, huddled inside the sand-battered tent, with each of them trying to get whatever sleep they could.

After seven days in the desert wastes, they at last came upon land that was not so desolate. There were shrubs for the donkeys to graze, and glimpses of life seen here and there – slender gazelles and long-eared foxes darting across the tufted plain. Finally, after another long day battling through the whirling sand, their guide Rudammon cried out.

'The Great Green!' he called back to them, fighting to be heard above the wind. Andromeda could see nothing through the haze, but as they journeyed on, the wind began to drop, and finally she saw a new texture emerge, between the orange earth and the darkening sky. It was her first glimpse of the sea.

Only when they had reached the white sand did they bring their donkeys to a halt. The sea stretched across the horizon, for as far as she could see in either direction. Andromeda was puzzled to find that it did not look green at all, but grey-blue flecked with gold where the rolling peaks caught the light of the setting sun. Though it was not as she had imagined, it was a beautiful sight nonetheless, and she took a moment to admire it while trying not to think of what must come next.

'It's getting late,' her father said, dismounting and taking a swig from his ostrich shell. 'We should set up camp and see to the sacrifice tomorrow.'

'No.' Andromeda slid from her own donkey and met her father's eye. 'While we delay the oasis will suffer. Give me to the god now. I am ready.' She meant the words she spoke, and yet she was surprised to find her voice so steady. Surprised and glad – she did not want her father to know that she was afraid.

'She is right, Kepheus.' Andromeda's mother had appeared at her elbow. 'The sooner it is done the sooner we can go home. But you must take refreshment first.' Her mother turned to her now, pushing plump dates into her hands. 'Drink all the water you can. Rudammon knows where to find more.'

Yes, it was wise not to be depleted before her ordeal began. So Andromeda ate and drank until she was satisfied. She realised that they had not discussed the particulars of the sacrifice, though it seemed her mother's thoughts were the same as hers.

'You must let me do this thing alone,' she said to them all. 'Once I am laid out for Ammon, you must stay away. It would only shame me to have you look upon me. Mother will help me, of course, on the beach, but you must promise me that no one else will approach. You must stay up on the land and keep any travellers away. Will you do as I ask?'

'You have our word,' said Phineus immediately. 'None shall see you but Ammon.'

She smiled at him, and they all nodded in agreement. She felt a little of her anxiety loosen, and a warmth spread through her limbs. It would be easier knowing that they were here waiting for her. Feeling her emotion rise, she took a deep breath and clasped her mother's hand.

'I'm ready.'

The beach was long and craggy, populated with large rocks that looked as if they had been dropped there by Ammon. Andromeda surveyed each of them as she walked by her mother's side, until finally she found a spot that was suitable – close to the water's edge and yet high enough that she would not drown if the tide came in. Their guide Rudammon had warned them of that, for he knew the sea better than they did.

With the sun setting there was no time to lose. Andromeda removed her billowing robe and the dress beneath, folding them neatly on a high ledge of rock. She had undressed before her mother a thousand times, and yet already it felt different. She was not only naked before her but before the world, not concealed in their tent but exposed beneath the open sky. She wrapped her arms around herself, her skin pimpling now that the warmth of the day had fled. She gave her arms a brisk rub before opening the little bag she had brought with her. Inside was a long strip of leather and a small stake of fire-hardened wood.

'You must fix me to the rock,' she told her mother, pressing the materials into her hands. Her mother blinked in surprise.

'Is it necessary, my child? We know you will do as you have said. There is no need to add to your discomfort.' She took the bag from her to put the items away, but Andromeda grasped her arm.

'Please, Mother. If I am to be a sacrifice I must be treated like one. Ammon must know what is given.' She did not add that she doubted herself. Not her intention, but rather her courage. When the dark night came, when she was cold and afraid and alone, would she be able to resist the temptation to run back to her family? She hoped she would, but she could not risk the fate of the oasis on that hope. It was better to be sure. Andromeda kept her expression hard as she looked at her mother, and eventually she relented.

'Very well. Though I will try not to bind you too tightly.'

Her mother did well. The leather felt secure around her wrists but did not pinch, and the stake was firmly wedged into a crack in the rock. Her hands were bound together above her head, just as she had requested, low enough that she could rest them on her head for comfort. Though fear rumbled in her belly, Andromeda was pleased that all so far had gone to plan. Despite her nakedness, her vulnerability, and the unknowable night stretching before her, she felt in control.

'I will come to you again at sunset tomorrow,' her mother said softly. 'And we'll have honey bread waiting for you.' Andromeda could tell that her mother was trying to smile, but her cheeks were too heavy. 'I'm so proud of you, my sweet one. You've saved us all. Your family, the oasis. All will be well because of you. Remember that when the night comes.' She kissed Andromeda's forehead and stepped down from the ledge.

Andromeda watched her mother until she was out of sight, then turned her eyes back to the swelling ocean. Though she knew those she loved were not far from her, she had never felt so alone.

CHAPTER 28

It was not long before the last rays of the sun had been swallowed by the horizon and the dark night descended. Andromeda listened to the sound of her own breath, shaking over the heave and sigh of the waves. She tried to calm it, to fall into rhythm with the great swell, to feel comforted and not menaced by those churning waters that she could barely see but which filled her ears like the roar of a hundred lions.

She looked up, admiring the countless stars that speckled the sky, and remembered the stories her father had told her about them. No one could tell a story like her father could. She remembered how proud it made her, to see their neighbours gathered under the citron tree outside their tent, ears turned with eagerness towards her father's soft voice, building the story line by line like the weaving of a basket.

She smiled at that vision of her home, full of colour and sound and texture, full of smiling faces that now felt so far away. As the waves rose to lick at her feet, as they crashed against the rock and sprayed her bare skin, she closed her eyes and thought of the oasis. What was one night of fear, if she could save all that she loved? By the next night Ammon's anger would be quelled and she would be with her family again. They would go home and she would be married and live her days in happiness. She only had to endure.

The waves rose higher, splashing her shins, her knees, her shivering thighs. Andromeda was afraid that they would not stop. She had to push away visions of her gasping mouth, her chin struggling to stay above the swell, the thought of her mother returning tomorrow only to find her limp body hanging from the rock. She realised that her heart was racing, that her skin had grown tight with that terrible image. But just as the sea foam began to creep towards her hips the tide drew back, the waves shrinking gradually until they slapped only hard rock and not her flinching flesh.

Though the worst was over, the long night still stretched ahead of her, and so Andromeda sang to herself, her voice thin and quavering in the darkness. It was a comfort to hear those undulating sounds, rising and falling just as the waves did, sounds she had heard and sung so many times before. It was the sound of home, here at the edge of the world.

Despite the ache in her limbs and the rough stone at her back she must have fallen asleep for a time, for when she next opened her eyes the glow of morning was on the horizon. It was a welcome sight, and although she knew her ordeal was only half done, she did not fear the day as she had the night. Already seabirds began to wheel in the sky, and she felt a little less alone.

But the higher the sun rose, the less grateful Andromeda became. The darkness, though terrifying, had been like a cloak for her nakedness. Now she felt utterly exposed, pinned to the rock, desperate to wrench her hands free and cover herself. She knew there was no real need to fear, that the beach was deserted and that she could trust Phineus and her father to keep it so. It was foolish to blush before the gaze of the gulls. She knew that, and yet she felt their sharp eyes upon her all the same.

It became easier, in time, as she followed the slow course of the sun and felt the moment of her liberty draw closer. The tide swelled again, but this time she knew that she would not drown, and though she braced herself against the waves she did not fear them. The day brought other challenges, of course, as Andromeda felt her mouth become drier, her head lighter, her skin more seared. She ran a stiff tongue over her cracked lips and tasted the salt of the ocean spray. She dreamed of fresh milk, of the clear waters of the oasis. *Soon,* she told herself. It would not be much longer.

The sun was halfway across the sky now, shining down with an unrelenting intensity. Andromeda found its reflection on the water so dazzling that she had to close her eyes, but when she did, she felt so unguarded that she compromised with a narrow squint. As she scanned the waters to the west, her sliver of vision caught upon something. A black shape far off on the water. A sail full of wind and the tiny figures of men moving back and forth upon the deck.

Her heart began to hammer, her skin suddenly cold with dread despite the sun. *They will not see you.* Andromeda willed every muscle to hold still, to draw no attention, to fight the urge to squirm and shrink. They were so far away that she could make out none of their faces. No, they would not, could not see her. She let herself breathe a little as the ship went on its way, following the horizon with no care for her. She supposed she had known that ships journeyed along the shore, but she had not expected to see one. She had been so concerned with warding off travellers from the land that she had not thought that the great expanse before her might bring forth its own threats. Andromeda scolded herself for her foolishness, but it mattered little now. The ship had passed her, and she told herself that she would be unlikely to see another. After all, the sea had been quite empty until now.

Just as her muscles had begun to slacken they tightened again. The ship was changing course. Its black prow turned until it faced the beach, and the broad sail grew larger and larger. Andromeda swallowed hard, her dry throat struggling with the effort. She began to pick out the faces of the crew. Were they looking at her? She couldn't tell. Suddenly the sail was rolled and there were several splashes as anchors were dropped. The ship had come to rest a way off from her rock, down the beach, but it was close enough to make Andromeda's breath rattle.

She watched as a slender figure jumped from the deck. She watched as he waded through the shallows, as he walked out of the waves onto the beach, and made his way towards her. And all the time her heart pounded, her wrists straining at their bonds.

He stopped below her rock, a boy barely older than herself, and spoke a greeting she did not understand. He smiled lightly, as if they were simply two travellers crossing on the road, but when her lips remained stiff his smile waned. Andromeda's stomach twisted as he beheld her, his eyes roving without shame, bright with curiosity, or with amusement, or with desire. It was the last she feared, and hardened her gaze as if her very eyes might hold him back. But he skipped easily from the sand up onto the ledge where she was tied, and spoke again in his strange language.

'I don't understand you,' she said, shaking her head and fighting not to be consumed by her fear. 'Please, don't come any closer.' She moved away from him, as far as her bonds would allow, but his expression did not change. He closed the gap between them, and extended a hand towards her.

'Please—'

But he stopped her lips with his thumb, tracing it over her chin, down her throat, towards her thumping heart.

She twisted herself violently and he stepped back. Though he frowned he did not look angry. He simply watched her, straining helplessly. She thought she saw the spectre of a smile pass his lips, and then his eyes followed her trembling arms, to the leather nailed to the rock.

He spoke again, gesturing to the bonds, and she saw his hand move to a curved blade at his hip.

'No, you mustn't,' she said suddenly, pulling away from him again. 'I must complete the sacrifice.' She found her fear abating a little, seeing his intention. If he had wanted her, he could have taken her. Why cut her loose? But she could not let him ruin everything. Not when she had come so far.

His face creased in confusion to see her resist liberty, but then he looked from her to his knife. It was clear he thought she feared violence, for he smiled reassuringly and spoke soft words. Then in one swift movement he raised the blade again and cut the leather as if it were butter.

Her arms suddenly free, Andromeda clasped them to her chest and rubbed her wrists. She was glad to be able to cover herself a little, to hide her breasts from this boy who had no right to see them. But as he watched her expectantly, she realised that it was not fair for her to be angry. He had done no real wrong. She could still fulfil her promise to Ammon. She shook away the memory of his fingers upon her skin, and reminded herself of how she must have looked to his eyes. He had tried to help her.

'Thank you,' she whispered. She inclined her head to make her meaning clear, and when she looked up again he was smiling.

She forced her cheeks upwards for a moment and then waited, holding her arms across as much of her body as she could reach. When he made no move to leave, she looked across to his ship.

He nodded with understanding, and she began to let out her breath in relief, but he wrapped his hand around her wrist. As he stepped down from the rock she realised that he meant to lead her with him. She tried to pull her arm free but he held it tight, pulling her onto the sand.

'No. I can't go with you,' she said firmly, planting her feet. But of course, he understood her words no more than she understood his, and continued to lead her along the sand. Unable to release herself, Andromeda found another idea forming in her mind.

'Stop,' she called, touching his forearm to gain his attention. He turned towards her and she pointed back towards the land, to where her family waited beyond the beach. She pulled him gently, smiling encouragingly. If she could take him to her family, he would see that she needed no rescuer. They would give him hospitality, as was proper, and then he would go on his way and tomorrow she could return to complete the sacrifice.

As his feet turned towards the land her smile became genuine. She led him over the rocks, stopping to dress herself hurriedly in the clothes she had left on the ledge. It was a relief to be covered, and she felt her stride grow steadier as they walked together. But as they left the beach and the salty waves grew quieter, Andromeda became aware of a foul smell on the air, acrid and sweet at once, enough to roll her stomach with each waft. With a surety she could not explain, she knew the source. A leather bag was slung over the stranger's shoulder, large and full, with a terrible weight as it swung against his hip. Andromeda found herself transfixed by it, drawn and yet repulsed by its pendulous motion, by the rotten-sweet smell that oozed through the leather. It was a smell she knew, impossible to forget, woven as it was with memories of loss. It was the smell of death.

CHAPTER 29

'Andromeda!'

Her mother's face barely had time to smile before it clouded with confusion.

'The sun has not set. I thought—' Kassiopeia's frown turned towards the stranger and she took a step backwards.

'Do not be afraid, Mother.' Andromeda put out a reassuring hand.

'Who is this man?' Her father appeared from behind the tent, fingers gripping the handle of his crook. 'Where has he come from? Has he hurt you?'

'No, Father.' She tried to smile, but her mind was still on the swinging bag. 'His ship was passing and . . . He does not speak our tongue. He thought that he was helping me.' She looked at the stranger, his eyes moving between them all, to the crook her father clasped. 'I thought we should offer him refreshment,' she said hurriedly, afraid the stranger would take their frowns for hostility. She was beginning to think it had been a mistake to lead him from the beach. 'It is not right, Father? That we should give hospitality, as we would to any traveller?'

He looked her over, as if to check that she was truly unharmed. Then finally his brow loosened.

'Of course. Yes, of course. We would not send him away with dry lips. Come.' Her father gestured widely with his free hand, beckoning them toward the fire. 'We must thank our guest for his . . . care.'

Andromeda knew that the stranger could not have understood the words they had spoken, but he smiled at her father's open arms and she felt her misgivings lighten.

Once they were seated in front of the tent her mother handed her an ostrich shell filled with water, which she gulped desperately. Remembering her manners, Andromeda passed it to the stranger, though her parched throat still cried for more.

'Is that the last?' she asked, watching a precious stream run down the boy's chin.

Her mother nodded. 'But Phineus has gone with Rudammon to fetch more. They should be back before long.'

'They are here already,' her father said, shielding his eyes from the sun as he stared out across the sand. Andromeda followed his gaze and sure enough she saw the silhouettes of two donkeys, and a man leading each.

'Blessings to Ammon,' her mother muttered, but Andromeda was not sure whether she was grateful for the arrival of the water or the men. Though she smiled pleasantly when the stranger met her glance, Andromeda saw her mother's eyes grow sharp when he looked away. She was wary of him. Perhaps because he was not of their land. Perhaps because she had noted the glinting metal at his hip. Perhaps because she knew the circumstances in which he had found her daughter, that he had seen what he should not see. Or perhaps she too had caught a waft of that rotting sweetness and discerned its source. Whatever the cause of her agitation, she seemed to relax upon seeing the men on the horizon.

'The dough is already mixed and risen,' she said brightly, her tattooed cheeks quivering with a forced smile. 'You must be hungry, my daughter. And our guest too. We shall see that he has a full belly before he goes on his way.'

Andromeda helped her mother with the bread, though her arms trembled with the effort after her night on the rock. Together they swept out a crater in the hot ash from the fire and laid the round dough in place, before heaping more ash on top. As they waited for it to bake, Andromeda could feel the stranger's eyes upon her, burning her cheeks like the unblinking sun, following her as she leant forward to replace fallen embers. It should not have bothered her. What harm was there in a look? He was a stranger in these lands and no doubt curious about their ways, and about the girl he had found in so strange a situation. And yet as he gazed upon her she felt somehow naked again, as if her flesh, now seen, could not truly be hidden from those eyes. As she watched the embers glow with each breath of wind, she wondered whether he saw her as she appeared, or as he knew her to be beneath her woollen folds. The thought made her shrink. *He will soon be away on his ship*, she told herself, fighting to keep her face smooth.

By the time the bread was baked the men were near. Andromeda's father strode to meet them and explain the presence of their guest. Meanwhile Andromeda brushed the top embers to the side with a stick and lifted the hot loaf with careful fingertips, shaking off most of the ash and sand. She began to raise the edge of her skirt to brush off what remained, as she had done a thousand times before, but stopped herself. Feeling the stranger's eyes on the bare skin of her leg, she dropped the hem and did her best to brush the bread with her sleeve. When the job was done she looked up to see Phineus and Rudammon tethering the water-laden donkeys and smiled. With relief she felt the stranger's eyes leave her, turned as hers were towards the new arrivals. She rose to her feet.

'Andromeda,' breathed Phineus, striding towards her. He looked as if he would keep striding but stopped himself, nodding respectfully with sand still between them. 'Are you all right? How was the night? How . . . ' He glanced at their guest, still seated on her father's mat. 'Kepheus tells me you were . . . assisted?'

She saw the question he was truly asking, in the crease of his brow, the concern of his gaze. And didn't he have every right to wonder? About what had transpired between this stranger and his betrothed? Andromeda thought of those uninvited fingers on her collarbone and drove the memory away.

'I'm quite well.' She smiled, hoping he had not seen her hesitation. 'It was a simple misunderstanding. We shall thank the traveller for his concern and then I shall complete my offering to Ammon.'

'You would expose yourself again?' Phineus stepped towards her, half raising an arm as if he would take her hand. 'The winds have dropped. You need not risk yourself any further.'

His pleading expression struck her chest like a stone, but it was not in her to go against what she had promised. Andromeda opened her mouth to argue but it was her father's voice that sounded.

'Rudammon may be able to trade words with our guest,' he announced across the narrow camp. 'He looks to be an islander, and our guide tells me he has traded with the people of the Great Green.'

Rudammon bowed to the stranger and spoke a greeting that Andromeda did not understand. Jolted into action, the stranger sprang from his mat and clasped their guide by the hand. He began rattling off unfamiliar sounds, just as he had when he had come to her on the rock, but Rudammon's head was tilted, his brow creased in concentration. When the sounds stopped, he nodded.

'He is a trader from across the sea, Lord Kepheus, as we thought. He gives his name as Perseus, and asks for yours. And for hers.'

Rudammon glanced across to where Andromeda stood, and she was surprised when her heart began to quicken. A name was no secret thing. It should be freely given. So why did she feel herself stiffen?

'Please give him our names, Rudammon,' her father replied. 'And tell him that he has my thanks and my friendship, for aiding my daughter.' Her father moved so that he was next to her and placed an arm around her shoulder, nodding graciously towards the stranger who called himself Perseus.

Rudammon conveyed it as requested and Perseus looked pleased, bowing towards her father and sliding his gaze to meet Andromeda's own.

'An – dro – med – ah,' he attempted, drawing out the sounds as if they were sweet on his tongue. At the edge of her vision she saw Phineus' shoulders tense, and was relieved to know she was not the only one made uneasy by the stranger's smile.

With the loaf baked and the honey pot opened, the meal could begin. They sat in a circle, the ashes swept away, and passed the jar from one hand to another so that each of them could dip their bread and share in its golden sweetness. Andromeda's stomach rumbled in anticipation, and when the pot reached her she took a generous plunge. For a moment, as the honey touched her tongue, she forgot all else. But once the edge of her hunger had been smoothed, she found her eyes falling once more upon Perseus, seated between Rudammon and her father, with his soft curls and his disquieting smile. What pleased him so? He was buoyant like one celebrating, talking animatedly to Rudammon – who looked like he was struggling to keep up – and swilling his water as if it were wine. Their meal was only simple fare, such as they had been able to carry with them from the oasis, but from the broadness of his cheeks you would think the boy had never tasted food so fine. It worried her, as if he were privy to a joke that might end at their expense.

Once the bread was all gone, Andromeda saw her father raise his ostrich cup.

'To our guest, Perseus. May we ever hold him as our friend.'

The words were customary on such an occasion, but they seemed to please Perseus when Rudammon repeated them in his own tongue. He raised his cup high, and everyone drank. Then Perseus spoke words to Rudammon, and Andromeda caught her name among them.

'Our guest proposes a drink to Andromeda,' announced their guide, though there was a wrinkle of uncertainty between his thick brows. Perseus leaned towards his ear again, speaking sounds that seemed to make as little sense to Rudammon as they did to the rest of them. More words were exchanged, before their guide turned to Andromeda's father.

'He wishes to drink the health of his bride.'

Andromeda's stomach dropped and she saw her consternation reflected around the circle. Whatever she had expected Rudammon to say, it had not been that. And yet she had seen it. She had known that something was amiss. Perseus revelled as if it were a wedding feast, for to him it was.

'Are you sure you have understood him?' her father asked, his face grave.

'No, perhaps . . . Or perhaps he has misunderstood me. The tongue is subtle and not fully known to me. Wait, I . . . '

Rudammon turned to Perseus again and words flowed back and forth between them, while the stranger's brow dropped lower and lower.

'He believed there to be an agreement,' said the guide. 'That he would take your daughter as his wife, since he had been the one to rescue her.'

'Rescue?' Phineus set down his cup, which tipped and spilled onto the sand.

'You must tell him that she is already promised,' her father said simply, gesturing towards Phineus. Andromeda could feel Phineus bristling on the mat beside her.

'I have already done so,' Rudammon murmured, throat strained. He swallowed but his voice grew no louder. 'He says that no worthy husband would leave his bride to be ravaged by the sea.'

At this Phineus snapped, and rose from his mat. Andromeda put out a hand to touch his leg, but she wasn't sure he felt it.

'We cannot entertain this,' he said angrily. 'The stranger has taken his refreshment and now I suggest we send him on his way, before he thinks to take anything else.'

Perseus was on his feet, his taut body mirroring Phineus' own. It made Andromeda afraid and she rose too, glancing between the two of them, and to the curved bronze shining on Perseus' hip, and the dread-filled bag swinging beside it.

'Be careful, Phineus,' she whispered, touching his arm. Her heart pounded like a warning drum.

Perseus looked annoyed and took a step towards her but Phineus blocked his path, guarding her with one arm while the other he raised before him, open palm, weaponless.

'Rudammon,' Andromeda called desperately. 'You must tell him that he cannot have me for his wife.' Perseus stepped closer. 'Tell him we shall give him gold for his reward. Ivory. Amethyst. Anything he would like, it is his.'

The guide began to jabber the strange sounds, but Perseus' eyes remained fixed on Phineus.

It happened slowly. Or it felt that way, as if her legs were stuck in the sand and her mouth choked with it. Perseus' hand went to his hip, raised its bronze claw. One pace was all it took and he swept the blade before him. For a moment all was still, and then Phineus staggered. He stepped back, eyes wide, and Andromeda saw the great gash across his belly. She gripped his arm, and he gripped back, pulling her as he fell. Thick blood was streaming, oozing over his beautiful skin. She could hear her mother cry out somewhere behind her, but her own voice was stoppered. She looked at Phineus' face and her heart quivered. He knew what was done. As surely as if he already lay in his grave. His dark eyes shone and his lips trembled, spit flying as he struggled to breathe. His grip on her arm was still strong and she stroked his cheek with fingers she could barely feel.

Around them words flew, known and unknown, all sharp as arrows. Andromeda dragged her eyes from the dying boy, and a new terror struck her chest.

Perseus was stood not a stride from her, with bloody blade outstretched. He glanced about him, pointing it in turn at her father, at her mother, at Rudammon, all outraged, all afraid, all undefended. The boy shook with a terrible energy, his muscles winding tighter and tighter just as she felt Phineus' grip slacken. He looked as if he might kill them all with that hateful bronze. And she had brought him here. This boy who smelled of death.

'Stop. Please,' she croaked, forcing herself to her feet. He turned at the sound of her voice and her stomach jolted as he looked her in the eye. She raised her hands before her, shaking, bloody. 'Please. Rudammon, please tell him. Tell him I will go with him. If that is what he wants. Let no more blood be spilled.'

'Andromeda.' Her mother's voice was broken.

'I won't let him harm you,' Andromeda cried. 'I can't. Rudammon, please tell him.'

Their guide hesitated, looking to her father, whose face was blank. He moved his lips but it was as if his cheeks were numbed.

'Father, I accept it. You are my heart. Both of you.' She looked between her parents, eyes burning. 'Go home and be safe. I beg you. It is as it must be.'

Her father seemed to find himself again and looked to Perseus, whose dagger was only a breath from her mother's throat. If it had been at his own throat, perhaps everything would have happened differently, but Andromeda knew him. She knew that he held his wife above all things, even over his children.

'Tell him, Rudammon,' her father rasped.

She heard her mother cry out, and it was as if the sound had been ripped from her own throat. But Andromeda pressed her lips tight, and watched as the words were spoken and her fate sealed. She could hear a voiceless gasp at her feet but could not bring herself to look down. She had to look at what she had saved, at what her sacrifice had paid for. She watched her parents for every second that she could, setting their faces into her memory. And then Perseus took her hand and she turned away, feet stumbling over the dusty earth.

CHAPTER 30

The boat was small. Barely twice the size of her tent in the oasis, and stuffed with eight men. In truth Andromeda had never seen another ship and could not know whether this one should be considered large or small, but compared to the wide oasis, the vast sands she had travelled through, and the endless waters they sailed upon, the wooden deck felt like the smallest of sheep pens. It even had a little fence running around its edge.

Andromeda did not know how many days it had been since her shaking legs first stepped onto the deck. No more than she could count on her fingers, but what use was there in that? Days, weeks, months – these things felt meaningless to her. Now there was only the light and the dark. The tolerable and the dreaded.

She had known what it would mean. From the moment he had looked at her upon the rock, traced his fingers across her skin, she had known. And still she had gone. She had given herself up as sacrifice for a second time.

The men slept above, under the open sky, while Andromeda was stowed away with the cargo, her narrow bed laid between cold copper ingots and splintery boxes filled with hippopotamus teeth. The pieces of ivory clacked against one another each time the hull tilted, and Andromeda had grown so used to the sound that it was almost a comfort, like the sighing of a friend beside her in the darkness.

Then the hatch would open. A glimpse of stars before his body blotted them, and the darkness returned. He seemed to prefer it that way, for he never brought a lamp. Perhaps he could not stand the hatred in her eye. Or perhaps he imagined another face, while his rough hands groped her.

She preferred the darkness too, for it made it easier for her spirit to wander. Though he took her each night he never had her, for she was not truly there. She was back in the oasis, weaving baskets with her mother and listening to the children play in the springs. When she closed her eyes, she felt the warm sun on her face, breathed the scented breeze as it rustled the palms. All his grunting could not pull her from that place. His rank breath could not overpower the smell of citron and dates and honey milk.

She made no sound when he came to her. Not a whimper, not a gasp. Even when he hurt her, she willed her throat to stay silent, and bit her lip until it bled. The first time had been the hardest, with the smell of Phineus' blood still upon her, the memory of his wide eyes burning in her mind. She hadn't been able to escape then. Her spirit was trapped in her trembling body, violated by his murderous hands. And still she had willed herself to silence. It had felt like a victory of sorts, to withhold something from this boy who had taken everything from her. Here was something she could control, a power she could wield. No maiden's cry for him. She lay there as if she were dead, and let him rut.

It was only afterwards, when he had gone and she was left alone, that Andromeda allowed the wall between body and spirit to crack, and the one would rush back into the other, licking wounds, sharing in the loss, vibrating together with pain and shame and fury. It was difficult to breathe, the air of the hold still choked with the smell of him, but in time her chest would stop rattling and she would lie down to sleep, and imagine that the sound of the waves was the whisper of palm leaves.

Andromeda stood on the deck, blinking in the bright morning sun. Her eyes stung after the dark of the hold, but she was glad to feel the wind pull at her dress. She tried to imagine that the wind was stripping away her sadness too. It felt so heavy about her, like a fleece soaked in water, dragging at her shoulders, buckling her knees. When she closed her eyes and breathed deep, she could convince herself that it was lifting a little, but when she opened them again there he was, leaning carelessly upon the rail, and her sadness came crashing like a boulder.

No, it was not sadness but anger. Anger at the life he had stolen. Perseus had not only taken her home from her, her family. He had taken her power. He had taken the future she had made for herself, the husband she had chosen, the freedom she had worked for. It had all vanished in the slash of his knife.

That anger burned her every time she looked at him. The memory of that moment was so raw that it still made her heart thump as if she were there, feeling the strength slip from Phineus' fingers, watching that boy point his vicious little blade at those she loved most in the world. She had known what she had to do, as clearly as she had seen the way to save her father from ruin. She had spent the last of her power making that choice, but only because Perseus had given her no other.

Now she stared at him, chest tight, imagining all the things she might say if only she could make him understand her. How she would curse him, shame him. No longer a silent, shivering thing locked in the dark, her words would be sharp like spears, her voice loud and fearless.

Her thoughts stuttered as her eyes fell upon the leather bag. He never brought it below deck – she would smell it if he did – but in the day it hung from his shoulder, full as ever. She did not know why, but the hidden evil of that bag made her more afraid than anything she had seen with her own eyes. She knew that Perseus was a killer, but that bag held more than death. The sight of it made her cold with dread.

It would take courage to confront her captor. She knew that. But she had always been able to summon her strength when it was needed. No, what she did not have were words. She might as well be a goat bleating in the paddock, for all the attention the men paid to her. Without words she could do nothing, change nothing. She could not curse or convince them, she could not plead with them to turn their ship back, to restore what was left of the life that was stolen.

Andromeda felt her mood begin to shift as she realised that the day was not simply an absence of the night, an escape from that dark place and the dark things she endured there. It was an opportunity, a time to gather knowledge, a time to regain control. From now on she would not waste a moment of it. She would listen to the men, peel apart their sounds like flesh from a stone, examine every piece and store it inside herself. Silence was strength when it was all she had, but words would be her true power.

CHAPTER 31

The ship was tilting more than usual today, but though Andromeda's stomach rolled with the waves she kept her mind focused. An unruly sea meant more work for the men, and as their words flew back and forth across the deck she honed her ears to their sounds.

'Pull up the sail!' she heard the thick-bearded captain shout, his hand gripped firmly on the rudder. She was satisfied to know that she had understood him correctly as she watched the men begin to pull on their ropes and the broad canvas folded.

With the sail shrunk the ship settled a little, though the wind still whipped Andromeda's braids across her cheek. She stood near the prow, out of the way of the men and their working hands, but on the small deck it was not difficult to hear them call to one another. It took great concentration to draw out any sense from their hurled remarks, but it was worth it for the moments of clarity, of confirmation, of new understanding. Worth it too for the space it took up in her mind, leaving no room for thoughts of home, of her parents struggling back across the sand, of Phineus' lonely grave so far from those who had awaited his return.

She knew the power she sought would only come with patience, and she had enough of that, but Andromeda was beginning to fear that her throat would close up before she had the chance to wield it. It was one thing to hear the words, to repeat them to herself in the quiet of her own mind, but would her tongue obey when she finally had need to call upon it? Would it bend to those foreign shapes? She began to flex it in her mouth, imagining how she might form the sounds.

'Pull up the sail,' she mumbled. Was that how the captain had said it? No, it had been more rounded. 'Pull up the sail,' she tried again.

'Are we to take orders from you now?'

Andromeda started, gripping the rail in surprise. On the deck nearby was one of the crew, young and squat, his brown back shining with sweat as he scrubbed the wooden boards. She had known he was there, had seen him scrubbing away all morning, but that was not what had startled her.

'You speak Egyptian.'

'Like a native.' He grinned, pausing his work to glance up at her.

Now that she looked at him, he didn't look much like an islander, though he dressed like one. His eyes were sharp, his features broad, his jaw bordered by a narrow beard. He spoke little to the other crew members, so she hadn't paid him much mind until now.

'What are you doing on this ship?' Andromeda was a little embarrassed to hear the keenness of her voice. Egyptian was not her mother tongue, of course, but it was well known to her from all the traders and travellers that passed through the oasis. Her own great-grandmother had been Egyptian, so her father had told her, and hearing those familiar tones after so long in a sea of unfamiliarity was like a warm hand upon hers.

'It pays me well,' the young man shrugged. 'And it pays them to have an Egyptian on board, to get the best price on their goods. They say I have a golden tongue.' He looked proud for a moment, before looking down at the grimy deck. 'Though recently it seems they've forgotten that.' He began scrubbing again, and she saw him glance over towards Perseus, leaning back on the stern as he shared a joke with the captain.

'I've seen you watching the men,' the Egyptian said in a low voice, seeing that her gaze had followed his. 'Planning your escape, are you?'

There was a curl of a smile about his lips, but his eyes held a sympathy that surprised her.

'I wouldn't bother,' he continued. 'Unless you happen to be half fish.'

'I'm not trying—' she began, but stopped herself. Should she really be talking to this stranger? What if Perseus should notice them? But there was no one else on the ship she could talk to – not yet, anyway – and though she knew nothing about him, somehow this boy made her feel a little less far from home.

'What is your name?' she murmured, keeping half an eye on Perseus.

'Seneb,' the Egyptian replied. He seemed to sense her worry and continued to work as they spoke, so as not to draw attention.

'I'm not trying to escape,' she said, turning her body a little as if she were looking out to sea. 'Where would I go? Libya must be far behind us now.' She felt her chest tighten but kept her voice steady. 'I want to learn their way of speaking. I can't change anything until I can be heard.'

Seneb paused for a moment, looking up at her with a curious expression. 'Yes, I suppose you're right about that. And it's served me well, knowing the foreigners' tongue. Just look at the honours heaped upon me.' He straightened his back, gesturing to his soaked knees, fingers wrinkled from the scrub water. His face spread with a wry grin, and she couldn't help smiling back. It was strange to feel her cheeks lift. They had been heavy as stone ever since Perseus had led her aboard.

'My name is Andromeda.'

'I know,' he said, continuing with his work. 'He tells us often enough.' Seneb's head jerked toward Perseus. 'The Princess Andromeda, that's what he calls you.'

'I am not a princess,' she murmured, her mouth tight at the thought of her name on those hated lips.

'And he's no Gorgonslayer, yet that is what they call him.'

Andromeda paused. *Gorgonslayer.* Yes, she had heard that word from the mouths of the men.

'Why do they call him that? What does it mean?'

'Well, if you're as gullible as our soft-minded captain, it means that boy with reeds for legs has slain a fearsome beast. At the Green Mountain back along the coast. It could turn a man to stone with as much as a glance, if you'll believe what he says.'

'You don't believe in monsters?' she asked.

'Of course I do. I just don't believe Perseus would be the one to slay them.'

She made a noise like half a laugh but found she could not smile while they talked of Perseus.

'Oh he's quite the hero by his own account,' Seneb carried on, his hands tight on the scrubbing brush. 'Lopped off the Gorgon's head and then rescued you from . . . What was it? Yes, a sea beast.'

'A sea beast? He did not rescue me at all! He took me and he threatened my family and he killed—' Hearing her voice rise she looked about to check that she had raised no one's attention, and dropped to a whisper. 'I was safe before he came.'

'Oh, I don't doubt it. And isn't it curious that not a one of us saw this beast from the ship?' He looked half bitter, half amused, but when Seneb's eyes turned to hers his face fell. 'I am sorry, truly, for your situation.'

Though he spoke sympathy, and she knew he meant well, Andromeda felt her cheeks burn. He knew what happened each night beneath the deck. All the crew must know, and yet they slept soundly above and did not stop it. To see that he knew her shame, that he pitied her, made her feel more wretched than ever.

'The Gorgon . . . ' she muttered, desperate to talk of something else. 'You say he cut off its head?'

'So he claims,' Seneb scoffed. 'Brought it back as a trophy. It certainly impressed the captain – soft-minded, like I say. Perseus claims it is hideous, half woman, half beast, but as none of us have actually seen it I wouldn't be surprised if it was the head of some poor village girl in there. He has a darkness about him, that one, though the captain seems not to see it. Do you know it used to be Perseus who scrubbed this deck? Captain barely gave the lad a sideways look, then he turns up with that stinking sack and it's like he's his own son. Close as plaited reeds they are. Now Perseus gets to take in the breeze while I'm up to my elbows in bird mess. Three years I've been on this ship . . . '

But Andromeda had stopped listening. Her eyes were fixed on the bag at Perseus' hip, just as they had been on that day she had led him from the beach, when she had first noticed its dreadful swing. Her stomach was churning, twisting like a wrung cloth, sending hot bile up her throat. She turned just in time, retching into the sea, gasping for air until her chest burned. She gripped the rail, legs shaking as she heard the crewmen muttering behind her. Though her mouth was silent her heart screamed, with sorrow for the woman whose head was stolen, and with terror for herself.

CHAPTER 32

The night had been long. Andromeda's eyes stung, barely rested, so she kept them closed as she sat on the deck, forehead pressed against the rail. She tried to enjoy the gentle breeze, the warmth of the sun on her skin, and reminded herself that she had a new reason to be thankful for the coming of the day: the company of a friend. She spoke with Seneb often. Sometimes they could only snatch words under their breath, if ears were too close or eyes too sharp, but she relished every exchange like a drop of honey in a bowl of thick gruel. She still missed her home, the swinging bag still made her heart clench, and Perseus' hands still made her spirit fly from her body, but without Seneb those feelings would swallow her up. The thought that they might share a few words, or even just a glance of understanding, gave her the strength to raise her head up out of the hold each morning and force herself back into its depths each night.

He helped her train her tongue, too. If she heard a word she could not understand she would keep it in her head and get the meaning from Seneb when they had chance to speak. Sometimes they even spoke in the islanders' tongue, so that she could try out what she had learned, practise the sounds, find her mistakes. This they only did when the rest of the crew were away at their duties. Andromeda thought it safer if the men did not know she had begun to understand them. An ignorant woman was no more threat than a donkey. But one with ears and a voice, that was one they had to watch. For now she would hide her new power. She would store it away and feed it and grow it, to use at just the right moment.

Things would not always be as they were. That was what she told herself. Change was coming, even if it took all her strength to drag it. Determined not to waste a moment, Andromeda tucked the frayed edges of her spirit and began muttering to herself – phrases she had heard that morning, words that drifted across her weary thoughts.

'Talking to the dolphins?'

Seneb's voice brought her eyes into focus, and she turned to see whether they were being overlooked. To her relief all the men sat at the other end of the deck. With the sea calm and the wind steady there was little for them to do. A group of them were throwing knucklebones, engrossed as the little pieces clattered on the deck. She watched their faces brighten and sour, at wagers lost and won. Perseus' face was the stormiest among them. Andromeda knew she should fear what his foul mood might mean for her, but instead she felt a flicker of satisfaction. Gladness, too, that she and Seneb could speak freely.

She turned herself so that her back rested against one of the struts of the rail and raised a weak smile. Seneb was smiling too, crouched by the rope pile he pretended to detangle. But as he surveyed her face his brow dipped.

'You look tired.'

'I'm well enough,' she murmured, avoiding his gaze.

'You're not.' His roving eye stopped on her bare arm, where Perseus' fingers had dug bruises. He looked uncomfortable for a moment, as if he regretted saying anything. Then he opened his mouth again. 'Is he . . . violent, when he comes to you?'

Andromeda felt herself bristle. How could it be anything but violent? How could he not understand that?

'He does not intend to hurt me,' she said stiffly. 'He simply does not care that he does.'

Seneb's head twitched as if he understood, though of course he did not. She wanted to shake him, to tell him what her spirit endured while his dreamed peacefully. But she knew that it would drive him away, her only friend.

'I wish I could help,' he whispered, and hung his head. He looked so pitiable that Andromeda found her anger distracted for a moment. She could see the weight of his words upon him. They were an admission of shame, of guilt.

'You do help,' she said softly. 'You didn't bring me here and you can't take me back. I just . . . I'm trying to endure. I'm biding my time.' But even as she said it a whisper of doubt scratched at her. Biding her time for what? Every day they sailed further and further from Libya. Though Andromeda had fortified herself with thoughts of the oasis, of how she would persuade the men when she had mastered their tongue, it was beginning to feel like a foolish hope. Seneb had already told her that the ship would not return along the coast. Once each summer they ventured as far as the silphium growers, and then back around the ocean's ring to their islands in the north. What use was patience or endurance, then, if it could not earn her the very thing she longed for?

'I tell myself that I can still win, but every night feels like defeat.'

She felt her voice cracking and swallowed the lump that had risen in her throat. She didn't want to look broken in front of Seneb. She could barely admit it to herself. But that was how she felt. Pulled too far, tearing thread by thread.

Suddenly she found laughter gasping from her throat, desperate and unnatural. Through blurry eyes she saw Seneb regarding her.

'Andromeda?'

'I should just kick him next time he comes to me. Hard. Right in his manhood. Wouldn't that be a quicker victory? He'd drop like an anchor.'

'Hush,' Seneb whispered, glancing to check whether the crew had heard her laughter. His face was dark with worry. 'You're not serious,' he said, though he didn't seem sure.

'Why not? All this time learning their tongue, but that would be a language he could understand, would it not?'

'Andromeda,' he murmured, his tone urgent. 'Promise me you won't. Don't resist him, don't anger him. Above all, don't embarrass him. I won't be able to protect you.'

'Embarrass him?' she scoffed. 'Can the great Gorgonslayer really be so fragile?' She laughed again, but her amusement had already turned bitter in her mouth.

'I'm serious, Andromeda.' Seneb gave her arm the briefest touch, and she met his eye. But then he seemed to shrink back. 'If it were me . . . ' He stared down at the deck, summoning his words, and then looked at her straight. 'Give yourself to him. Make him feel as if he has won you. Make him feel like a man. That is what he wants.'

Andromeda felt her folded body harden. 'No, I can't. I . . . What do you know about it?' she flared. How could he say that? Because it was not his body, not his spirit.

'I have watched him longer than you. I know what he is. I have known men like him before. If he cannot have you one way, he will take you another.'

She sobered at that. Though he did not say it, she read Seneb's meaning in his eyes. The bag. The awful, dread-filled, sickening bag. Her gaze drifted towards it, drawn across the deck as it so often was. She imagined another bag beside it, heavy and reeking. That was her choice, then. But was it any choice at all?

'Please, Andromeda,' Seneb urged, putting a hand towards her knee. 'Play the game a little longer. Be cautious. Be clever.'

It reminded her of something her mother had said to her once, but before she had thought of it a shout broke her attention.

'– my wife!' was all she understood, as Perseus strode across the deck towards them.

Seneb moved back from her but it was too late. Perseus dragged him up by his armpit, puffing his chest like some ridiculous bird. Seneb's head was bowed, murmuring apologies.

'I thought she looked thirsty,' she heard him say. 'Please. I meant no disrespect.'

Andromeda saw her friend's cheek tense with anger, and she knew it must gall him to beg forgiveness from this boy who was even younger than he was. *Play the game*, he had said.

Perseus looked towards the rest of the crew, his hand still gripping Seneb's arm, and Andromeda saw a flash as his curved dagger caught the sun. And once again she felt utterly powerless. If she spoke she would likely make things worse. So she closed her mouth and forced her face to indifference, looking cluelessly upon the scene as her heart hammered in her chest.

Between Seneb's bowed head, her gormless mouth, and the mild curiosity of the crew, Perseus' bluster ran out of wind, and he released Seneb with a scornful look. As he walked away she let out her breath and tried not to look at Seneb, who made himself busy on the other side of the deck. But at the stern Perseus was speaking with the captain, their heads close together, their brows heavy. And with every nod of the captain's head Andromeda felt the rope around her chest wind tighter.

CHAPTER 33

They had stopped at many ports since Perseus had brought her aboard the ship. At each one Andromeda saw only a glimpse of the land, the town, the people, before Perseus shut her into the hold, and she heard the heavy bar thud across the hatch. She wondered if he thought it normal for a husband to lock his wife away, for fear that she would run from him.

This stop was no different, though Andromeda had learned ways to make the time pass more quickly. Alone in the dark she traced her fingers over the cargo that remained, and tried to remember what had been there before. The glass beads were missing, she realised, finding empty air where their jar had been. She hadn't known what colour they were, of course, though she imagined a vibrant blue, like the ones her mother always wore about her neck. She had liked to roll them in her fingers, to calm herself while she awaited the inevitable, and was sad to find that they had gone. No matter, she told herself. The crew would bring another item to fill the space the beads had left. Some sweet-smelling resin, perhaps, or some fine cloth she might wrap about her in the cold night. She could not think about what was lost, but what she might still be able to gain.

She sank onto her bed, hard despite the woollen blanket, and curved with the shape of the hull. The hippopotamus teeth were still there beside her, a strange comfort if they were one at all, but in the still waters of the bay they lay silent. Instead she could hear distant voices, too indistinct to know whether they spoke the tongue of the islanders, or the Egyptians, or some other one entirely. The salt of the sea was too strong for her to learn anything from her nose. What incense did they burn here? What spice did they sprinkle on their meat? She knew she would never find out, but it gave her a kind of painful satisfaction to think of those people on the other side of the wood, living in freedom and happiness. That was what she hoped, for their sake and for hers. The further the ship sailed from that cursed rock where Perseus had found her, the more Andromeda realised that she might never see her home again. She had to believe that another happiness was possible, that joy and safety were not bound to those lonely springs in the middle of the desert, that with patience and bravery and cleverness she would be able to find those things elsewhere.

She forced herself to smile in the darkness. Though she had avoided speaking with Seneb over the last few days, she knew he would still help her. He had already helped her so much. When once she felt as if every word of the islanders' tongue had to be dug out from a great pile of mud, now they rose to the surface like bubbles in a spring, there when she bid them, clear when she heard them. With a little more practice she would command them as the men did.

There was a thud above her and Andromeda knew the gangplank was being put out. The men who had gone to trade were returning. A mercifully short stop, she thought, wondering how far the sun had gone across the sky. Even a little while in its light would be a blessing – a chance to breathe, to see, perhaps to speak with Seneb while the crew were busy handling the new goods. Her tongue was feeling as stiff as her cramped legs.

It was not long before she heard the bar slide back and stinging daylight streamed in through the hatch. While she was still squinting a hand came to pull her up to the deck, and she stumbled to the rail as the men began to pass jars and boxes down into the hold.

Though she was thankful for the sun, it was dazzling after her morning in the dark, and it took her a moment to adjust. With blinking eyes she scanned the deck, trying to find the squat figure of Seneb among the moving men. He was not one of the chain carrying goods from the gangplank to the hatch, nor was he with the men readying to haul the first anchor. The captain stood not far from her, overlooking the work while Perseus spoke beside him. She didn't catch what he said but he looked buoyed by something, and as the captain turned to clap Perseus on the back she strained her ears and focused her mind.

' . . . better off without him, now Egypt's behind us.'

It was like a fist in her gut. She glanced about her again as if Seneb might appear, but she knew now that he would not. Anger battled panic as she stared at Perseus and his satisfied smile. He had done this, said something to make the captain leave Seneb behind. She knew it instantly. He had robbed her of her only support, and already she felt herself collapsing. How would she master the words now, with no one to help her? How would she face the descent into the hold, without the promise of a friendly face when she arose again? She felt sick. She couldn't be near that hateful boy who had taken everything and would continue taking until there was nothing left of her.

She stumbled backwards and would have fallen if the rail had not held her up. She turned and gripped the wood, dragging the wind into her lungs as her chest shook. And that was how she stayed, fighting to keep herself whole as the cargo hatch thudded behind her and the stone anchors were heaved out of the water. She did not even turn to watch the port disappear, as she usually did. It was not her town, not her people. She had never felt farther from home than she did in that moment, and she knew the distance would only grow. She would never see her father's face again, never hear her mother's laugh, never raise her nieces and nephews up on her shoulders or bathe her own children in the salty pools.

Andromeda's arms trembled in front of her, still grasping the narrow rail. She leaned forward, letting her waist press against the wood, and stared down at the sucking waves.

She had saved her family. That was what she told herself when despair took hold. Her parents were safe because she had boarded this ship. They were home even if she would never be. She tried now to soothe her fracturing heart with that thought, but it was not enough. She felt herself unravelling, dark thoughts tearing at the walls she had tried to build. She remembered the blood, and the fearful gasps of that kind boy whom she had not saved, and everything felt painful and wasted and hopeless. Her heart was so heavy, dragging her down against the rail, towards the grey water. It would be so easy to let herself fall. It would be a release, to let herself be sucked beneath the waves where nothing could hurt or haunt her. She felt her heels lift from the deck, watched herself begin to tip as if it were not her body at all. The waves were loud in her ears, slapping the hull as if urging her on. She would be gone in an instant. The men could not stop her.

But something made her brace. It was not her heart, for that was ready to fall. Her spirit, perhaps. Something gripped her gut and would not let go. It whispered that death was not a victory but only another defeat. Her life was all she had left, and no matter how wretched it was she could not bring herself to throw it away.

As she straightened, slowly, Andromeda felt a strange new power ripple through her. She had held the decision in her hands. And though she did not want to die, she realised that she did not fear death. She let herself breathe with that knowledge and what it meant. She did not have to fear Perseus, she realised, or his murderous hands or his glinting knife. She did not even have to fear the dreadful bag he carried. There was nothing he could hold over her now, nothing left that she had not lost or relinquished. Not her parents, not Phineus, not the hope of home, nor the care for a friend. Not even her own life.

CHAPTER 34

When Perseus came to her that night, everything felt different. When the hatch clattered open she did not tremble; when it closed her breath was steady. Her tongue was taut like a bowstring. Her heart pounded, but not with terror. Her spirit would not fly away tonight. No, it would stay just where she needed it.

The wood creaked and she knew that Perseus was beside her. She heard him crouch down, felt his sleeve brush her arm, his fingertips touch upon her dress.

'No,' she said, quietly but firmly, in his own tongue.

He stopped, hand hovering over her breast. She imagined the surprise on his face, felt the uncertainty in his quivering fingers. Then his hand pressed against her.

'No,' she said again, louder than before. 'Do not touch me.'

His hand froze but did not lift. She hated the feel of it there and pushed him away. She heard him fall backwards.

'I do not want you,' she shouted clearly, taking care with each word. She was sure she had it right. She had practised what she would say as she lay waiting. But he said nothing in reply.

Andromeda sat up and gathered her knees against her. In the silence a dark anticipation began to grow. Not fear – she was done with that. But she imagined Perseus' rage, saw his fists clench, his jaw tighten. She braced herself for his violence. But it did not come.

Suddenly there was a sound, like a breath sucked too quickly. And she realised he was crying. She listened as his chest heaved, as little whines escaped those lips she so detested. Of all the things Andromeda had prepared herself for, she had not imagined this. She had rehearsed more words to speak but they hung silent in her mouth. What use in shooting a beast already downed? So she waited, blinking in the dark, as Perseus wept like a beaten child.

She remembered what Seneb had said to her the last time they had spoken. *Don't resist him. Don't embarrass him.* He had seen Perseus' fragility, warned her of it. But Andromeda began to real- ise that she could use it. With a little water the brittle reed could be made pliable and put to better purpose. That weeping boy was not fragile but soft, like potter's clay not yet fired. She thought of how he puffed his chest, how he hovered by the captain's side, how he looked to the men for approval at every word he spoke, how he fingered his shining blade as if that hardness were somehow his by extension. Here was a boy who did not know who he was, who was trying so desperately to be what he thought he ought to be. She did not pity him, even as he wept. She could not pity a spirit that had done such evil. But for the first time she felt that she understood him a little, and that understanding was something she could use.

Heart racing, she realised that this was the moment. Here, now, while his spirit was bruised and hers was fearless. She thought of all she knew, all she had learned and observed. She thought of the terrible bag with its terrible contents. She thought of how he had found her like a glinting shell on the beach, and gathered her up and made her his. How convenient that she could not reject him then, with hands and tongue bound tight. It was plain what he feared. She had seen now how her simple words could cut him. But there was no gain in fear. One cut would be met by another – perhaps the girl in the bag had learned that too late. No, if she were to survive this boy, she had to know what he wanted. To prove himself, yes. To be praised and respected, she had no doubt. And he wanted her, too. She had felt his desire at the first touch, she had known then his will to possess her, but now that she heard him sniffling in the dark she knew that what he truly wanted, what he craved, was to be wanted in return.

She hardened herself until she was like a stone, and forced her limbs to move, crawling cautiously over the boards. Perseus must have heard the creak, for he fell silent, his ragged breaths stoppered. Then when she had found his foot in the dark, she followed it to the knee and the hot hand she found there, and kissed it. He seemed to flinch and for a moment she thought she had it wrong. She waited for his hands to grab her, for his anger to fly out. But instead he took her hand and pressed it against his wet cheek. It took all her strength not to pull away, to just let him hold her, breathing his warm breath over her shaking arm.

She had already given up her body. She had had no choice. If the price was paid, why not gain something from it? She could suffer to submit that part of herself if her spirit would remain free, if she could regain some control, if she could carve out a place for herself that wasn't filled with fear and defeat. This time it would be different. This time it was a choice. If she must have this man as her husband, she would shape him to be one she could tolerate. She would build a life she could survive.

CHAPTER 35

They stood on the deck, the two of them, looking out across the waves. Their hands were on the rail, a narrow strip of wood between them. There was a time not long past when it would have made Andromeda's skin tight to stand so close.

'Are you hungry, my wife?' Perseus asked casually.

He liked to call her that, especially when the other men were nearby. No doubt some of them had wives too, waiting for them in some little town across the sea, but Perseus spoke the word as if it were a unique accomplishment.

'A little,' she replied. 'My stomach is making a rumble like the storm.'

He turned to her and gave a quiet laugh, and though she lifted the corners of her mouth her lips were tight. 'Did I say something funny?'

'No, it's just the way you speak sometimes.' He smiled, looking over her face. 'It's . . . quaint.'

'Quaint? What does that mean?' she asked, holding her own stiff smile.

'Unusual. Charming,' he told her, and turned back to the waves.

Andromeda let her face sour. She did not want to be quaint.

'You must tell me,' she said sweetly, 'when I say something . . . unusual. You must tell me so that I know what is the right way.' It irked her, that smiling face. Her husband had shown no great surprise that she had been able to learn his tongue so quickly. All her proper speaking drew no comment, but he seemed to find amusement in her mistakes. 'You must help me improve,' she said earnestly.

'There is no need, my wife,' he said, glancing at her. 'You speak well enough. We understand one another, do we not?'

Andromeda forced herself to smile again. It was not enough to be understood. That had been the first barrier, yes, but to gain the power she desired, the influence she needed, she had to be respected.

'A great man should have an elegant wife, should he not?' she went on softly, determined not to lose the opportunity. 'What if I should embarrass you with my . . . "quaint" speaking? They will say, "That man cannot be great, for he has an ignorant wife."' It made her lips twist to say such things about herself, but Andromeda had learned that to master her husband's fragile pride she had to sacrifice a little of her own. Her words seemed to strike the nerve she had aimed for.

'Mmm,' he said, ruminating like one of the goats in her father's paddock. 'Yes, perhaps you're right. I will make sure to tell you if you say something inelegant.'

Andromeda smiled, and stretched out a hand to rest upon his.

When they stood this close together she could smell the rotten-sweetness of the bag. She had put her terror away the day that she had stood tilting over the rail, but her stomach was not as strong as her spirit and it kicked in protest, thankfully empty. That disgust, that outrage at the smell of him, the sight, the touch – that had been harder to overcome than her fear. It was rooted deep, in hatred and pain. But what use was hatred to her now? It served no purpose other than to make her own heart heavy, to rake her from the inside while doing no injury to him. So she had closed it up. She had squashed it small and hidden it within herself, not gone but buried enough that its cold fingers did not choke her. It was what she had to do, it was all that she could do, to survive.

And so she squeezed his hand, that hand that had done unspeakable things, and felt his response. His warming. His softening. Like wet clay in her fingers.

The nights were different now. When Perseus came to her it did not feel as if she were losing a part of herself, but rather she felt her power grow, with every touch, with every sigh, lips no longer silent but encouraging. She inflamed his desire, his need for the things she gave. Perhaps one day she would convince herself that she could find comfort, even pleasure, in those embraces, but for now she was thankful that he did not hurt her. Her husband's new gentleness felt like a victory. It was proof that her circumstances were not immovable, that this new path might lead to more hopeful ground.

Andromeda's mind was brought out of the dark hold by a shout from the sailors. They were approaching the port. She looked towards the prow to the shore beyond and saw little square buildings clinging to a hillside, one atop the other like boxes of stone. As the ship glided into the shallows the buildings grew larger, until she could see figures moving between them, climbing steep steps, carrying sacks and jars, leading animals on thin tethers or herding them with sticks swinging back and forth. She took in as much as she could, knowing that she would soon be sent below.

When the anchors were dropped the men began to lift goods from the hold. The great ingots that had lain beside her were brought out one by one, so heavy they needed the strength of two men to lift them. Then came the hippopotamus teeth, rattling in their box as if bidding her farewell. Perhaps Perseus saw her frown, for he put a hand on her shoulder.

'They will fetch us a good price here,' he said, as if that should please her. She knew it would be foolish to miss them. They were dead things, white like bone, sharp like stakes. And yet they had travelled all the way from Libya as she had. They almost felt like a piece of home.

When the goods were ready to be carried ashore Andromeda waited to be ushered into the hold, but instead Perseus took her hand.

'We'll be back before the sun is set,' he said with a light smile, before stepping away to help with the lifting.

Andromeda opened her mouth in surprise, but what should she say? *Aren't you forgetting to lock me away?* So she stayed silent, watching as the goods were carried along the gangplank onto the jetty. As the men made their way towards the town Perseus looked back at her, and something in his steady glance told her that he had forgotten nothing. This was simply part of the change between them.

There were two men left behind, to guard the ship and the remainder of the cargo. They were islanders like Perseus, though she did not know their names. She had avoided speaking with the rest of the crew, after what had happened to Seneb, but she felt the eyes of the two men upon her now. She held the rail and avoided looking in their direction. No doubt they were curious as to why she had been allowed to stay above deck, she told herself, but an uneasiness began to grow in her stomach. She did not like the way their eyes stuck to her, the way they made her skin prickle. But as her chest began to tighten she realised that there was nothing to fear. They would not dare to touch another man's wife, not when he was so soon to return and had such a violent temper. For once she found herself thankful for her husband and his shining dagger – for what other protection did she have?

As the men's attention drifted elsewhere, Andromeda let herself take in the scene before her. She watched the people of the town go back and forth, examined their little houses daubed with paint – white and blue and yellow. She could see ribbons of smoke rising and wondered what the women were cooking. She could see men pushing carts full of goods and wondered which might be brought back to fill the hold. And before the town there lay the beach, pale sand stretching across the bay, and before that the long jetty and the gangplank still laid out.

Andromeda felt a curious twitch in her chest. She could leave, she realised. She could run now, down the gangplank and along the jetty before the men on the deck had even seen her go. They would chase but she was fast. This was her chance.

She felt her feet tense, ready to spring like a gazelle from a lion. Her tongue was dry in her mouth. What was she waiting for? She felt like a root that could not be pulled, held fast to the deck. She could run, or try to, but what would she be running into? Not the old world she longed for, but a new unknown. What if it was crueller than the life she had? Here she had a little power at least, and it was growing. There she might have none. She might be captured and sold, passed around like a jar of palm wine, beaten and whipped. She had no wealth, no family, no protection. What would she be able to gain for herself, and what more might she lose?

Her chest was still churning when the men returned. Though she had made her decision she could still see the door open, and felt as if her spirit were split in two. Even as the new goods were loaded, as the anchors were hauled one by one, her calves were tight. The gangplank was still out. A few leaps and she could be on the jetty. As she stood glancing from deck to beach, she felt Perseus take her hand.

'I brought you something,' he said quietly, and she dragged her eyes towards him. In his open palm was a small piece of ivory, with a thong of leather threaded through the top. As she looked more closely she saw that it was carved into the shape of a fat-bellied hippopotamus. 'Do you like it?' he asked.

Her eyes flicked upwards and then back to his palm. She reached out a finger to touch the smooth ivory and felt her cheeks lift with a smile she did not need to force.

'It's beautiful,' she said, and was surprised when her lips trembled. How could it mean so much to her, this little piece of tooth? When she looked up again Perseus was smiling. He gestured for her to turn around and she felt his hands lift her braids as he tied the thong around her neck.

Andromeda saw that the gangplank had been lifted and felt the ship begin to move away from the jetty. A moment ago her heart might have lurched at that rift of water, growing wider by the moment, but as she ran her finger over the grooves of the pendant she felt her chest loosen. The opportunity had come and it had passed. No doubt there would be more, but she did not think that she would need them. If she was to build herself a new happiness, this is where she would do it.

CHAPTER 36

Perseus was agitated. Andromeda could see it in the tightness of his jaw, the tapping of his fingers on his dagger's hilt, his standing and sitting and standing again. He had not been still all morning, and there was a fixed line between his brows. It made her nervous to see him unsettled.

The sky was clouded like his mood, and a chill wind raised the hairs on her arms. The days were growing cold, and the nights even more so. Andromeda had begun to appreciate the warmth of Perseus' body when he came to her in the creaking hold, and no longer dreaded that he would fall asleep beside her instead of returning to the deck. It was a strange thing to welcome what she had once despised, what she still despised in the truest part of herself, but at least it kept her limbs from shivering.

Andromeda saw that Perseus had moved to the prow, his brown curls tossed by the wind as he scanned the horizon ahead. She joined him there, but seeing his fingers once more upon the curved blade she kept some deck between them.

'Is something wrong?' she asked softly.

His eyes did not leave the sea.

'We reach port soon,' he murmured.

'And that troubles you?'

Perseus half turned towards her, and she saw the weight of his brow. But then he twisted back again with an impatient breath.

'It is not any port. It is the port of Seriphos. My home.'

Andromeda's face crumpled in confusion.

'Should you not be happy, then, to return to the land of your fathers?' She felt her heart twist a little, with the knowledge that she might never have that chance.

'I have no father,' Perseus said, his tone flat. 'This was never my land, not truly.'

'But your mother waits for you?' she asked, swallowing her own pain. Perseus had told her little of Seriphos, or of the life he had lived there before coming aboard the boat. But he spoke of his mother sometimes, with a tenderness that gave her hope for herself. 'That must give you cause for happiness.'

He gave a stiff nod.

'How pleased she will be to see you return,' Andromeda said brightly, determined to blow away whatever darkness pulled at him. The twitch in his cheek began to rouse her old fear, long buried. His gaze was fixed ahead, unblinking, and she saw that the muscles of his bare arm were set hard. She could not lose the channel she had opened.

'Your mother will surely be impressed at the man you have become,' she said warmly, stepping forward to touch his arm. 'I see how the crew admire you. Gorgonslayer, they call you. Monster killer. And soon your people will admire you too. A hero returned to their shore! And with a wife by your side.' Andromeda smiled to see him turn towards her, to see his face unfold a little. She knew the words to say, the ways to warm him. 'What a welcome you shall receive.'

His eyes were on hers, shining, searching. She kept her gaze steady, and when his arm relaxed beneath her fingers she knew that he had found what he was looking for.

Perseus let out a sigh.

'A hero. Yes.' He spoke almost to himself, his gaze drifting back to the waves. 'There!' he suddenly shouted, startling Andromeda so that she gripped his wrist. 'There. Do you see it? That is Seriphos.'

She followed his gaze to a smear of grey on the horizon. With the sky so milky she could barely make it out.

'Not far,' he breathed. 'Not far now. I shall be pleased for you to meet my mother. She is a fine woman. Very fine. She will be a great example to you.'

Andromeda smiled crookedly, wondering what fineness this woman could impart that her own mother had not. But she felt a relief too, that Perseus seemed lighter, that his face was smooth and boyish again. It would be comforting to spend some time on the land, she told herself.

Seriphos was barely a port. The ship sailed into a wide bay with long rocky arms on either side to welcome it, while Andromeda took in the view around her – fishing boats bobbing in their wake, children running unclothed along the beach, huts scattered on the hillside. And there above them all a large house caught the sun, gleaming like a white stone atop a pile of grey.

'Who lives there?' she asked, but Perseus did not hear her. His gaze was fixed ahead, his stance set. Not tense as it had been before, but filled with an expectant stillness.

The short jetty looked as if it might come apart beneath them. Andromeda watched her feet to make sure they did not drop between the slats, and when she reached the beach she looked up to find that Perseus was already speaking with a local man further ahead. The man put down his basket, filled with glistening fish, and pointed a little way up the hill. As she approached she heard him say, '. . . where I would look. My wife tells me she is seen there often.'

The stranger smiled mildly, but Andromeda could see his eyes drifting over Perseus, perhaps trying to discern the source of the rotten-sweet smell that lingered about him.

'Have you any cumin aboard that ship of yours?' he asked hopefully. 'We have sponges to trade if that would interest you.'

But Perseus did not answer him. He was already striding in the direction that the man's arm had pointed, and Andromeda could only give an apologetic smile before hurrying after him.

The dirt path was wet from rain and she slipped a little as they climbed up from the beach. Perseus' strides did not shorten and she struggled to keep up. They turned onto a side path, lined with houses made from piled stone.

'This is where your mother lives?' Andromeda called, taking in the little smoking fires, the racks hung with fish. It was nothing like the oasis, but the people she saw seemed contented enough, giving friendly, curious nods as they passed.

'I do not know where she lives now,' Perseus called back to her. 'But we may find her at the shrine of Poseidon. It is only a little further along . . . '

His voice trailed off, his feet suddenly stopped in the mud. Before them stood a tall, narrow structure – four elegant pillars of wood supporting a pointed roof, its front carved with the curling crests of the sea. Beneath the roof, open to the air and to their eyes, there stood a great stone and before the stone, with back turned and head bowed, there knelt a woman.

Her head was covered with a scarf, her shape obscured beneath a thick mantle. It could have been anyone kneeling there in the dirt, but Perseus had stiffened, his chest rising and falling from their rush up the hill. He stepped forward, pace by pace, his boots making a wet crunch, and Andromeda stepped with him.

'Is it her?' she whispered. Andromeda did not know if it was the shrine or Perseus' manner that made her drop her voice. She felt as if she were upon sacred ground.

'Mother?' he called.

Andromeda saw the woman's head move, saw her covered form rise. And as she turned, Perseus let out a choked breath.

The pale face beneath the scarf opened wide in surprise.

'Perseus,' the woman gasped. There was a crack as the clay bottle she was holding slipped from her fingers and broke upon the ground.

'You've been away so long. I prayed for you every day. I begged the Lord Poseidon to keep you safe.' She glanced down at the cracked bottle, and the dark wine spilling into the mud. 'And now here you are.'

The woman smiled, and Andromeda thought how beautiful she was, with her eyes so full of love. It made her ache for her own mother.

'You must tell me everything,' she went on. 'All you have seen and done. You look so strong now. Come, let me see you.'

Perseus strode forward and she put out her arms to embrace him, but as she did her mantle fell open and between the folds a great swollen belly emerged. Perseus stopped as if struck by Ammon.

Seeing his gaze fall, his mother's smile vanished.

'Is it not a blessing?' she asked. Though she made her voice bright, Andromeda heard it quaver. Her eyes were set on Perseus, whose face Andromeda could not see. His mother watched him as one might watch a wild dog.

'He took you,' Andromeda heard Perseus murmur.

'He did not take me,' his mother said stiffly. 'We are married.' Her face was smooth, but her eyes still wary. She stepped forward to take Perseus' hand, but he withdrew it.

'He had no right.' The hardness was back in Perseus' arms. Andromeda thought she saw him shaking. 'You swore that you would not give yourself to him. He had no right to marry you without my word.'

Whom did they speak of? Andromeda knew she did not understand all that passed between them, but she felt the tension in the air like the coming of a storm. Her heartbeat crept into her throat.

And then Perseus turned. He was running back along the path, and Andromeda could do nothing but run after him.

'Perseus!' she heard his mother cry behind them, but her voice was already drowned in the slapping of their feet on the gravel.

CHAPTER 37

Andromeda knew where they were going, even though she had not the breath to ask. She followed Perseus as he climbed higher and higher, towards the gleaming white house upon the hilltop. Her legs shook beneath her, shocked by the effort after so many months on that narrow deck, and every breath burned her lungs. Ahead of her Perseus' heels flicked mud, while the leather bag slapped wildly against his hip. Was it madness to chase him? A part of her felt as if she were following death itself up that track, but what other path was there?

By the time they reached the white house Andromeda was bent over her knees. But Perseus was already hammering on the wooden door.

'Polydektes!' he thundered.

There was quiet for a moment. Andromeda unfolded herself and put a hand on Perseus' elbow.

'Why are we here? If they were wed, then no wrong has been done.' She kept her voice low, hoping to soften him. 'Your mother looks well and happy. Come, let us return to speak with her.'

But he pulled his arm away. 'Do not speak of what you do not understand,' he growled, and hammered the door again. 'Polydektes!'

The door opened, revealing an affronted face.

'Lord Polydektes is entertaining most esteemed guests—' the stooped man began, before Perseus pushed past him.

Andromeda followed, pulled as if they were bound together. Her heart, already racing from the climb, began to pound as they reached a brightly coloured room, with five men lying on couches about the edge.

'Perseus,' said the one at the centre. Though he was clearly surprised, he did not seem alarmed. His eyes were glassy, his bearded jaw relaxed as he reclined upon his elbow. 'What an entrance you have made.' He glanced in her direction. 'I am glad to see you safely returned, and in such . . . colourful company.' The man smiled at her, and she saw his eyes trail over her tattoos, her braids, her dress. Though his tone was affable, there was an amusement in it that bristled her. Her hand drifted to the carved hippopotamus hanging at her throat. The feel of its notches kept her calm.

'Come,' the man said – Polydektes, she presumed. His attention was back on Perseus. 'We are drinking. Let me pour you a cup and you can tell us of your travels.'

His words dragged a little, making it more difficult for Andromeda to pull them apart. She wondered whether Perseus had noticed, as he stood rooted in the middle of the stone floor.

'You have bedded her,' he said quietly.

'You mean my wife? Yes, I should hope so!' Polydektes laughed heartily, and his guests laughed as well. He turned to the man on his right, who raised his cup as if to toast their union.

'You had no right to wed her,' Perseus growled, a little louder.

'No right?' Polydektes seemed to sober a little and raised himself higher on his elbow. 'I had every right. I asked her and she accepted. I have shown her kindness. I have kept her safe. I have given her a home and everything she needs. Eileithyia smiles upon the match and fills her womb with life.' He splashed a little of his wine on the floor, as Andromeda had seen the sailors do for good fortune. 'I have done all according to what is proper, and invite you to share in our happiness. The gods despise those who spit on generosity,' he added, with an edge of warning to his voice.

'You married without my consent,' Perseus murmured. 'You asked her when you should have asked me.'

'Asked *you*?' Polydektes scoffed into his wine cup. 'You were a child. I see that you are still a child, for all your travels. I had hoped a year at sea would season you. Come, stop this nonsense.'

Perseus' body had taken on a new energy. Andromeda felt it beside her, as if his spirit were fighting to escape his limbs. But he remained still.

'I am not a child.' His jaw was like a stone. 'I have done things you could not. I have fought monsters. I have rescued the Princess Andromeda and made her my wife.' His head twitched towards her. 'I have slain the dreaded Gorgon.'

There was a ripple among the reclining men, as heads turned and tongues murmured in curiosity.

Polydektes raised a dismissive hand.

'A Gorgon? I have never heard of such a creature. Though I'm sure it makes a frightening tale for young maids.' His eyes slid to Andromeda again. 'A man is not made by what he claims but what he does.'

'It is not a tale,' Perseus snapped back, his voice rising. He looked from one man to another and seemed to expand under their gaze. 'I have the proof.'

Suddenly Andromeda's stomach rolled, for she knew what was coming. Perseus' hand went to the bag and he unslung it from his shoulder. He untied the leather that bound it, lifted the dreaded flap. She wanted to close her eyes, to shield herself from that terrible evil that had haunted her for so long. But she could not bring herself to do it. She had to see. She had to know.

Perseus opened the neck of the bag wide, bent down, and tipped the contents out onto the floor.

The head hit the stone with a sickening thud and left an oozing trail as it rolled. Andromeda gagged at the smell, already so familiar but now unleashed in full. It was sweetness masking rot. Though the head had been soaked in honey it had done only a little to stop the decay. Eyes bulged, cheeks were swollen, lips were pulled back in a terrifying grimace while a black tongue poked out between glistening teeth. It was an image of death, of her husband's violence written in flesh. She had tried to put it from her mind, to bury it like she buried her hatred and her fear, but she could not deny it now. Here exposed was the evil Perseus had done.

Around the room the men recoiled. Polydektes' mouth was open in disgust, his dark beard quivering in outrage.

'How dare you pollute my hall with this . . . this . . . '

'It is the Gorgon's head,' Perseus declared proudly, taking a deep breath as if the stench were nothing to him. 'I have brought it all the way from Libya. Will you call me child now, with this trophy before you? You should speak my name with glory and call me hero.'

Polydektes was looking at him as if he were mad.

'Hero? And what great deed have you performed? I see only that you have slain one barbarous woman and brought back another as your bride.' Polydektes raised a hand to his mouth, as if he might be sick. 'I have tolerated you for your mother's sake, but you go too far. Remove yourself from my hall, and do not return until you can sit among honourable men.'

Polydektes glared at him with eyes sharp as flint. But Perseus did not move. His legs were stiff but his arms were shaking, his breaths quick and shallow. Andromeda began to tremble too. The words had cut him. She knew that. They had sliced his pride and left him bare before these men, frowning at him over their cups, wrinkling their noses in disgust, sneering in derision.

Stop it, she wanted to shout. Didn't they see the danger they coaxed? It was there before them in those bulging eyes, that dead tongue. She wanted to reach out a hand to Perseus but her arms were stuck by her sides, her own tongue seized in her mouth.

As Perseus remained rooted, Polydektes spoke again.

'Must I have my slave escort you? Do not disgrace yourself further, boy.'

And that was enough. One movement and Polydektes was choking, hand clutching his streaming throat as Perseus held his curved dagger high. The shock in those wide eyes reminded Andromeda of another face, and she stepped forward as if to help, but there was nothing to be done. His fine tunic was soaked red, his head lolling back to pull the pulsing gash wide.

'Perseus,' she breathed, but when she turned she saw his wicked blade flash again, down across one of the other men, half risen from his couch. She stood frozen as she watched him leap and slash. They were old, unarmed, slow from the wine, while he was quick, with the strength of a beast enraged. Whether they grappled or cowered he cut them down. And Andromeda watched. Helpless. Useless. Voiceless.

By the end her breath was so shallow she thought it had stopped. She was surprised when she heard herself scream.

No. It was not her voice.

Andromeda forced herself to turn, and there in the doorway stood Perseus' mother, clutching her belly as she fell against the frame. Her chest was heaving, her pale lips quivered, as she took in the horror of that hall.

'My son,' she croaked, looking as if her face would split with anguish. 'What have you done?'

CHAPTER 38

Perseus turned, blood-spattered, at the sound of his mother's voice. For a moment he didn't seem to see her, his shining face fixed with a satisfied grimace. But as she cried out again his eyes cleared and he looked down at the knife in his hand. One of the men was still gasping on the floor behind him, but they were all beyond help.

'We should go,' Andromeda croaked, her legs desperate to carry her away from that place, towards air that wasn't thick with death.

Her words seemed to spur Perseus into action. He slotted the still-bloody knife back onto his belt and stooped to put the rotting head back into its bag. Then he strode forward, seizing his mother's wrist as her wide eyes darted between her son and the crumpled bodies. Sounds leaked from her horrified mouth but she spoke no more words. Perseus pulled her from the room, and Andromeda stumbled after them.

They passed the aged slave as they came through the courtyard but he did not stop them – only shrank at the blood on Perseus' tunic and the wildness in his glance. When they were past him Andromeda looked back to see the man hurrying towards his master's hall, her own heart stiff from knowing what he would find there. She quickened her pace.

They were halfway down the hill when the shouting started. Andromeda could hear the cries erupting behind them, violent with outrage, ragged with sorrow. Perseus broke into a run, the bloody bag clutched under one arm and his mother dragged by the other. Andromeda had to clasp the poor woman's elbow to stop her from falling, and her own chest quaked to hear the breathless sobs that broke from her. She tried to ask Perseus to slow his pace, but her words were whipped away by the wind. He would not have heard her anyway. He charged down the muddy track like a bull on the run, and she could only follow.

The captain was carrying a basket along the jetty when Perseus collided with him. He saw the blood, heard the shouts, and it seemed barely a word was needed. They were on the deck and raising anchors before Andromeda had sucked the breath back into her lungs.

As she watched Seriphos begin to shrink into the horizon, she found her legs could no longer hold her, and she sank against the rail. Her heart was pounding so hard it made her head pulse, and her stomach rolled with each tilt of the waves. But as she looked across the deck and saw Perseus' mother on her knees, pressed against the mast with one arm wrapped around the thick wood and another thrown across her belly, Andromeda felt her own fear dissolve. The woman's face was pale like the moon, her eyes shut tight and her lips muttering. The wind was high now, whipping her dark hair, and she looked so frail that she might be blown away.

An instinct filled Andromeda's limbs and she crawled across the boards towards the mast. The touch of her hand made the woman's eyes snap open.

'The waves,' she whispered. 'They are so loud.' She raised a hand to cover her ear and Andromeda saw that she was shaking.

'You will grow used to them,' she murmured, putting an arm around those shuddering shoulders. 'They roar and they rock, but they cannot hurt us. We are safe now.' She tried to smile but it was difficult when her own lips were trembling.

'I swore I would never go upon the waves again,' Perseus' mother said, gasping tightly. Suddenly tears filled her pale eyes, quivering in the wind. 'Where will we go now? All that I had is gone. I built it for both of us. And now Polydektes is dead and my son . . . my son . . . '

She spoke mostly to herself, and Andromeda realised that Perseus had not even introduced them.

'My name is Andromeda,' she said softly. 'What is yours?'

'Danae,' the woman croaked, and she blinked as if she were seeing her properly for the first time. 'You were there. With my son.'

Andromeda nodded stiffly. 'I am his wife.' Her lips still resisted those words, but they were true whether she spoke them or not.

Danae nodded slowly, taking in her face. But she said no more. She drew her scarf tight around her head and looked down at the deck, shaking again with fear or with sobs – Andromeda was not sure which. Now was not the time for words. They had both seen the same evil atop that hill. She knew what horror Danae's mind was battling, or at least some part of it. It was different for her. Andromeda had seen that violence before. She had felt it coming before the shining blade was out of its sheath.

And she had not stopped it.

Her eyes fell upon her sandals, dark with blood that had spilled over the leather, spread between her toes, dried and cracked on her skin. The sight of it made her feel ill. But beneath that, deep in her gut, there was the heavy stone of guilt. She should have done something. Said something. Instead of standing paralysed as she had stood before. Would those men's faces haunt her as Phineus' did? She shook her head, as if to ward them off. What could she have done? He would have cut her down as easily as the others. So why did her heart feel so knotted?

She thought of Perseus stood before the reclining men, demanding respect they would not give. Their words had cut him and he had cut back. But she remembered words she had spoken too, of the glorious welcome he would receive. They had been meant to please him, to soften him, to keep her safe. But they had inflamed him too. She had built his spirit high and given it further to fall. That had been her part, she realised. Her fingers had not held the dagger, but her words had helped to raise it. She saw it now but could not have known it then. She could not have known.

Andromeda felt her heart racing, her skin hot and cold at once. It was a dangerous power she wielded, when every word might grow safety or danger, peace or violence, tenderness or hate. She would not torture herself with what had passed. Her spirit could not endure it. But she knew now that her voice was a heavy thing.

Her arm was still around Danae, trembling in her mantle. Over at the rail Perseus stood with several of the crew, his face lit bright as he told them a tale of what had happened on the hill. As Andromeda watched them her brow became hard, her fingers tight. The men exclaimed in awe as Perseus showed them his bloodied dagger. Their hands clapped upon his back. It was not right, Andromeda thought. How could they celebrate him? But then, had she been so different? *Hero,* she had called him. *Gorgonslayer.* What glory could there be in that rotten head? The very word made her gut squirm, but she had spoken it.

Perhaps the men feared him as she did. Perhaps they simply spoke the words he wanted to hear, made him their hero so he could not be their enemy. But she would not do it. Not now that she knew the horror it might breed. There were other words he needed to hear, and no one else to speak them.

She waited until the sun was going down and a steady calm had fallen upon the waves and the men. They were out of sight of Seriphos now, and there was no ship to be seen on the horizon. If the crew had feared pursuit they had forgotten it now, and rested lazily about the deck, throwing knucklebones and enjoying some of the fresh fish the captain had acquired. Perseus stood alone at the stern, and she knew that this was her opportunity.

She prised Danae gently from her shoulder and left her by the mast, silent and dull-eyed. The night air was setting in, so Andromeda wrapped her arms around herself and made her way to the back of the boat, legs stiff after being folded beneath her for so long. Perseus smiled when he saw her, and it made her shrivel.

'Is my mother well?' he asked lightly, glancing towards the mast as if he had only just seen her there. 'She is not used to the sea as we are.'

'You should ask her yourself.' Andromeda tried to keep her tone soft, but there was a bite in it that she could not hold back.

A wrinkle appeared on Perseus' brow, but it soon smoothed.

'She will not have to endure long. We will reach Argos by tomorrow's light.'

Argos. That was their destination, then. It was little more than a name to Andromeda, though she recalled that Perseus had spoken of it before – soon after they had first begun to speak together, when every word between them was so desperate, so cautious. While she had been straining to survive each day he had talked of oracles and inheritances, things so far from her she had barely noted them. And they felt far still. Her mind was still on Seriphos, in the painted hall and its red floor.

'I go to reclaim my kingdom,' he said. His green eyes were fixed on her, glinting with expectation. 'Does it please you, my princess, to know that you will be soon be married to a king?'

'I am not a princess. I have told you so.'

The wrinkle returned to his brow. 'You should soften your tongue,' he said, with an edge of warning. 'Come, we should be celebrating my victory.' He moved to pull her toward him, but she set her body hard.

'Victory? Is that what you call it? You murdered an unarmed man. Many men, when the wine was upon them. You must see that it was wrong.' Her voice was low, her eyes sharp as she watched his face, heart hammering.

She knew he had heard her, but his expression was strangely unreadable. 'Wrong? By what measure? I have saved my mother and taken revenge upon a man who wronged me. No man would condemn me for it.'

'Saved her from what?' Andromeda asked, pressing on while her nerve held. 'From a gentle life? She was happy, I think, and safe. Now she weeps alone. And her belly is full with a child that will have no father.'

She felt her temper rising. She spoke for Danae, but for herself as well. They had both been ripped from happiness by Perseus' hand. She had to make him understand.

'A child needs no father,' he said, lips stiff. 'They will both have all they need. They will have more than I have had. You'll see. I will win it for them.'

'What if she already had all that she wanted? Did you ever ask? Did you stop to think before taking what *you* wanted? Did you ever ask me?'

She knew she had let herself go too far and braced for his anger. But Perseus only looked confused.

'Ask you what?' She could not fathom the blankness of his face. 'I rescued you. I married you.'

'You raped me,' she choked.

He frowned and shook his head. 'No. You didn't push me away. You never said no. Not until—'

'I didn't say yes either.' Her cheeks were so heavy now, but she wouldn't stay silent. Not now that she had a voice she could use.

'I rescued you,' Perseus said quietly. 'I have never beaten you. I have kept you safe.'

'I was safe before I ever met you.' The words tore from her lips, vibrating with anger. 'I went with you because I had no choice. You took me from my home. You threatened my family. You killed Phineus when he had done nothing.'

'Him?' Perseus threw a hand down as if slashing Phineus all over again, and Andromeda lost some of the breath that fired her.

'How can a man protect his women if he cannot protect himself? A real man takes what is his, and he defends it.'

He had raised himself to full height, but she could feel herself shrinking. How could she argue against such surety? With every word he believed himself right. And with every violence his arm grew more confident. It felt so unstoppable, the wheel that turned within him. She had thrown her truth against him, and it had clattered uselessly.

'Please,' she murmured. 'Do not hurt your mother further. That is all I ask. Whatever you strive to gain in Argos, make sure it is truly for her good.'

Andromeda had shielded her own spirit long ago. Though she had hoped to make Perseus see the wrong he had done her, it would make little difference now. No, it was Danae who was in peril. Her wounds were raw, her heart split open. One more cut and her soul might fly out and never return. She could see it in those hollow cheeks, in her shivering body slumped against the mast.

As she watched that pitiful figure, she felt Perseus' gaze turn upon it too. She glanced across and saw his eyes shine with something that had not been there before. Perhaps her words had moved him after all. The tiniest nudge, she did not doubt, but it was a start. He kept his lips silent, and she did the same. Enough had passed between them today. Andromeda could only wait for the dawn and hope that even a little of what she had spoken had been heard.

Part 4

Danae

CHAPTER 39

Danae blinked in the thin morning light. She thought she had slept a little, for she remembered dreams filled with horror, but her eyes were dry and swollen as if they had not closed at all.

They had tried to lead her into the hold where that other woman slept, but Danae had clung tight to the mast. She could not bear to go down into the moonless dark, to hear the waves slosh in her ears, to have the creaking boards above her head. There were some memories that stayed as sharp and terrifying as the day they were made. Her first voyage across the sea had been one of them, and now she felt another one buried in her heart like the tip of an arrow, pricking her with every breath.

Perseus stood at the back of the ship, talking with a thick-bearded man beside the rudder. Though Danae knew she looked upon her son, she felt as if she were squinting through a veil, trying to catch a glimpse of the child she had raised. How changed he was from the figure she had watched shrink away from her not even one year ago. There was a hardness to him now, in his body, in his gaze, in the way he set his chin. Was this what Polydektes had intended when he had urged her to send her son away? Perhaps he was a man now, or perhaps only a hardened boy. Danae was not sure she wanted him to be either, not when the cost was so great. Where was the boy she had raised in gentleness? Gone, with the husband who had loved her. Both spent to gain this stranger who filled her with fear.

The longer she looked at Perseus the more twisted her heart became, as love battled revulsion – the one deep-cut and slow-shifting, the other fresh and searing. They tumbled through her like writhing beasts, churning her chest until she thought she would be sick. She let out a shaking breath and told herself that she only needed time. Time to grieve. Time to find her son again. Time to gather the pieces of herself and settle them anew. She had done it before. She had been shattered and she had rebuilt. But that only made it harder. This was all too familiar, like opening a wound barely healed. She cradled her belly and hummed a faltering tune. Here she was, once more, about to bring a child into a world she did not yet know the shape of.

Danae had not even summoned her voice to ask where they were sailing. What use was it, if she could not change the course? She had made her harbour at Seriphos. Now it lay ruined behind her, that cherished home she had built in Polydektes' hall. He had been a good husband to her, and she had cared for him. Not in that flaming way she had felt once before, with skin hot and heart racing. But he had made her feel safe. That was all she wanted, truly. To root herself in soil that would not slip away. And she had felt that, for a time. As the child began to grow inside her she had not been afraid. She had imagined the life it would have, the life they would all share once Perseus returned. Now her stomach rolled and dropped as if there were no bottom for it to reach.

But even as she watched her son with his violent hand upon the rudder, and felt her anger rise at all he had ruined, Danae knew that Perseus was all she had left. He had made it so, by his will or by fate, and now the two of them were adrift once more with only the other to cling to. For two decades he had been her constant, bound by love and blood. But now for the first time Danae felt the weight of that bond about her, a chain as much as an anchor. And she could not remove it. She could not leave him. Whatever he had done, however distant he felt from the boy she had nurtured, he was still a child of her own body. He was fixed to her as surely as the one that now dragged at her hips. And she was fixed to him. Where else could she go? Who would she be, without him?

That knowledge sat like an immovable weight in her chest. Danae knew that she would have to accept it, and that in time she might even find it a comfort to have this one certainty amid so much devastation. But for now the sight of her son's triumphant face made her shudder, so she turned her eyes away. As they swept the deck they fell upon Andromeda, swaying a little with the rock of the ship. They had spoken yesterday, she thought, though her memory was thick like fog and she could remember little but the girl's name. She thought she recalled a warm hand about her shoulder but it might have been her own. Now that she looked at the girl properly she realised how strange she was. Her hair, uncovered, was plaited like black snakes, and her dark skin patterned here and there with lines and symbols. Even her face was marked, her fine chin etched with black ink. Was she a priestess, bearing the signs sacred to her god? Danae had never seen such a woman and she found herself frightened, imagining what uncanny powers she might wield. Had she woven her influence upon Perseus? Had she made him love her and driven him to do terrible things? She had been there, hadn't she? Yes, Danae had seen the girl standing in that bloody hall. The memory of it seized her heart and she had to drive it away. But as she watched Andromeda watching her son, she found herself wanting to believe that it was true. That Perseus had not done what she had seen him do. Not truly, not in his true mind.

Andromeda's face turned towards her and she looked away, gazing out instead at the blue sea and the pale sky and the green hills climbing to meet it. She thought that something in their peaks and ridges seemed familiar, and as she turned herself about she realised that there were hills to either side of the ship, and more emerging from the haze ahead. It settled her a little to know that land was not far away, but at the same time a new feeling began to knock in her chest. No one had told her where they were sailing, but as the hills grew clearer she knew.

'The Gulf of Argolis,' one of the crew announced behind her.

She turned back to see Perseus clasp the thick-bearded man around the shoulder before meeting her eye.

'Did you hear that, Mother? We are going home.'

Home. She wondered whether he saw her wince. These hills had not been her home for half a lifetime. There was no comfort for her here, only painful memories. Her comfort was back on Seriphos, soaked in blood. How could Perseus be so eager for a place he had never known? The light in his eyes made her fearful. It had been there before, as he stood in Polydektes' hall with his dagger dripping. But now it burned with a new intensity, and with a jolt of dread she realised what had ignited it. It was the spark of destiny.

Not for the first time, Danae wished that she could unspeak the truth she had told him. But those words could no more be taken back than the oracle itself. Even after all these years the memory of Aristides' dark face still plagued her, his words fixed in her mind like letters scratched in stone. *The Pythia foretold that your daughter Danae would give birth to a son, and that he would be your death.* The future the Pythia spoke of had seemed so unlikely when she had first heard it, and even more so in all these years spent on Seriphos, far from her old life. But now she found herself carried back towards it, her sweet son blooded and hungry.

She pulled herself up against the mast, but the ship was already turning, the thick-bearded man pulling at the rudder. She had no power to stop it. It was not only the wind that pulled them on but unrelenting fate.

'We make our landing at Nauplia,' the bearded man called.

That name beat her chest like an ancient drum, throwing up dust long settled. To think of Nauplia made her think of Argos, of her father, of Myron and the glistening rain turned to gold, of Perseus heavy in her belly and that dark beach where her first life had ended. Now the same sand was so close and she felt her dread drag her towards the deck.

A great rock rose out of the water ahead, like a titan of stone stretching out into the gulf. As the ship sailed around it, the port came into view. Other boats already floated on the sparkling water, some larger than theirs, others smaller, and on the shore there was the movement of men. One of the distant figures must have noted their approach, for he began to wave with wide arms and drew them to an open jetty.

When the anchors had dropped and the gangplank was laid out he stepped aboard with the long strides of a man who had made the same steps many times before.

'You are welcomed to the harbour of Nauplia,' he announced with a hasty smile. 'You may hold your ship in our safe waters for as long as you need to trade and refresh yourselves. We only require that you make your trades with the great city of Tiryns before taking your wares any further inland. You may do so here at the port and will find our merchants fair and well stocked.'

When he had reeled off his words he smiled again and turned towards the jetty, but Perseus stepped forward.

'Tiryns? Our business lies in Argos. Is this not the harbour of that rich city?'

'It was the last time I sailed here,' said the bearded man, whom Danae took to be the captain. Her mind had been filled with too many things to wonder at why the man had called Tiryns a great city. In her girlhood it had been little more than a small town in Argos' shadow.

'You have been on the sea some years, I see,' said the officious man, with a curl in his lip that almost looked like pity. 'Nauplia is under the protection of Tiryns now, and serves her before all others. You are free to journey to Argos, but if you wish to trade your goods there you must seek permission from King Proitos.'

Danae's heart jumped.

'Proitos?' She pushed herself forward, legs unsteady. The man's gaze turned upon her. 'Was that the name you spoke?'

'King Proitos, indeed. He rules at Tiryns. I can request an audience if that is your need, but I doubt he will be able to see you until tomorrow at the earli—'

'You must take us to him,' she cried, surprised by the loudness of her own voice. Argos, Nauplia – these places held only fear. And Seriphos was like a smouldering wreck behind her. But the sound of her uncle's name was a torch in the dark.

The man's face wrinkled. 'As I said, I doubt that he will—'

She clutched his tunic before he could step back.

'I am Danae, daughter of Akrisios. You will take me to my uncle.'

CHAPTER 40

They left the harbour by a road scored deep with wagon tracks. The land here was flat, as if washed that way by the waves, though in the distance hills crowded, and straight ahead there rose a crag of rock breaking out from the earth. The closer they came the higher the crag seemed to rise, an island of grey in a sea of green. Danae's heart pounded with every step she took, but for the first time since she had dragged herself up the hill towards Polydektes' house it was not heavy with fear. This feeling was different, filling her limbs and driving them on, building and building as the grey rock loomed before her. It was anticipation. She could barely breathe with the thought of seeing that face she had so loved, that she had thought she would never see again. The promise of it pulled her onward, out of the storm and into something like safety, like home.

It was strange that she should feel this way, as she looked upon a place she did not even recognise. As Danae drew closer to the crag, she realised that its grey face was not the cliff she had taken it to be. Though the base was raw stone the top was orderly, shaped by men not gods, a great wall that sat upon the rock like a towering crown. It was a wall unlike any she had ever seen, great boulders piled so high she felt her shoulders tense as she walked beneath them. She was relieved when their group began to climb a narrow stairway. Better to be upon the acropolis than beneath it.

'You will need to wait here,' the harbour master said when they had reached a gate in the great wall of stone. He glanced between Danae and her son, seemingly uncertain as to which of them he should be addressing. 'I must speak with Lord Proitos before you can be permitted to enter the citadel.' He nodded to a guard clad in polished bronze and disappeared through the gate.

There were only three of them on the stairs – Danae, Perseus, and the girl Andromeda. The captain and his crew had remained at Nauplia, with the promise that they would keep their ship in port for three days. Danae knew they would not need it. If her uncle was truly lord at Tiryns then they would have safety here. A place to set themselves. That was all she wanted or needed.

As they waited for the harbour master to return, Danae's attention was drawn to her son, shifting on his feet with an impatient energy.

'How far is it to Argos?' he asked, scanning the plain and the hills beyond. Danae followed his gaze. Would she be able to see it from here? Would she know it if she did? Everything seemed so different from a distance, and yet the shapes of the land did look familiar.

'Not far,' she said, pulling her eyes away. There was a part of her that didn't want to see that place, and another that could not yet rest comfortably upon her son's face. She stared at the rough stone of the wall instead.

'Then why do we waste time here? You must know why I have brought us to Argolis.' She could feel Perseus' gaze on her but did not turn. 'It is time for me to reclaim my birthright.'

'Uncle Proitos is your kin,' she said stiffly. 'He will protect us. We are in great need of allies.' *Now that you have driven us to exile.* Why could she not speak those words aloud? They were true and he should hear them. But her lips resisted, and she realised that it was fear holding her back. She kept her eyes on the stone.

'I need no protector,' Perseus said, and she saw his brown shoulders shrug at the edge of her vision. 'My destiny lies in Argos, not Tiryns.'

Destiny. The way he spoke that word made her shiver, and she did not have to look into his eyes to know that the spark had returned. She forced herself to turn, but before she could speak again there was a movement ahead of them as the guard stepped aside.

'Danae!'

Her uncle strode forward and wrapped his great arms around her, filling her open mouth with his tunic. She had barely seen his face but she knew it was him. His shape, his voice, his smell. They were just as she remembered. She let herself fall into his broad chest, throat suddenly choked with tears. It was as if all the weight had been lifted from her, and she clung to him like a drowning man to a rock.

'It's really you,' he said gruffly. She heard him suck in a breath and when he pulled away from her his eyes were sparkling. 'I never thought that . . . ' His eyes darted across her face, as if they still did not believe what they were seeing. 'I never forgave myself, Danae,' he said, his voice thick. 'I should have protected you.'

'You tried,' she mumbled. 'You did more than—' But the lump in her throat was too large. She swallowed it and shook her head. 'Let us not talk of the past. I am here and you are here. That is all I care about.' She reached for his hands, but as he squeezed them a noise beside her made his head turn.

'And this young man.' Proitos beamed, eyes wide. 'He must be . . . Can he be?'

'My son, Perseus,' she said, with lips tighter than she ever thought they could be with those words upon them. 'And his wife, the lady Andromeda.'

'And another child soon to come!' Proitos exclaimed, touching her belly with gentle fingers. 'I am honoured to welcome you all. Honoured indeed. I will order a bull to be sacrificed, in thanks to the gods, and this evening we shall dine and drink and you shall tell me all that has come to pass.'

Though his smile lit an old fire in her chest, she found she could not enjoy the warmth of it. How could she speak of the things that had brought her here? Her tongue was like lead at the thought of it, and perhaps Proitos saw her cheeks grow pale.

'First you must rest,' he said, his hearty voice suddenly soft. 'You will be in want of comfort after your voyage, and we have plenty to offer. Soft beds, warm baths. Come. Come.'

His smile was so inviting that she followed without another word and did not allow herself to think about what she would tell him, or about Perseus' hard brow or the strange woman's watching eyes.

Danae had eaten well this past year, grateful for all that she received at Polydektes' table. But the food before her now was something else entirely. Wild mushrooms with garlic, tender artichokes glistening in oil. Fresh blackberries and pickled strawberries. Pears and plums and pomegranates – more than they could possibly eat. Cattle were rare on Seriphos and she could not remember the last time she had tasted beef. Now here it was in abundance – grilled, stewed, spiced – and yet the smell only turned her stomach.

'Come, Danae,' her uncle said, helping himself to a spoonful of chickpeas with saffron. 'What is your fancy? The plums are perfectly ripe. Here, try one.'

He held it out to her and she took it from him with hesitant fingers. She could not disappoint that expectant gaze, so she put her teeth against the smooth skin and bit until juice ran down her chin. The flesh was so sweet on her tongue that it made her choke. How could she take delight in it when Polydektes lay cold? She should be tearing her hair and beating her breast. She should be anointing his body, singing beside his tomb. Instead she had fled, rushed to find comfort from the next man who could give it to her. Her lips began to tremble against the half-bitten fruit, her eyes stinging with tears of shame.

'Danae? Oh, my dear.'

She felt Proitos' hand on her arm, heard the concern in his voice, but she could not turn to face him.

'I have upset you. I should have known that something was wrong, for you to arrive here with a round belly and no husband. Come,' he murmured, taking the plum from her shaking hand. 'The food will wait. First you must tell me what has happened.'

She closed her eyes and sent tears spilling down her cheeks. 'My husband,' she began, but her tongue was stiff, unable to speak the words.

'He is dead,' came Perseus' voice from across the table. It made her cold to hear him say it. Danae opened her eyes to see Proitos nod.

'A terrible misfortune,' he said gravely. 'How lately did he pass?'

'Very recently,' her son said flatly, as if he were talking of nothing more than the changing weather. She noted that he did not say precisely how recently, for then he would have to explain why they had fled before the rites were performed. Though it made her angry to hear him skirt the truth, a part of her was relieved, to know that he was ashamed to speak of what he had done. He had some conscience, at least.

'Who was he, your husband?' Proitos asked, turning back to her. 'A good man?'

She nodded stiffly. 'Lord of Seriphos, where I landed after . . . after . . . '

But her uncle saved her from speaking what he already knew.

'Seriphos. Yes, I know of it,' he said slowly. 'And to think that you were so close all these years. Forgive me, Danae. I should have searched for you, but I was sure you were dead. Akrisios tried, so I'm told. He sent men all along the coast, hoping you had washed up somewhere. He must have realised his madness – too late, I thought, but here you are.' He beamed at her, but she was too surprised to repay his smile.

'He looked for me?'

Proitos nodded his silvery head.

'I imagine he was desperate to get you back, once he saw what he had cast away. I fled with my girls that same night, and he has been alone in his crumbling hall ever since. No heir, no kin. He has brought himself and Argos into ruin.'

Danae was silent. For many years she had tried not to think of her father, and now hearing these things she wasn't sure how she felt. Should she pity him? No, the feeling that squeezed her chest was not pity, but neither was it satisfaction. She could not yet feel its shape, but perhaps that would come in time.

'But you have thrived,' she said, letting her lips relax into a smile. The proof was in the feast before them, in the bright colours of the freshly painted hall, in the fine weave of her uncle's tunic and the gold that gleamed at his wrists. 'I am pleased to see it.'

'Yes.' He nodded, with a humble touch of his brow. 'The city of Tiryns welcomed me in my exile, and I have thanked her by making her great. The gods have granted me much good fortune.' He smiled, though Danae thought she saw a sadness ripple across his cheek. 'I have a son, not much younger than your Perseus.'

'That's wonderful. I should like to meet my cousin,' she said warmly.

'Of course. Though he is at Mycenae presently, seeing to our affairs there. Iphianassa too, with her husband and two sons. I visit them often, for it is only across the plain. Lysippe is married as well, of course, and happy, though she is far away in the north.'

The brightness was back in her uncle's eye as he spoke of his children.

'And Iphinoe?' she asked, and saw his face fall.

'She has gone beneath the earth,' Proitos murmured. 'Not long after we arrived here, she was struck by a fever.'

Danae felt her heart twist. So long ago, and yet she had not known. Somehow it seemed as if she should have felt her cousin's spirit slip from the world. They had been so close once, and Danae had not even felt the thread snap.

'Her mother has joined her now, in the realm of the Thirsty Ones. Two winters have passed, and yet sometimes it feels as if I buried her only yesterday. A terrible sickness it was.'

His robust voice was suddenly thin, close to breaking. Danae saw him shudder as he splashed a few drops of dark wine onto the floor.

'Oh, Uncle,' she whispered, reaching towards him as if she might absorb some of his pain.

'Terrible,' he said again, with a shake of his head. 'But we cannot thank the gods with one mouth and curse them with another.' He looked at her steadily and shaped his lips into a smile. 'I have enjoyed much happiness, and now I find my family grown again.'

He took her hand and looked about him, at Perseus, at Andromeda, and finally to her own swollen belly. 'Pain fixes to our hearts too easily. We must remember to fix our joy there too.'

She felt his thick fingers squeeze her palm and let his words sink like water over parched earth. She had been close to cracking, but now sitting in this smoky hall Danae began to believe that everything could be healed and whole again.

They sat like that for a moment, before Proitos cleared his throat.

'Now, Perseus, I am glad to see you so well grown. It is rare I have such a fine young man in my hall, and I would hazard to say you have seen further shores than I.' He turned a pleasant smile to Andromeda. 'You must tell me how you came to have such a lovely wife.'

Perseus had been quiet until now, picking at the meat and fruit with half a wary eye glancing across the table. But now his face opened into a smile as he leant back on his chair.

'It is a long tale indeed,' he said. 'And worth the telling.'

So he began, and Proitos listened, and so did Danae. Her son's eyes were bright as he spoke of foreign lands and dreadful beasts, and for a time Danae let herself be absorbed by his words, desperate to find some understanding in them, of the man her boy had become. But as the tale went on Danae found her gaze sliding to Andromeda, who stared into her cup with silent lips. It barely seemed as if she was listening, and yet sometimes her face would twitch, almost a wince, and she would open her mouth as if to speak, but form no words. If Danae had not heard her speaking Greek aboard the ship she would wonder if she knew how. No, here was a woman who had chosen silence. But the longer she watched her, the more Danae wished she could know what those lips would say.

CHAPTER 41

The next morning Proitos insisted on giving them a tour of the city. They began at the citadel, where he had provided them with guest chambers and where his grand Hearth Hall stood as an imposing centrepiece. They had seen it last night, of course, but her uncle seemed keen for them to view its painted walls illuminated by the sun's light, streaming in through the square hole above the hearth. On every side there danced beasts and fishes, leaping through blue sky or gliding through blue ocean. Danae might have sat there all morning taking in the detail, but Proitos had much he wanted to show them.

'The Great Court,' he announced, as they went back through the anteroom and into the open air. They had already passed through it, criss-crossing from chamber to hall, but now her uncle stood smiling as he looked about, and his smile broadened as he saw hers.

'It is wonderful,' Danae breathed, her eyes trailing from the neatly laid slabs beneath her feet to the great gateway that stood ahead of them, with columns rising towards the sky. She had never been surrounded by so much stone, so finely worked. Proitos must have seen her gaze stuck on the towering walls.

'Thick as ten men, shoulder by shoulder,' he said proudly. 'Thicker, in some places.'

Danae's mouth opened in awe, imagining how many straining arms would be needed to raise just one of those boulders.

'Why so deep?' she asked. 'Are there men who would do you harm?'

He only shrugged. 'We have much to protect. Better to be prepared. But . . . ah. I see you are worried.' He stepped forward and put a light hand on her shoulder. 'Don't be. I keep the peace as well as I can. These walls are a symbol as much as a shield. What man would dare assault us? Come now, we are safe here. You will always be safe here.' He drew her into his chest and she was glad he could not see her eyes glisten. He spoke those words so lightly and she knew he could not know what weight they held for her, nor how desperately she hoped they were true. By the time his thick arms had released her she had blinked her tears away.

'Over there is where we keep our finest cloth, and there the wine,' he went on, pointing to a row of squat buildings shadowed by the great wall. 'And there our arms.'

'What is that building?' Danae asked, pointing to a small but handsome-fronted structure beside the Hearth Hall.

'Ah.' Her uncle swallowed as if something had caught in his throat. 'The Women's Hall,' he said with a thin smile. 'I had intended it for my wife and her ladies, but the sickness took her before it was finished.'

There was pain written in every line of his face, and Danae wished she had not spoken.

'I'm sorry, Uncle,' she said softly.

'For what, my dear?' He turned to her and his cheeks seemed to fill a little. 'It is the same loss that you yourself have suffered. The gods leave no life untouched by sorrow.' He looked about at each of them, and back to the hall. 'I grieve, but I live too. Bitterness is a consuming fire and I have lost enough already.' He looked back at her and smiled. 'Come, let us visit the lower town. There is much more to see.'

Danae smiled back, and as she was led through a gate in the thick wall her mind was full with her uncle's words. His pain was clear, and yet it almost seemed to drive him. His face beamed with pride as they walked through the town, past smiths and potters, weavers and dyers, tanners and carpenters. All this he had brought together, like the colossal walls that circled the citadel, laying one stone upon another until he had created something extraordinary.

She watched Perseus walking ahead of her and saw the dagger glinting on his hip. It made her stomach clench to think of what her son had done, but she saw his pain too. She had been there when those wounds were made. She had watched them deepen, year after year, at every slight, every embarrassment, every rejection. Though she had brought him into this world she could not protect him from it, not she alone. *Son of Danae,* they had called him. *Bastard. Fatherless.* And she had watched her child cringe and stoop. Now he stood tall, but that only made her more afraid. His pain was not gone but hidden within, filling his heart, driving his hand. It was a hungry pain, a devouring pain. Her uncle's pain had made him hungry too, but for life, not death. As they walked the crowded streets Danae looked at all that he had accomplished, all he had gathered about him, and found herself hoping that here among the fresh-cut stone her son might learn how to build rather than destroy.

When they had walked beyond the craftsmen with their busy hands and sweating brows they came to an open place, where the walls ended and the wide landscape spread towards the hills. Danae smiled gently at her uncle.

'Tiryns truly is a wonder,' she said, turning back towards the town. 'Are we to return to the citadel now?'

Proitos smiled. 'Soon, if you wish. Though there is one more thing I would show you.' He looked down and tapped his foot. Danae had thought there was nothing here but grass. Now she saw that amid the green-brown tufts there was a round hole, edged with stone. She took a step towards it, peering into the unfathomable blackness.

'A well?' she asked.

Her uncle shook his head. 'A cistern. A great vault of stone, beneath the earth. Ever full with fresh water, so that my people may never find their throats dry.'

Danae nodded, imagining what might lie beneath her feet and stepping back a little.

'It is a well, then,' said Perseus, glancing at the hole. 'I daresay we have all seen one of those.'

He looked around as if he had said something amusing, but Proitos was the only one to smile.

'Not a well,' he said quietly, his lips strained. 'No, the rock goes too deep here. A well would not . . . Ah, listen to me, boring you all with my projects and keeping you ladies out in the sun.' His face softened and he looked about at each of them, until a thought seemed to strike him. 'Perseus, tell me, do they keep hunting dogs on Seriphos?'

Her son shrugged. 'Not that I ever saw.'

Proitos' eyes lit up. 'Ah, then you must see mine! I keep a fine pack. Harehounds, deerhounds. I have just had two bitches brought from Krete. Beautiful creatures, though they need some breaking in. Come, I will show you. And another day we shall take them into the hills with us. A noble young man such as yourself must learn to hunt.' Her uncle's smile was warm, genuine, and a little of it seemed to reflect itself on Perseus' face.

'All right,' he said. 'We will see these hounds, if it pleases you.'

'Excellent.' Proitos beamed, clapping his great hands together. 'The kennel is in the lower town, just behind the tannery.'

He started towards the sprawling buildings and Perseus followed.

'Come, Andromeda,' he said, taking her by the wrist.

'Uncle,' Danae began, taking quick steps to catch his long strides. 'Hunting is the sport of men. By all means take Perseus to see the hounds, but I fear I have had enough of the sun, as you say.' She drew her veil close about her face, smiling delicately. 'I think it is time for me and the lady Andromeda to return to the citadel.'

He stopped his stride and looked at them both. 'Yes, of course. I shall escort you.'

'There's no need,' Danae smiled. 'We know the way, do we not?' She turned to Andromeda, who looked a little surprised to be addressed, but nodded politely.

'Very well,' her uncle agreed, glancing at the path back to the high citadel. 'No one will harm you here. And please, will you sit in the Women's Hall? It should see some use.'

'Of course, Uncle,' she said softly. 'It will be our honour.'

Danae took Andromeda's arm, but as she drew her away from Perseus she felt him resist. He opened his mouth but she filled the air before he could.

'Go, see the hounds. Such things are not for women. We will be waiting in the shade for when you return.' She held his gaze lightly, and though his brow creased a little he let go of Andromeda's wrist.

Danae set off along the central street, leading the girl beside her. Her heart felt uncomfortable in her chest, but she kept her feet moving. A part of her wished that Perseus would not see the hounds, was glad that there had been so little game on Seriphos as to make its pursuit futile. She remembered how her father had brought bloody carcasses back from the hills, thrown down on the stone floor of the Hearth Hall, their necks limp, eyes fixed wide. She had tried to keep her son's hands clean from violence, but they had found it anyway. Fish bellies split open, goat blood spilt over shaking fingers, and now the blood of men too. It was as if his hands were made for it, just as a dog's teeth were made to tear. How could she bind such a nature? Let Proitos teach him to kill rabbits and deer. Her son had done worse already. What she needed was some time away from him, so that she might speak with Andromeda alone.

CHAPTER 42

Danae was still a little afraid of the woman from across the sea.
Her large, dark eyes had an inscrutable quality, an intelligent light
that watched but did not reveal. On the boat Danae had avoided
that gaze, but she felt stronger now. She was in her own land, under
her uncle's protection. And she needed to know what those dark
eyes had seen. Not tales or trophies, but the truth. She needed to
know who her son was and what he had done, and she knew that
this girl could tell her.

They sat in the Women's Hall, the two of them alone. Though
the sky outside was bright, winter's chill was beginning to close
in and it was cold in the shade, with the hearth fire unlit. Danae's
arms began to pimple and she tried to rub them smooth. Andromeda, on the other hand, sat perfectly still, her own brown arms
resting lightly on her lap. Once again Danae found her eye drawn
to the patterns that punctuated her skin.

'Your people do not mark themselves as we do,' Andromeda
said suddenly.

Danae's eyes flicked away from the girl's arms, and she felt her
cheeks flush a little.

'You paint your houses instead,' Andromeda continued, looking
around at the bright walls.

Danae looked about her too, at the delicate birds swooping
among flowers of yellow ochre. She nodded. 'And your people
do not?'

Andromeda shook her head with a curl of a smile. 'Our
homes are not so . . . permanent as yours. They are built for
moving with the herds, though my own home had no need for
it.' The smile that hovered on her lips seemed to dip a little.

'My people make our marks on our bodies, for they are with us wherever we go.'

Danae nodded, allowing her gaze to pass over the patterns once more. 'And what do they show?' she asked quietly.

'Many things,' said the girl, her tone aloof. But after a moment she pressed her finger to a hash of lines on her forearm. 'This one is for my father, to show that I am the daughter of a great man. And this one for my tribe,' she continued, raising her leg to show the dark lines across her ankle. 'And this one is for my first blood,' she said, pointing to the marks that dotted her chin. She fell silent, her finger still pressed into the smooth skin. 'I should have more, now that I am married. But who will make them?' She smiled with twisted lips.

And there it was, the crack in the mask. Danae had seen it before as they dined together in the Hearth Hall. She knew there were words the girl did not speak, that sat behind her teeth making her tongue bitter.

'And how did you come to be married?' she asked slowly, like a hunter trying not to startle his quarry. 'My son has told his tale of it, I know. The rock and the sea beast. But I wondered . . . Can that really be the truth? Perhaps it is some part. But I would hear your tale, if you would tell it.'

Andromeda looked at her levelly, but Danae saw a glint of surprise in those dark eyes.

'He found me upon the rock, as he says,' Andromeda said slowly. Danae thought that might be all that she would say, but there was depth to her gaze, as if the girl was weighing her up. Her lips twitched and she let out a sigh. 'Is this what you want? If I tell you the truth it may hurt you. I do not wish that.' The girl shook her head. 'Forget I have spoken. Let us talk of other things.'

But Danae leant forward. 'Please. I must know,' she whispered.

The look on Andromeda's face was pity mixed with pain. 'He found me upon the rock,' she said again. 'But there was no beast. Your son did not save me. He *stole* me.'

There was a coldness in that word, and its icy fingers reached out to touch Danae's chest. 'He stole you,' she said, but there was no question in her voice, no doubt, no denial. She knew it was true. Perhaps a year ago she wouldn't have believed it, but she could not close her eyes now that they were open. 'Go on,' she murmured. 'Tell me.'

And the girl did. She told her of the sandstorm, of the oracle, of the sacrifice she had made to save her family. She told her of the boy she was supposed to marry, how Perseus had cut him down, how he had taken her from her home and kept her in the hold like a jar of oil. And all the while Danae felt her stomach sink lower, and lower, until it had dragged her head down with it, and she could no longer meet those dark, angry eyes. Parts of Andromeda's story were so much like her own, but it was not only sympathy that pressed her heart.

'I'm sorry,' she tried to say, but her voice was too cracked. She swallowed uncomfortably and tried again. 'I'm sorry for what you have suffered, for what my son has done.'

'It is not you who should be sorry.' The girl shook her heavy head. 'You were half a world away. What have you done to me?'

'I brought him into this world. I raised him, and look what he has become. He has brought so much pain, so much death. My hands are stained as much as his.' Danae held them before her, pale and trembling. That feeling, that guilt, had been circling her these past days, she realised. Too terrible to acknowledge. And now that it was spoken she felt herself being consumed by it. Suddenly she felt the weight of the life inside her, heavier than it had ever been. She had failed to protect Perseus from the world, or the world from him. How could she trust herself to raise another child?

Danae closed her eyes and heaved a breath into her tightening chest. But as she let it out she was surprised to feel warm fingers fold over her own.

'You made him, but you did not shape him,' Andromeda said quietly. 'Not you alone. Many hands worked at that wheel, not least his own. And I have tried to shape him too, for my own sake. To temper him, to protect myself. So that I may tolerate the intolerable.'

Danae looked at her, still unable to read all that the girl's face held, but finding a sincerity that calmed her. And something else that she recognised.

'You are a survivor, Andromeda. Like myself. We do what we must and endure what we can.' She forced her cheeks to lift and squeezed the girl's slender fingers. 'I am sorry, truly, for what you have lost. But happiness can be found again. We're safe here, I promise you. I will keep you safe.'

She did not speak for Andromeda's sake alone, but as the girl returned her gaze there was doubt in her eyes.

'You fear him,' Danae went on, feeling her heaviness drag at her once more. In her honest heart she feared him too. 'Is that why you stayed silent last night? I watched you as he told his tales, and I know now the words you could have spoken. Why didn't you?'

'I feared him once,' Andromeda said, staring at the cold hearth. 'But it is different now. I fear what my words will make him do.'

The girl glanced at her, as if she were looking for something – understanding, even forgiveness. Danae did not know what to say, and stared back dully.

'His pride is fragile,' Andromeda went on, shaking her head and turning her eyes back to the hearth. 'There is a time to speak and a time to be silent. What harm can his stories do me now? At least I am still here to know the truth, even if I do not speak it. But that head . . . the woman he carries . . . Who can know her truth? Who lives to remember it? Her fate is not mine, and if I have to keep a silent tongue sometimes, then I will. I speak when it matters.'

The girl's face was creased as if she were in pain, and Danae knew she did not understand all that filled her troubled mind, but she nodded anyway.

'You know how to survive,' she said quietly. 'We are the same—'

'Perhaps it is not enough that we survive,' Andromeda said suddenly, fixing Danae with shining eyes. 'I could not help that woman, whoever she was. I could not help Phineus, or your husband. If anything I . . . ' Her voice began to break, and she took a long shaking breath. 'I cannot let Perseus do more harm. Please –' suddenly she grasped Danae's hands – 'you must help me. Together we might stop him.'

Danae pulled back, though she could not release her fingers from that desperate grip. The sharpness with which Andromeda said her son's name made her afraid.

'You must know that I still love my son,' she said, searching the girl's face. Her trembling expression was part anguish, part resolve. 'No matter what he has done, or what he will do, I am his mother. And there is more between us than that. When I was broken and alone, he put me together again. I could not have survived on Seriphos without him. He has told you of how we came to that island?'

The girl began to nod, but then shook her head. 'He tells me things, sometimes, but I cannot know what is true. He says he is the son of a god, that he is heir to a great kingdom. Argos, yes? For that is why we are here. But he spoke little of Seriphos.'

Danae saw the question in her young face, but some things were still too raw to speak of. 'There is some truth in what he has told you,' Danae said quietly. 'My father, King Akrisios, cast us out from Argos before Perseus was even born. And so we have spent our years on Seriphos. The two of us together, do you see? He has kept my heart beating, even when I was afraid for him, or when he hurt me. The bond between us will never break. I just need to find him again. There is gentleness in him still. I have to believe that.'

Andromeda looked at her for a long time, but Danae could not know what she was thinking. Had this girl seen anything of the kind boy she had raised in Diktys' smoky hut? Would she ever be able to see him, through her pain? Danae's own pain lay thick upon her, but she had lost so much in her life that she could not help holding tight to what she had.

'I do not mean to harm your son,' Andromeda said eventually. 'I'm not even sure that it is within me. Please, do not misunderstand me.' She pressed Danae's hand again, gently this time. 'I only meant that I cannot see another life stripped away by his hand. I will use all that I have to prevent it, even my own wretched life. But I fear it will not be enough.'

Danae could hear the truth in Andromeda's pleading voice, and her fear fell away.

'You are not wretched,' she said gently, pulling the trembling girl to her with shielding arms. 'Not any more. I will not let it be so. You are my daughter now, by the laws of gods and men.' She felt Andromeda's rigid body give way a little, and held her tightly. 'I will help you,' Danae whispered. 'We will do what we can.'

CHAPTER 43

Their dinner that evening had a different texture, Danae thought, as she ate spiced lentil stew from a steaming bowl. The food was just as rich, but it did not stick in her mouth as it had the night before. Across from her sat Andromeda, and whenever their eyes met she felt the new bond between them strengthen. It was an understanding that ran deeper than words, cut by shared experience, like two channels now flowing into one. It was a comfort to sit with her, and to sit with her uncle too, to sit in this so-solid hall in all its permanence, as Andromeda had described it. She felt sheltered here, like a bird too long in the sky when it has found a safe place to land. Proitos had built this place for himself, for his children and for his people, but somehow Danae felt as if it had been built for her too. As if her uncle had somehow known she would need a home to return to.

'What did you think of the hounds, Perseus?' she asked tentatively, looking between him and her uncle. She thanked the gods that her son had come unladen to the hall this evening, and her nose thanked them too, to be able to breathe without the rotten-sweet stench of that bag filling the air between them. It was only now that he sat here without it, and without that sharp bronze hanging beside it, that Danae realised how tight it had made her heart. To know what the dagger had done, to know what horror the bag contained, was a darkness that had hung about her these last days. But now finally she felt it begin to lift. And she hoped that something might have shifted within Perseus too, for him to put those dark things away from him.

'Fine beasts,' he said with a nod, pulling a piece of beef from its skewer. 'I should like to see them in action.'

Danae smiled stiffly and looked to her uncle, who was nodding too.

'Of course, of course. You cannot get the true measure of them until you have seen my bitches run down a stag. We shall go into the hills, as I said. Tomorrow if the weather is fine.' Proitos smiled and Danae felt her darkness lift further. Above all she wanted them to spend time together, for her son to learn something from his uncle's nature, for him to take it into himself.

'It is some time since I have eaten venison. And the hunt will be thrilling, I'm sure,' she said with forced brightness, trying to hold her smile as she thought of the ravaged carcasses her father had brought home. 'Will it not, Perseus?'

But her son's face was flat. 'Perhaps we shall go hunting together,' he said. 'But not tomorrow. I have more pressing business. In Argos.'

Danae felt her stomach tighten. She knew those words might come, but a foolish part of her had hoped they would not. She stared down at the wooden table, as if she could pretend that they had not been spoken.

'Argos?' she heard her uncle ask. 'There is little for you there, my boy. Only a bitter old man in his crumbling hall. Some things are best left alone.'

Danae looked up and saw that her son's jaw was tight. She wished Proitos had not called him *boy*.

'Everything is there,' Perseus said, his voice taut. 'My fatherland. My kingdom. I will take back that which was denied to me. To us,' he added. He reached a hand out towards Danae's own, but she did not take it. He barely seemed to notice. 'Akrisios cast out a girl and an unborn babe. Now he will have a man to reckon with.'

Danae's tongue was stiff in her mouth. She glanced at Andromeda, whose eyes were already upon her, but it was Proitos that spoke.

'If it is a kingdom you desire, you need not go to Argos to get it. I had a mind to tell you when we were out on the hunt, but it seems the gods make their own time for things.' Her uncle smiled amiably, but Perseus only looked impatient. 'I wanted to ask if you would take over my affairs in Mycenae. That is, the city would be yours to rule. And a rich one, in time. My son has already set about improving it, as we have done here in Tiryns, but I am not as young as I was and I will need him to return as my heir. I know of no man better to carry on the work he has started. I would be here to guide you, of course, but Mycenae will belong to you and your descendants.'

Proitos' smile passed over each of them at the table, and Danae did not think she had ever been so thankful to another human soul. Though she had never been to Mycenae, it already shone like a beacon in her troubled heart. A place to call home. A place for Perseus to prove himself, and to grow in the same lines that her uncle had, to build and improve and prosper. A place for the child she carried, too. The weight of it inside her was so heavy, begging for a place to be set down. A safe place, that would not be ripped from them by fatal words or bloody hands. They could all begin again in this new kingdom. She and Andromeda would raise their children together, and her uncle, her cousins, would be close by. Her mind swam with visions of family, of the wholeness she longed for.

Danae looked across to Andromeda, whose eyes reflected a little of the hope she felt, though it seemed edged with caution.

'Your proposal is generous,' said Perseus with a respectful nod. 'And I shall think on it. But my soul is bound for Argos. The Fates have spun it so. From the moment I was born, before then even, my destiny has been in that place and with that man. My mother has told me of the oracle that was spoken. Akrisios will die by my hand. That is what the Pythia foretold. I cannot turn from the path laid out for me, not now that I have come so far.'

His face was set with such conviction, the words coming as if he had spoken them to himself a hundred times or more. Proitos' mouth hung open, his brow heavy.

'It is a grave thing you speak of, Perseus,' he said in a low voice. 'To slay one's kin, even a man such as Akrisios . . .'

Danae's chest was filled again with the creeping dread it had harboured since they sailed into Nauplia.

'Please, Perseus,' she whispered. 'Listen to what your uncle is offering. You do not need to go to Argos. Not now, not ever. Everything we need has been given to us. Please, accept it and be content.' She reached out and forced her hand around his, squeezing hard. She threw a desperate glance at Andromeda.

'You should listen to your mother,' the girl said in a smooth voice, leaning her lips toward Perseus' ear. 'She does not want to go back to that place, you see? It holds an evil for her. And perhaps for you too. I know something of oracles, and they are not always as they seem.'

'You know nothing,' he said, shaking his head violently as if to throw off her words. 'There are things a man must do. He takes what is his. I ask no one to come with me. My mother may stay in Tiryns if she wishes, and you as well. I have no need of twittering birds when there is a man's work to be done.'

'No.' The word was so sudden that even Perseus jumped a little. 'No,' Andromeda said again, more softly. 'I am your wife. Your fate is mine. I will go with you.'

The girl's dark eyes slid across to Danae, though she could not tell what they were saying. There seemed to be an acceptance in that gaze, but the girl she had seen yesterday – finally, truly seen – had not been one to nod and follow. She had been sure and strong, determined to stop Perseus' violent hand at any cost. And now Danae understood. If they could not persuade her son to stay in Tiryns, they would have to leave with him. Like the leash on a straining hound, they would hold him back from destruction. Or at least they would try. Better than letting him run loose.

She saw Andromeda's head give the smallest twitch, as if she were telling Danae not to follow her. But she had promised to help, hadn't she? She had held her in that cold hall, wrapped that girl in her arms and felt her strong body tremble. If Perseus's fate was bound with anyone's, it was with his mother's.

'I will go too,' she said with a tremor. 'We shall go to Argos together.'

CHAPTER 44

They left the citadel soon after dawn and set out across the fertile plain. They barely passed another traveller on the road, though here and there stood lonely shrines or a goat stretching to reach the leaves of a twisted olive tree. The early-morning sun warmed Danae's cheek and gave a vibrancy to the green and gold fields where men worked with bare backs. She found her eyes drawn to them, her countrymen, as if she might see some face she recognised.

It was foolish, she knew. Even as a child she had barely left the Golden House. She had never known the faces of the men whose labour made her father rich. She had never watched them at work, seen the sweat glisten on their tanned skin, or touched the calluses on their hands. She had known so little then. But Seriphos had changed her. To lose all that she had, to work her fingers sore for every meal, to learn the true value of comfort, to regain it, to cherish it, and to lose it once again – that was what her heart had learned there. Those things had shaped it, its fears and its longings. They sat heavy in her chest, just as her baby dragged at her hips, making her steps slow. She did not want to walk this road. She did not want to look upon what was so long lost. Her feet urged her to turn, to go back to comfort and hold on to it with all that she had. But ahead of her the confident boots of her son crunched on the dusty track, and she knew that she must follow.

The sun was still far from high when the first houses came into view, square and squat. Danae braced herself for a city full of curious eyes, but as they walked through the winding streets she found only one or two dull stares. The houses, like the people they passed, had a huddled quality as if waiting out a storm. Half of them seemed abandoned, hearths cold, doors swinging open unchecked, clattering against their frames with the next gust of wind. They came to the main street, and though it was the merchants' hour few had come to trade. Whom would they sell to? Danae remembered the last time her feet had crossed these cobbles, how the throng had pressed so close around her, how she and Korinna had held hands so as not to lose one another in the streaming crowd, how their voices had been lost among the swell. That had been the last day of her first life, she realised. The day of the oracle. The memory squeezed her chest and she forced herself to keep walking.

Perseus had never seen the Golden House before, but his feet stopped when hers did. Perhaps he would not have known it otherwise, for though larger than any other house in the city, it had lost its radiance. The ochre walls were cracked and faded, crumbling at their corners and pockmarked where the paint had fallen from the plaster. Danae glanced across to see her son's face and thought it had dropped a little. Was he disappointed, to finally see his inheritance? She turned back to the great doors that had once felt so welcoming and raised an unconscious hand to her belly. All at once she felt jolted, split between past and present. Though she knew Perseus stood beside her, it was as if he were in her belly again, and she the girl who had borne him. How young she had been. That girl had known happiness here, and desperation too. Love and family, loneliness and betrayal. Those memories all swam together, bound to that golden hall. She remembered things she had shut away. The smell of coriander in her cramped cell. The lyre's arm pressed to her sobbing chest. Myron's young face, smiling beneath wet curls.

Would she recognise him now? She did not hope to find him here. No, she could not picture his beaming face amid these sad streets. But would she know it if she did? Would he know her? Her hand was drawn to her cheek, as if to feel whether she was still the same Danae. Just as Perseus' birth had left its stripes across her belly, so his course through life had lined her face. With worry, with guilt, with fear, with horror. So much time had passed, so much life. The girl who had skipped up the hill to glimpse the sea felt like a stranger to her now.

She realised that Perseus had gone on ahead, but her legs stood stiff beneath her. It was not her memories that held her back, but the present reality of what lay beyond those doors. She had imagined this moment a thousand times, thought of what she would say to her father, how she would curse him with words honed over decades. Yet somehow she was not ready.

Perseus was at the doors now. She lurched forward, as if remembering how to move. His fist was raised, ready to hammer on the wood. She had to be there. She had promised Andromeda. Her stomach rolled as she drew beside him. And the door creaked open.

'Korinna!' Danae gasped.

She knew it was her, as surely as if she had seen her yesterday. But the woman only blinked. Then slowly her gaze drifted between the three faces that stood before her, and came to rest on Danae once more. She blinked again, and her eyes widened.

'Mistress.' Korinna took half a step back. Her sallow face became sickly pale, as if she were looking upon one of Hades' shades.

'Don't be afraid,' Danae hurried to say. But Perseus' hand was already on the door, pushing it open further.

'Where is Akrisios?' he demanded, peering into the dark atrium before fixing Korinna with sharp eyes.

Danae grasped her son by the arm, though she knew she could not truly hold him back.

'Do not be afraid,' she said again softly. 'We will do no violence against you.' Though she looked at the slave woman, she squeezed Perseus with pleading fingers.

Korinna's mouth gaped dumbly. When she found her voice
it was high and cracking. 'I'm sorry, my lady,' she cried out.
'I'm sorry for all that happened. I didn't know what your father
would do. If I had known, I . . .' She gasped a lungful of air, a
tear breaking away down her cheek. 'I didn't know. I swear by the
gods. I wept to Hera when I heard what he'd done. I begged her
to save you, and your little—' Her eyes flicked to Perseus, with
his arm still braced against the door, and she looked as if she had
swallowed her tongue. 'By the gods. Is that him?' Her face was
frantic, trembling. 'A son, just as the oracle said. And now he's
come to . . .'

She started muttering a prayer, grasping a stone bead that hung
around her neck.

'Where is Akrisios?' Perseus asked again, but Korinna was
avoiding his gaze.

'He's not here,' she mumbled.

Danae felt something loosen in her chest. The woman might
have been lying, but she didn't think so. She had known that face
well enough in its younger years to believe it held no falsehood
now. What surprised her was the relief she felt, that she might not
have to look upon her father after all, that Perseus might not be
able to confront him.

'We should go, then,' she said quietly, pulling at her son's sleeve.
'Perhaps we might return another time.' But in truth she hoped
they never would. If she could only get Perseus back to Tiryns,
and on to Mycenae, he would see what he had and forget about
Argos. What had it ever been to him?

'No,' he said firmly, wrenching his arm away. 'The kingdom is
ours by right. Akrisios must pay for his crimes.' He swelled to full
height, bearing down upon Korinna, who was shrivelled against
the door frame. 'And what was her part? Where was she when we
were cast into the sea?'

'She did nothing, Perseus. Please, leave her be. Akrisios is not here.'

But his muscles were tense, his hand lowering toward his belt.

'He is at the temple,' Korinna said suddenly. 'The temple of Apollo and Artemis, on Larissa Hill. That is where you will find him.' Her wide eyes were on Perseus and the bronze glinting at his hip. But now they flicked to Danae. 'Will you forgive me now, mistress? I should have helped you.' Her eyes were full again, her voice hoarse. 'The gods know I have been sorry for it. Please, Danae. Say that you forgive me.'

'I never blamed you,' she said, feeling her heart sink into her gut. 'There is nothing to forgive.' And yet she wished Korinna had not spoken. Already she felt Perseus' energy rising beside her, like a wave she could no longer brace against. 'Go back inside,' she whispered, and the slave woman needed no more urging. She nodded, and Danae saw Korinna's face spread with relief before the heavy door was pulled shut.

'Which way to the temple?' Perseus asked as soon as the three of them stood alone once more. His heels were already raised, though he did not know which way to turn.

Danae glanced at Andromeda and saw the warning in her dark eyes.

'Please, Perseus. Let us return to Tiryns. Look around you,' Danae said, flinging her arms at the empty street, the crumbling buildings. 'What inheritance is this? You can build your own king-dom, greater than Argos ever was. Please.' She felt tears begin to rise but blinked them back. She did not want her son to think she spoke from fear alone.

'Which way?' he asked again, his voice hardened. 'If you cannot tell me I will find someone who can.' He looked back to where they had passed the street sellers, and she saw his hand drift once more towards his belt.

'No,' she said, grasping his arm. She looked to Andromeda and saw the same fear reflected on the girl's face. Who knew what he might do while his blood was so high? It felt as if there were a spike in her chest, and whichever way she turned it only drove itself deeper.

'Come, Danae,' Andromeda said softly. 'Our path leads to the temple. Will you show us the way?' There was a reassurance in her tone, a steadiness in her gaze, and Danae had no choice but to trust it.

'We must go back through the town,' she said, her voice half stolen by the dryness in her throat. And so the three of them set off towards the hill.

CHAPTER 45

Danae's legs were like bronze as she dragged herself step by step up Larissa Hill. She had walked this path before, of course. Many times, in those days before everything changed. She remembered how she had been pulled onward in her eagerness to gaze at the shimmering gulf, how she had rarely felt so light in all her life. Now it was as if she were stepping upon the black earth of Hades, and her heart quivered with every breath.

How would they stop him? She kept glancing across to where Andromeda took her measured steps, but she could read nothing on that face. The girl stared straight ahead, at Perseus perhaps, or at his shining dagger, or at the leather bag with its sickening swing. Danae had to hope Andromeda had a plan. For right now she felt as if they were leading the lion to the fold. How could they cry horror at what it did there?

Danae had never felt strong. She had survived, yes. She had endured fear and pain, lived through hardship, done what she could to protect herself and her child. But she only ever felt as if she were keeping her head above the waves. She could not control the tide – that was for the gods. They had set her life in motion and told her where it would lead. *Your son will be the death of your father.* The Pythia had said so all those years ago. And she, Danae, had been torn by those words, from home, from family. Why now should she hope to deny them? And yet she knew that when the deed was done she would be torn anew. Her son, a kin-killer, would be barred from the world of civilised men, and she would have to rip herself either from the world or from him. She did not think she could survive either loss. What more was there for her to do, then, than to cast herself into the path of the inevitable?

Andromeda was ready to do just that. She had said so. The silent girl walking beside her radiated a strength that seeped into Danae's heart, hardening it to their shared fate. Whatever awaited them at the top of that hill, they would face it together.

As she saw the path begin to level ahead, Danae felt her blood grow hot, and she realised that it was not only Perseus who had come to confront Akrisios. If the Pythia's words had ordered her torn, it was her father's hand that had seen it done. The years had only deepened the wound of that betrayal. She had her own child now, and soon another. To know how fiercely she wanted to protect them, to cling to them, to love them, it made her burn to think that her father had not held that same feeling for her. Even now, after all the pain Perseus had caused her, she had not abandoned her son. Suddenly old tears were fresh in her eyes, brought by the memory of how easily her father had cut her away.

A feeling sprang from her heart to her lips, and was out as soon as it had formed.

'Let me be the first to speak with him,' she said to Perseus, widening her steps to draw level with her son. 'There are things I would say, before . . . Please. Allow me this.'

He looked at her, and his pace slowed a little. Perhaps it was the tears still glistening in her eyes that made him pause.

'He may be dangerous. What use are words now? No, I think—'

But Andromeda's hand had taken his, and she saw the girl press his palm.

'She will be quite safe, with you there to guard her.' Andromeda gave the hint of a smile, but her eyes were serious. 'This man wronged you both. Give your mother a chance to find her peace. She has suffered enough for it.'

Danae expected Perseus to argue, but he simply looked at Andromeda with his lips parted. The two of them were still for a moment, as if having a conversation Danae could not hear, before Perseus turned back to her.

'Very well,' he said. 'But I will keep close.'

The temple was in sight now, its round walls growing with every step. Was her father inside? Only the priests had had that privilege when she was a child, but everything was so different now. She found herself peering into the dark doorway, heart in her throat as if her father might step from the gloom at any moment. She almost tripped over her skirt when a pale face appeared.

'What is your business with the divine twins?' the young man asked, still half covered by the shadow of the doorway. He raised a hand to shelter his eyes from the bright midday sun.

'We seek Akrisios, Lord of Argos,' Perseus called, stepping forward boldly with his dagger in hand.

The man in the doorway seemed to shrink a little. 'It is forbidden to bear sharpened bronze on sacred ground,' he said with forced firmness. 'Leave this place, or the shining god shall rain his arrows upon you.'

But Perseus did not move. 'We seek Akrisios,' he said again, raising the curved blade by a fraction.

The man's eyes widened, though Danae could not tell if it was with fear or affront. He stood silent for a moment, regarding the three of them, his hand tight around the door post, and swallowed before answering. 'Behind,' was all he said, with a flick of his head, before disappearing back into the gloom.

They soon heard voices from inside the round temple, low and chattering like a flock of startled doves, but Perseus ignored them. He marched onward and would have carried on if Andromeda had not caught his hand. 'You agreed your mother would speak first,' she said softly, and his stride shortened.

Danae walked ahead of them, glancing between the uneven gravel and the plateau ahead, edging around the temple wall half afraid of what she knew she must see. Her mouth was sour, her tongue thick. She could feel the others behind her, their steps crunching at a distance. She thanked the gods that Perseus had kept his word, that Andromeda was here to hold him back with her gentle fingers. Danae knew there were wounds she must close, and she needed space to do it. But somewhere in her fluttering heart she found herself grateful, too, that her son was here with her. They had weathered these eighteen years together, each drawing comfort from the other. And though a part of her still feared him, still dreaded the things his shining blade might do, she was glad she did not have to face the past alone.

She forced her unsteady legs over the stones, already forming the words she would speak, the blame she would finally breathe, the curses, the questions.

And then she saw him. It must have been him, for there was no one else in sight, only this bowed figure seated on a rock. His thin robe hung loosely from his shoulders, like a cloth caught on a tree branch, flapping in the breeze and pulling at the bones beneath. His hollow face stared dully at the ground, but there was something in its shape, in the hard nose and the thick brows turned white that was unmistakable. It hit Danae like a blow to the chest, to know that this pitiful creature had once been her father.

The words she had formed stuck like pebbles in her throat, but her legs carried her onward, closer, closer, until the bowed head looked up.

His eyes were like clouded glass at first, but then they seemed to clear and she saw some of the man she had known.

His lips cracked open, his wrinkled skin shifting in confusion, disbelief, wonder.

'Danae,' he croaked. And he was on his feet, stumbling towards her with legs like brittle clay, juddering over the stones as if they might crack. 'Is it really you?' He reached out as if to touch her but she flinched, recoiling from those hateful hands, and he dropped to his knees.

She stood frozen, watching his wasted arms shudder.

'You've come back to me,' he cried, staring up at her with his dark eyes glistening. 'I prayed to Apollo. I asked him where I could find you, but you have come back to me. And so full with life,' he added, stretching a hand towards her round belly. 'Just as when you left.'

She stepped back, and he fell forward onto the stones.

'I did not leave,' she said, frustrated by how small her voice sounded. 'You cast me into the sea. You hoped the dark-haired god would drown me.'

He was silent at first, his dry lips pressed into a crooked line. Then he said, 'Yes. I cannot deny it. But that is in the past. We all must make our choices, and I have had my punishment for it. See how I am undone?' He pulled at his faded robe, drawing a thread from its frayed edge. When he looked at her again he was smiling. 'But the gods have forgiven me. They have delivered you back to me, with an heir in your belly.' He glanced at it as he spoke, eyes alight. 'I shall prosper again, just as the gods have willed. And you shall be beside me. So all has come good, you see.'

He stared up at her, still kneeling on the gravel. His expression was hopeful, almost joyful, and yet his words filled Danae with bitterness. How could he say that all had come good, when he knew nothing of what she had endured? He had not even asked. There was no apology waiting on those lips, she knew. There was no shame in his gleaming eyes. He thought only of what he might gain, and not of what she had lost. She put her arms across her belly, shielding it from his grasping hands. But what could she say? She saw now that he had not changed. What use would her curses be?

He must have felt the anger in her gaze, for his smile drooped.

'Come, Danae,' he said. His tone was almost admonishing, as if she were a child again. 'We each betrayed the other. I have put it behind me, and you must do the same. Here, now, before the gods. You must say that you forgive me.'

'I must do nothing,' Danae said, keeping her voice level even as she felt her cheeks grow hot. 'I cannot forgive you.' She knew the truth of those words as she spoke them. Like a staff broken and repaired, her heart would no longer bend. She could no longer afford to believe the best in him. 'You cannot offer anything that is not already mine. I have a home. I have a family, as you did once. I owe you no part of it. I do not forgive you, but neither do I wish the gods to curse you any more than you have cursed yourself. I do not wish anything for you at all.'

As she finished speaking, she found that her anger had slipped away, and she stood quite still, not stiff, not trembling, as she drew in a long breath of fresh hilltop air. It was as if a burden long carried had been lifted from her shoulders.

'Danae,' her father murmured, reaching out to clasp the hem of her mantle. She tried to step away but his bony fingers dug into the cloth, fixed like hooks.

'Let me go,' she began, but behind her there was the hurried scuff of boots.

'Enough.'

Perseus' voice was like the thrum of a bowstring. Danae did not need to turn for he was already beside her, dagger drawn, its tip inches from her father's grey cheek.

'You do not touch her,' he said, but Akrisios' hands had already dropped. He was staring at Perseus with haunted eyes that grew wider and wider as she watched. He swallowed, but when he tried to speak only a little spit escaped onto his hanging lip. He knew his grandson, then. Perhaps it was by his eyes, so like hers, or he saw something of himself in the set of her son's hard jaw. Or perhaps it was simply the surety of fate, resisted all these long years and now here in the undeniable flesh.

'You have said your piece?' Perseus asked, without turning one muscle away from Akrisios.

Danae hesitated. She had no more to say to her father. All she wanted was to turn from him, finally, and let her new lightness carry her away. But she knew what would come next.

Perseus took her silence for an answer.

'Then I must do my part,' he said.

What surprised her was the breath that followed, as if he were bracing himself for it. Had he not been charging towards this moment? He lifted the curved blade so that it gave a flash of sunlight, but then it hung above them. Suspended. Quivering.

Akrisios was muttering prayers, eyes closed, bargaining for his tattered life with whoever would listen – Apollo, Zeus, immovable Atropos. He said nothing to Perseus. Even now her son was not a person to him, not a feeling soul but only the sword of fate. He had thought himself rid of it, sent to the bottom of the sea while it was still only a swell in her belly. Now here it was, just as appointed. Her father would not argue with the implement of his death, only its senders. But they had already spoken. Danae felt herself heavy with the inevitability of their words, rooted to the ground, arms fixed, tongue stuck. She had been foolish to think she could change anything.

But then there was a movement beside her. Andromeda stepped in front of Perseus, between his hovering knife and the kneeling figure of Akrisios. Danae's heart leapt.

'Do not do this,' the girl said. Though her voice was low it had a firm authority. Her dark eyes did not flicker.

'Stand aside, wife.' Perseus set his own voice firm to match, and yet Danae heard a waver as he went on. 'It is my destiny. My vengeance. There are things a man must do.'

'Are there?' she asked, unmoving.

Perseus' hand seemed to tighten on the dagger's hilt and Danae's chest swelled with fear to see the dreadful blade hover so close to Andromeda's skin. But the girl only blinked.

'Is this what makes a man?' she asked. 'You must cut down those who are weaker than you?' Danae saw Perseus' eyes flick to Akrisios, his aged limbs folded on the gravel, his thin cloak trembling. 'Is that a hero's task?'

Perseus looked back at Andromeda, limbs tense, dagger still hanging as if the winds had fixed it in place. He looked divided, with one ear to her words and the other still hearing the call of destiny. He closed his eyes, as if he might shut one out.

'There are some who call you that,' the girl went on, her voice quiet but unshaken. 'Hero, they call you. Gorgonslayer. Beast-killer. What will they call you now? Kin-slayer? Killer of old men? Temple-defiler?' His eyes opened at that, set upon Andromeda's, and she raised a hand to his chest. As she pressed it there his arm seemed to slacken and the blade dropped a little. If the girl noticed she did not show it, but went on in her low tones. 'Word of what happened on Seriphos has not yet spread. That story is yours to tell. Mother-defender. One against five. But here? What will they say of this? Youth against age. Dagger against open hand. Kin against kin. What tale will those priests tell?' She glanced to the temple, where a cluster of pale faces looked on through a narrow window. 'Or will you slay them too and curse yourself before your gods?'

Her hand stretched up to touch the fist that held the dagger, and Perseus let her fingers close around his.

'There is no glory in slaying the defeated,' she said softly, and for a moment Perseus stood fixed in her gaze.

But as his eyes slid back to the cowering figure behind her, he shook his head.

'I have glory enough. What I want is justice.' Suddenly there was a new energy across his face, a fire of anger, and his arm was tense again. 'I want to strip his life from him, as he tried to strip mine. It is a deed in kind, and less than he deserves. He has had his life. He has lived in power, while I was thrown into nothingness.'

His lips began to quiver and he pressed them shut, prising Andromeda's hand from his. 'You know nothing about it,' he said, pushing the girl aside. He raised the dagger to its full height once more, as Akrisios cried out like a strangled beast.

Danae felt her heart knock. One beat. Another. And before she had thought about what she was doing, she was stepping forward into the space Andromeda had left. The girl's courage was hers now, filling her limbs and forcing them out of their stiffness. Now was the time for her to act.

Perseus' eyes widened, his body teetering just as he had braced himself to bring the blade down. He looked as if he would push her aside too, but she gripped his free arm before he could.

'I know your anger,' she said, chest pounding. Though she could feel the deadly blade above her, she kept her eyes on her son's face. 'I know it because it was mine too. The world is cruel and I tried to protect you from it. I gave you all the love I could, though I know sometimes that was not enough. I kept you safe but I hurt you too, I know that. When Diktys died, when you needed me most, I sent you away. I should have held you then. I should have kept you with me and taught you to cry and to love and to build a life that would bring you joy.' She felt her eyes sting, but she had to speak. There had been too much silence between them, but now the words came like a river bursting its banks, spilling over cracked earth. 'You are angry with me. You were angry with Diktys, with Polydektes. You hate Akrisios for throwing you away. And I hated him too.' She could hear her father's ragged breaths behind her, but they did not stick to her heart as they had before. She pressed her fingers around her son's taut arm. 'I am free of him now, do you see? I will walk away from this rock and not think of him again. And you can walk with me.'

He did not thaw as she had hoped, but stood frozen in his anger, paralysed by it and yet vibrating with halted energy. His gaze drifted to Akrisios, but she pulled his arm and drew him back to her.

'What happened to the boy I raised? Where is the Perseus who loved to tie nets with his mother? Who used to sing so happily, who wept when he found a dead bird upon the sand? Is he still there somewhere, in the man you've become?'

She raised a hand to his cheek as if she might find him beneath that glaring face. And as she held it there, the hard jaw seemed to soften. She kept her eyes on his, looking at her son more deeply than she had dared to since they had left Seriphos.

'You don't have to do this,' she murmured. 'You don't have to do anything.'

He swallowed, brow tight, lips curved downwards. When he spoke his voice was strained. 'Apollo,' he croaked. 'The oracle said that I would kill him. The god cannot be wrong.'

Though he spoke bluntly, Danae felt a fracture in his tone, as if the tail of a question were wrapped around his words. It gave her hope and she seized it with desperate hands.

'No,' she said, 'Apollo cannot be wrong. But perhaps he may be right in a way we did not expect.'

Perseus' eyes seemed to sharpen, and his frown took on a different shape. Danae's heart was racing. She knew that her words were important. She must choose the right ones.

'You have been Akrisios' ruin, without laying a single hand upon him. He sent me away because of you. He drove his brother away because of you. He has destroyed all that he had, because he feared that you would take it from him. The shining god gave my father just enough of the truth that he would make it so himself. Look at what he has become.' She stepped aside then, but she knew the sharp bronze would not be brought down. It hung almost forgotten as Perseus looked upon the crumpled wreck of his grandfather. 'Here is a man brought low by destiny. Do not waste your life as he has.'

As she finished speaking her voice broke. But she wanted Perseus to hear it. To know how she meant those words, how she longed to have her son returned to her. The oracle had cursed them both, but she would not be ruled by it any longer.

Her chest burned as she watched him – his trembling lips, his shaking arm. Suddenly there were tears in his eyes, and she saw his cheek twitch as if some part of him had been released. He didn't speak. Neither of them did. Danae just held him in her gaze and in her hands, as the dagger came slowly down from its precipice.

'I would have made you proud' was all Perseus said to the folded pile that was Akrisios. Her father's grey face stared wordlessly, eyes wide and quivering. But in the next moment Perseus had turned from it, drawing in a slow breath that seemed to fill Danae's chest as well.

'Let Argos crumble,' he said eventually. 'And its king too.' Then he strode away across the plateau, putting the dagger back upon his belt.

CHAPTER 46

All the way down the hillside path, Danae barely breathed. She was afraid to speak, to sigh, to do anything but shuffle steadily down the sloping track, lest she should tip the balance of what they had achieved. They had stopped him. She and Andromeda. Not with their bodies, or their lives, or with desperate straining hands, but with their voices. And yet even now she was afraid that Perseus would turn around, that he would shake off their soft words and march back towards the violence he had abandoned.

He kept walking, though. And as they reached the bottom of the hill and began to wind through the quiet city streets, Danae finally felt her racing heart settle. They did not return to the Golden House, nor speak with anyone they passed. They left as if they had never come, and began along the flat road back to Tiryns while the sun was still shining in the autumn sky.

Danae draped her veil across her head, but Andromeda left herself uncovered as usual as she strode silently beside her. The girl seemed almost to be smiling, or at least there was something that rippled across the smoothness of her cheeks. Perhaps it was simply relief. Danae felt it too, washing over her in waves, filling her chest with every new breath. But then the wind would change a little and her nose would wrinkle as a waft of rotten-sweetness dragged her heart down again. She had stopped her son from polluting himself further, but he was still stained by the evil he had already done. It hung around him in that nauseating stench, in the trophy he clung to, in the awful weight of the bag he carried. It would always be a part of him, she knew. No soft words could change that. But if she and Perseus and Andromeda were to build a new life in Mycenae, there were some things best left behind them.

'May we stop?' she asked, as they passed a flat rock beneath a tree. 'I should like to sit a moment. Please.' She cradled her belly as she looked at her son, but she did not have to feign her discomfort. Her feet ached terribly and her back begged for rest.

Perseus nodded without protest, his expression distracted. He seemed to be looking past her, back towards Argos. Danae regarded him carefully as she relieved the weight on her swollen feet.

'It is behind us now,' she said gently.

Perseus stood silent, his brow still folded. But then gradually it began to smooth, and finally his heavy head nodded.

Danae let out a silent sigh, but her chest was still tight. Now was the moment, the reason she had taken the risk of delaying.

'Perseus,' she said softly. 'There are other things we might leave behind us here.' Her gaze fell to the bag at his hip and his eyes followed.

He took half a step back.

'What use is it now?' she asked. 'You have proven yourself. From here to wide Libya men are telling tales of your deeds.' She swallowed, and kept her gaze fixed upon him though she could feel Andromeda watching her. 'It is against the laws of gods and men to carry the dead with us, to bring them into our homes or near our shrines. It was wrong of you to bring such a thing to your uncle's hall, but it will be worse still to pollute your own kingdom with it. We cannot take it to Mycenae.'

Her voice was firm, and Perseus looked as if he were bracing himself against it. His shoulders were tense, his stance defensive, his face frowning. But he did not speak.

'Let us bury it here, beside this rock,' she went on. 'Then it shall stand as a marker, should men want to seek the resting place of the legendary Gorgon's head.' Danae watched his face closely, and it seemed to lose some of its hardness. 'Come. Set it down. You need not carry it any more.'

Perseus was still for a moment. His mouth cracked open and she thought he was going to argue.

'Very well' was what he said. It seemed as if his energy had left him, and he bore an uncertain look. It had been written across his brow ever since they had left the hill. But it did not make Danae afraid. It was not the look of a man about to change his mind but of one who had had it changed for him, and was still trying to find where it would settle.

'We should bury it deep, so that a dog may not carry it away,' he said quietly.

Danae nodded. 'We shall do it.' She glanced across to Andromeda, who extended her arms. 'Give the bag to your wife. It is the duty of women to tend to the dead. Though perhaps we might use your blade for the digging.' Danae looked at her son expectantly, and he passed first the bag and then the dagger into Andromeda's hands.

'What shall I do?' he asked.

'The river is only a short way ahead. You could fetch some water for us.'

He nodded, and walked away along the road almost instantly, as if he was suddenly eager to be far from the rotting head. Danae watched him shrink away from her and for an instant she was back on Seriphos, sending her son to the fish racks or to wash out pots in the surf.

Danae allowed herself to breathe, and was grateful when Andromeda set to digging – she wasn't sure her own shaking hands could grip the dagger. The curved blade was not made to cut through dirt, but it turned itself well enough to its new purpose. She watched the girl work away at the hole, scooping out the loose earth with her gentle hands, sweat beading on her brow.

Once her nerves had settled, Danae turned herself to the bag. She was afraid to touch it. The leather flap bore a stain of dark blood, cracked and dry, from where Perseus had stuffed the head back inside, there in Polydektes' hall. Was it her husband's blood? She could not be sure. That hall had been so full of horror it had all run together. Now the sight of that stain brought the whole scene fresh into her mind, twisting her heart until she realised that Andromeda was touching her hand.

'Are you all right?' the girl asked, but her concerned face showed she already knew the answer. 'Come, the hole is deep enough, I think. Let me take care of that,' she said, reaching for the bag.

'No,' Danae murmured. Despite her fear, despite all that the bag meant, the way it pulled her skin tight and set her heart pounding, she knew that she could not let Andromeda do this alone. She had not been there to tend to her husband's body. She would not forgo her duty this time. Her son's hand had cut this woman down, and hers would lay her into the ground.

'Together,' she said, and Andromeda gave a nod of understanding. Danae's shaking fingers untied the knot, and they each lifted a corner of the bag so that the honey-covered head rolled softly onto the grass.

The face was as twisted as she remembered, foul and frightening, and yet as Danae looked upon it now she forced herself to see the woman beneath those bloated features.

'What do you know of her?' she whispered.

'Nothing,' Andromeda replied. 'A village girl, I would guess. One of the northern tribes near the coast. See? Her chin is marked. She had a family who cared for her.'

Danae nodded, wondering whether they knew what had happened to her. The black shape on the woman's chin, though distorted, was not unlike Andromeda's own. But the hair was cropped short, stuck flat by the honey.

It was then that Danae saw it. Half buried in the black hair, a twisting band of gold shone beneath the filth.

'She had power once,' she said, with a sudden surety.

Andromeda's gaze had found the golden snakes too, and she nodded silently. Neither of them moved to take the crown from its place, and no more words were spoken as they lowered the awful head into the hole. Danae's heart was heavy as they piled the earth on top, but she told herself that the woman was at rest now. They had done that much for her, at least.

When she sat upon the stone once more she felt as if some weight had been removed from her. She arched her back, stretched out her shoulders, and closed her eyes as the wind cooled her flushed cheeks.

'I wasn't sure that I could do it,' she breathed, bringing a hand around her belly. 'I didn't want to bring another child into the world. How could something so innocent survive among such terrible things? I was so afraid. To be alone again. To have to fight for everything. I couldn't imagine finding that strength. But now . . .' She looked at Andromeda, sitting on the ground beside the pile of churned earth. 'It's different now. The air is fresh and I feel as if I can breathe again. And this child inside me, it feels like a gift. I know that I can raise it and love it and—'

There was a choked sound and she realised that Andromeda was crying. A tear spilled down her still cheek and the girl closed her eyes in pain as if it had cut her.

'Oh, my dear. What's wrong?' Danae reached out to the girl's shoulder and felt it tremble beneath her fingers.

'I will have a child to raise too,' she stammered between sharp breaths. 'But it does not feel like a gift. It feels like a betrayal, as if my body has betrayed me. It has chained me here. To Perseus, to this land.' The girl looked up at her, and her dark eyes were so sorrowful that Danae felt her throat tighten.

'You're certain?' she whispered.

Andromeda nodded as if her head were made of stone. 'I know it was foolish, but a part of me still hoped that I could go home. Even when my blood stopped I pretended not to know what it meant. There was so much else to think of. I did not even know if I would step onto the land again. But now I am trapped more than I ever was on that ship, and I know that I will never see my family.'

Danae was quiet, watching the girl's bitter face, the tears dripping from her chin.

'Never is more than we can know. Who can say what the Fates will spin for us? So little of my life has happened as I thought it would.'

Andromeda shook her head, lips tight. 'My home is so far from me now. My parents will never even know what became of me. I may as well be that rotten head in the ground, for all they know of it.'

Danae reached down to take her hands and pressed them tight. 'The world is small when there are ships to sail it. Perhaps you will cross it again, or perhaps we will send a message with one of the merchants. We can tell them that you are safe, that there are people here who care for you. We will tell them of your beautiful children and the names you have given them.'

Andromeda squeezed her eyes shut and drew in a ragged breath. 'And Perseus?' she asked. The girl looked at Danae and she knew what that question meant.

'We will manage him,' she said steadily. 'The worst is done. I feel that now. The shadow that haunted him, that cast itself across our lives, has passed. We need not fear the Pythia's words any longer. Perseus has walked away from that path, and we will help him find a new one.' She held Andromeda's hands, feeling their warmth as those dark eyes searched hers. 'Things will be better. Mycenae will be a new home for us all. Not mine, not yours, and not his. But something we can make together.'

Danae found herself as desperate to believe her own words as she was for Andromeda to believe them.

It was not long before Perseus returned with the full water-skin, which Danae took gratefully. The water tasted sweet on her tongue and she savoured the small pleasure of it. He said nothing of the fresh-churned soil, or the stripes across Andromeda's cheek where tears had fallen, though Danae thought she saw his brow wrinkle with concern. It was a sign, she thought, that the tender boy she had tried to raise was not altogether lost. Already his face seemed softer, more like the one she had known. In trying to become a man, he had turned himself into a monster. Perseus the hero had been a figure to endure, one that she was relieved to have survived. But now she hoped that he could drive his energy towards being a son, a husband, a father. And as the three of them began along the road once more, she found each step a little easier.

Author's Note

In writing *The Shadow of Perseus* I wanted to retell the myth of Perseus through new eyes and have done so through our three protagonists: Danae, Medusa, and Andromeda. The skeleton of the ancient myth, which is preserved most completely in the accounts given by Pseudo-Apollodorus and Ovid, provides the backbone of my retelling and can be traced through the events of the novel. However, readers may also discover that my narrative deviates from the mythical frame in some aspects – a choice I made for several distinct reasons.

First, there is the issue of realism. As with my first novel, *Daughters of Sparta*, I wanted to reimagine this myth within a historically authentic setting, without the intervention of gods or supernatural forces, and so create a story driven primarily by human decision. Therefore you will find some of the fantastical elements of the myth reshaped into real-world alternatives, and others left out entirely.

Second, there is the issue of truth and memory. In *The Shadow of Perseus* we see how the events as they happen can be different to the events as they are told. Who controls the narrative which is passed down through generations, and whose account remains a silent truth? In retelling the myth from new perspectives, I wanted to imagine some of these lost narratives and give a voice to characters who might have had more to say.

And finally, I have exercised some creative licence in trying to tell a version of this much-revisited myth which is fresh, thoughtful, and satisfying to myself and to my readers. The power of myth is that it can be reworked, re-examined, and recontextualised. Ancient writers and artists found myriad ways to imagine the legendary events surrounding the life of Perseus. I hope that you have enjoyed my contribution to this tradition.

A Note on Setting

As mentioned previously, my intention was to set *The Shadow of Perseus* within an authentic historical context, based on my research and understanding of the Bronze Age Mediterranean world. The Perseus of myth belonged to the original generation of heroes – being the legendary founder of Mycenae, the great-grandfather of Herakles, and predating the Trojan War by multiple generations – and so I imagined my 'historical' Perseus existing sometime around 1400 BCE (to align him with the beginning of the so-called Mycenaean age and the fortification of the citadel at Mycenae).

In terms of the geographical settings of the novel, some of these are more obvious than others. The Greek locations – Argos, Nauplia (Nafplio), Tiryns, Seriphos (Serifos) – are still recognisable by their modern names. The North African settings are also based on real geographical locations, which I will clarify here.

Medusa and her fellow Gorgons, when they are mentioned by ancient writers, are almost invariably placed in 'Libya'. This word had a different meaning in the classical world than it does for us, and generally referred to the portion of North Africa that was not Egypt, or sometimes to the continent of Africa as a whole. I chose to locate my Gorgons in the region known now as Cyrenaica, on the north-east Libyan coast, and specifically imagined them inhabiting a large cave known as Haua Fteah at the base of Jebel Akhdar ('Green Mountain').

Andromeda begins her story in her oasis home, which is intended to be the Siwa Oasis in what is now western Egypt. It was sometimes called Ammonium by classical writers and was famous in antiquity for its oracular temple and its curious springs. When Andromeda journeys north to complete her sacrifice at the coast, I imagined the setting of this scene to be the rocky beach at modern Marsa Matruh, known as Cleopatra Beach.

It should be noted that both Pseudo-Apollodorus and Ovid tell us that Perseus finds Andromeda in 'Ethiopia'. Again, this word had a different meaning for ancient writers and loosely referred to the part of Africa south of Egypt, or again could sometimes refer to the continent of Africa in a more general sense. Some ancient writers appear to use 'Libya' and 'Ethiopia' interchangeably in referring to Africa. For my version of the myth to make practical sense, I decided to locate Andromeda within North Africa so that she might encounter Perseus on the Mediterranean coast (as my historicised Perseus is without magical flying sandals and constrained to travelling by the sailing routes of the Bronze Age Mediterranean). There is another ancient tradition which places Andromeda's sacrifice at the city of Joppa (modern Jaffa, Israel), but this appears to be a later variant of the myth.

I have tried to recreate all settings in accordance with the limited archaeological and written evidence which exists for them, though of course some degree of imagination is required when telling stories set in the distant and sparsely documented past.

Acknowledgements

Sincere and grateful thanks are owed to my two fantastic editors, Lily Cooper at Hodder and Lindsey Rose at Dutton, whose care and insight have helped to make this book what it is. Thank you for your patience, your reassurance, and your faith in the story I wanted to tell.

Warmest thanks are also due to my agent, Sara Keane, whose continued support and advice are invaluable to me in this vast world of publishing. In addition, I'd like to thank Sara for putting a title to this novel – something which was not easily done!

As always I'd like to thank my partner, Andrew, for his unwavering support, for all the times he has held me together, for every time that he makes me laugh, and for being the first person to read this novel.

Thank you to my parents, my friends, and my family, for all the love and support you have shown me over the last few years. It's been a pleasure to share this journey with you.

And finally, thank you to everyone who supported the release of my debut novel, *Daughters of Sparta*. Thank you to all the readers, the reviewers, the booksellers and the librarians, to everyone who bought a copy or borrowed one. Thank you to everyone who has taken the time to reach out and tell me that you enjoyed the book. It really has made all the difference.